PRAISE FOR ST. M̶ ̶ ̶ ̶ ̶ ̶ ̶ ̶ ̶ AND DRINKING CLUB

St. Michael Poker and Drinking Club is a look into the lives of a handful of clergymen chosen by an unlikely hero, Father Thomas of St. Michael's. The unusual pairing for ongoing poker games is an attempt on Father Tom's part to alleviate some measure of the inevitable loneliness associated with men of the cloth. Randle skillfully pulls us into the psyche of these honorable, albeit flawed men. The innocent attempt at fellowship takes a turn when Father Tom becomes infatuated with a fellow poker playing clergyman's wife. We slowly learn about what really makes these men tick, and perhaps understanding them better helps us understand, with greater clarity, our own motivations where right versus wrong and good versus bad. Ultimately, Randle unravels our inner fears about love, hope, and faith while masterfully weaving a tale regarding the complexities of each intricate and life altering concept.

– Kathryn Mattingly, award-winning author of novels *Benjamin, Journey, Olivia's Ghost, The Tutor*, and short story anthology *Fractured Hearts*

I loved the touching scene in the opening paragraph and was pulled in. Seen through the caring eyes of Father Tom, the world of *St. Michael Poker & Drinking Club* is painstakingly detailed, precise—enveloping. The many layers of each character are laid bare as though done by a skilled surgeon. Readers join these people at the card table and feel the heat of the story.

– Michael Loyd Gray, author of *The Armageddon Two-Step, The Canary*, and *Exile on Kalamazoo Street*

St. Michael Poker & Drinking Club is a contemplative and ultimately hopeful story exploring what happens when a lonely Catholic priest, desperate to avoid sinking into melancholy, gathers a group of clergymen to play cards. With unflinching honesty and touches of wry humor, Ned Randle deftly draws us close to heartsick Father Tom Abernathy as he and his new acquaintances learn more about each other. When illness strikes, they confront hard truths about themselves and their ordained place in the world.

- Heather Bell Adams, author of *Maranatha Road*

St. Michael Poker & Drinking Club

Ned Randle

Regal House Publishing

Published by
Regal House Publishing, LLC
Raleigh, NC 27612
All rights reserved

ISBN -13 (paperback): 9781646030033
ISBN -13 (epub): 9781646030309
Library of Congress Control Number: 2019941543

Interior and cover design by Lafayette & Greene
lafayetteandgreene.com
Cover images © by Sergio Foto, Alenkadr, and AR Images/Shutterstock

Regal House Publishing, LLC
https://regalhousepublishing.com

Printed in the United States of America

For my wife, who maintains the faith.

The wilderness and the solitary place shall be glad for them: and the desert shall rejoice, and blossom as the rose.

Isaiah 35:1

CHAPTER ONE

When Father Thomas Abernathy, pastor of St. Michael Catholic Church, found the cat dead in the alley, he sat on gravel and cinders amid the trash cans and wept. As a lifelong believer in signs, he looked up and asked God, "What sign is this?"

The loneliness of his office had been weighing on him when he first found the cat, alive in the rectory garage in late winter, mewling and hissing. The cat was lodged behind the vertical rungs of a wooden extension ladder lying prone along the west wall, and Father Tom thought the animal looked like a forlorn convict, which made him chuckle. As he considered the cat's position, he figured it got into the garage, perhaps as refuge from the cold wind, and hunkered down behind the ladder, not imprisoned, but feeling it sanctuary. Or perhaps the cat chased a mouse or a rat into the garage; the olio of stinking garbage cans along the alley was sure to attract game for an intrepid hunter. In either event, the cat may have appreciated the asylum provided by the sturdy building and the protection of the heavy rungs and decided to remain as a squatter.

And why not his garage? It was old but serviceable, cluttered but cozy, sized to fit one vehicle, with a cranky overhead door and a single utility door which, due to settling, defined a capacious gap of about three inches between the bottom edge and the sill. Father Tom surmised the gap was the point of entry.

At their first meeting, Father Tom let the cat be, huddled behind the ladder, wary and skittish, as he slowly backed his automobile out of the garage. Thereafter, he'd look for the cat each time he entered the garage, and when he saw it, found a measure of spiritual awe in the fact the animal settled in his

1

garage out of all the garages along the alley. He knew something of cats and liked them; his mother always had one or two around the place, ostensibly to keep her gardening shed free of mice but more likely because she appreciated the feigned affection and disingenuous displays of dependence they showed her. He admired their capricious independence, which compounded the pleasure he took from the cat choosing his garage in which to settle.

After about a week, he realized the cat was in his garage to stay, and he was very careful moving his car in and out lest he harm the fuzzy incomer who appeared to present no harm to him or his garage. After days of skulking behind the ladder, the cat finally made its way out of the garage, and the first time Father Tom saw it in sunlight he chuckled, as he often did at his own irreverent jokes: a mackerel tabby had decided to impose itself on a Catholic priest.

Nonetheless, the appearance of the stray was a godsend, Father Tom accepted, which offered him companionship and diversion and an object for his storehouse of moldering affection. The priest built trust between the cat and himself by setting small portions of food and drink just inside the utility door, while the cat crouched cautiously along the wall. Slowly, the cat acceded and would greet him at the door to accept his morning offerings. After a couple more weeks, the cat permitted Father Tom to cradle him in the crook of his arm and scratch his neck and feed him chunks of oily sardines out of the can.

As their friendship and trust grew, Father Tom allowed the cat access to the rectory at night, where it would curl around his ankles while he sat at his large mahogany desk, sparsely decorated with a desk lamp, a framed photograph of his mother, and a small statue of the Virgin Mary, writing his homily. As the arrangement progressed, Father Tom would read aloud to the cat to test the sound of his words and elicit an objective reaction, which generally was a generous yawn disclosing a bright pink tongue and needle-like teeth, which the priest accepted as biting criticism.

When his evening work was done, Father Tom would treat himself to a glass of wine and the cat to a small dish of whipping cream and when satisfied, the cat would leap onto the priest's generous lap, and the priest would hold it under its chest and forelegs with one hand and scratch its ears and neck with the other. He delighted in the cat's purring. Although he knew purring was an understandable anatomical phenomenon, he preferred to think of it as a spiritual manifestation of peace and contentment. It was in this posture, cat in one hand and glass in the other, that Father Tom sipped his evening wine and read his Catechism and Bible before bed.

Around the time the priest invited the cat into the rectory, he decided it needed a name. One doesn't usually invite a nameless stranger into his house, he reasoned, so after considering various fashionable and cutesy options, he simply called the cat Tom's Cat, but referred to him openly only as Cat, not wanting to exhibit airs or a pretense of ownership.

He'd been mildly concerned when the cat hadn't bawled at the back door around dinnertime as was its habit, but its habits could be irregular, and he understood cats and appreciated the animal's charming aloofness and assumed it had chosen its evening meal from among the vermin of the alley, as he had chosen his own from the array of fast food joints near the church, and he would find his pet when he took his carry-out cartons to the trash cans behind the garage.

And find him he did. As he sat in the alley at sunset staring at the dead cat, Father Tom could see from the tracks in the cinders and gravel and the condition of the body that Cat had been assaulted by an automobile. The right side of its head was shallowly caved in and bloody. There was a trickle of maroon blood from its nose down its left foreleg and the right eye was cocked and senseless. Father Tom assumed the cat was struck by a car driven by one of his reckless neighbors who often used the alley behind the rectory as a shortcut between Third Street and Garfield Avenue. He'd seen them speed, spinning their tires, sending sprays of cinders and gravel against the garages that lined the alley. He didn't recognize any of the drivers as parishioners, or spawn of parishioners, but his parish was large, and the young ones rarely attended Mass, and he dolefully accepted that one of his own flock might have killed his cat.

Father Tom leaned on a trash can and pulled himself up, an exercise that took no mean effort, considering his middle-aged bulk. He brushed the dust off his trousers, took out his handkerchief, dabbed his eyes and wiped away the bead of snot hanging from the tip of his nose. He'd dealt with death—the one undeniable inevitability—many times and would deal with this death as well. He spread out his handkerchief on a garbage can lid and gingerly placed the cat on the cloth. He folded the corners inward, like a crab Rangoon, and shook his head to rid it of the dark-humored reference to cats and Chinese food. He went into the garage and rummaged through his gardening supplies until he found a hand trowel. He went back out and picked up the cat in the kerchief (a cat's cradle? he mused) and rubbed his left eye on his shoulder to rid himself of the impious play on words as much as the last tear clinging to an eyelash, blurring his vision. He trudged toward his rose garden with the cat swinging in his left hand and the trowel in his right.

The priest got down on his knees at the border of the garden and used the trowel to scrape away mulch and dig a hole about two feet long, about eight inches wide, and about a foot deep. The grave was within the shade of an old willow tree adjacent the Bourbon roses. Father Tom appreciated the comforting presence of the willow tree which grew in a low spot in the rectory yard where rainwater gathered and provided ample shade for working in the garden in hot weather. He knew willow trees weren't indigenous to the area and that this particular one was not a voluntary. He figured a prior occupant, perhaps an old priest with a predilection for supple greenery, had planted the tree many years before to shade the back lawn and to sop up the runoff after a good rain. The Bourbon roses were in bloom and had deep pinkish-red petals that emitted a pleasant fragrance he could smell as he dug. As he prepared the grave, he breathed rapidly and deeply through his mouth, not to ingest the sweet air but because digging even in the soft earth of a turned flowerbed made him winded, and he perspired heavily, and his heart pounded, palpable reminders he was woefully out of shape.

He gently placed the cat in the kerchief in the hole and shoveled dirt over it, patted the dirt smooth. Still on his knees, he straightened his back and looked around the rose garden in the twilight, the scent of the fresh soil stirring his memory of the original planting of the flower bed, which he never considered at that time would become a burial ground for stray cats. When he'd moved into the St. Michael rectory in the autumn ten years earlier, one of the first things he did was till a small patch of yard to make a rose garden adjacent the willow tree. He was a decade younger and not so far removed from his days as a manual laborer, and he worked the ground with a spade until it looked as if it had been tilled with a power tiller. When he finished, his shoulders and back held the satisfying soreness that only a laboring man knows, and that evening, tired and aching, he carried out a kitchen chair and sat next to the garden site, sipped his wine and inhaled the organic smell of the raw soil until it settled in his belly and, along with the red wine and the sunset, filled him with a sense of well-being and wonderment at God's finest creations.

The next morning, he drove to a local nursery and bought large plastic bags full of topsoil, compost, organic fertilizer, and landscaping sand, all of which he worked into the tilled earth with a pitchfork until the soil had the familiar texture and fecund odor of his mother's rose beds, as best he remembered. The following spring, after the rose bed cured over the winter, he planted the Bourbons and some Wichurana roses, both hardy plants that thrived despite inattention and bore flowers redolent with rosy fragrances. He also planted Mister Lincoln roses, which produced velvety red flowers and a persistent damask scent. Mister Lincoln roses were his mother's favorite. He planted each bush evenly spaced apart from adjacent bushes in offset rows, so to the casual observer, his garden appeared orderly but not overly systematized.

For ten years, his rose garden added balance to his life. His days were filled with the innumerable chafing responsibilities of pastoring a congregation: preparing for and conducting mass; hearing confessions; suffering through tedious committee meetings; counseling drunks and addicts and wayward spouses, and recommending obvious, but ignored, interventions; performing the occasional funeral mass and absolution of the dead; lecturing catechumen; proctoring Pre-Cana sessions, and reassuring the wide-eyed-but-soon-to-be-disillusioned intendeds marriage mirrors the relationship between Christ and his church, hence the forced solemnity of oft-broken vows; attending meetings of the diocesan priests with the bishop; worrying over church finances; supervising the upkeep of the church and rectory properties; and attending to the other items on the never-ending list of matters of greater or lesser consequence which required his immediate attention. However, in the evening during amiable weather, he could remove his collar and loosen his belt and visit the rose garden, where he'd crawl among the plants, weeding and pruning, with a glass of wine near his knee. He hand-tilled around the plants, refreshed the mulch and pruned errant shoots to keep a proper distance between the plants, which facilitated airflow and helped retard the blackspot and rust that could tarnish the luster of the leaves.

He'd methodically inspect the petals for signs of aphids, which would occasionally invade in hoards overnight to gorge themselves on drops of honeydew that oozed from the velvety flowers. Occasionally, he'd spot a thrips, which he picked off the plant and crushed with great satisfaction between his forefinger and thumb. He was not bothered by the incongruity between his beliefs regarding the immortal souls of pets, such as his cat, and soulless bastards such as aphids and thrips. He refused to kill moth or butterfly caterpillars, however, believing their enhanced life cycles—larvae to pupa to butterflies or moths—augured a higher order. Besides, he thought chrysalis a religious term. If he found a caterpillar, he would carefully pick it off his rosebush and relocate it to a willow leaf.

Early on, he tried to control marauding, low order pests by introducing ladybugs, which have a taste for aphids, but they failed to propagate in his garden and disappeared with the first frost. So he resorted to other means to control the bugs. He refused to use chemical rose dust or sprays, so he mixed up a concoction his mother used comprising orange oil cleaner in water and sprayed the rose bushes. Her mixture appeared to control the insects well enough, but he didn't like the way orange scent adulterated the fragrances of the roses. He finally settled on another recipe: a half teaspoon of dishwashing soap and a teaspoon of cooking oil in a quart of water, which he sprayed on the plants religiously. At first, he was concerned the scent of the soap would be overpowering, so he spent a half hour at the local Wal-Mart sniffing bottles of dishwashing liquid in his quest to find one with a mild or innocuous odor. In the end, cheap dishwashing soap and Wesson Oil filled the bill. And at the first sign of fungus, he'd add baking soda to the mixture and applied it liberally to the leafy foliage. His homemade treatments worked well to control the aphids and thrips and fungi and still left the rose petals edible, albeit with a slight soapy flavor if the roses had not been rinsed with a freshening spray before he plucked a petal and tucked it inside his cheek.

Now, as he looked over the garden ten years after he first put a spade in the soil, he figured he'd planted dozens of rose-bushes, but he'd never planted a cat. And kneeling there, dirty and sweaty, he wasn't quite sure what was proper for his office under the circumstances. He'd often been dogged by theolog-ical questions regarding the place of pets on the sliding scale of insentient creatures to domestic animals to human beings. He not only posed questions on the matter to himself over the years; such questions also were raised by parishioners heart-broken by the loss of a family dog or cat. They were profound questions which contemplated the place of all living creatures in God's world and His plan for salvation and everlasting life. He didn't blithely dismiss the idea that we had a spiritual duty to creatures other than humans as some priests did. He wor-ried over it. He knew from scripture God gave man dominion over all the beasts of the earth, but for himself, that teaching only begged the question: do we have a responsibility for the disposition of the immortal souls as well as the husbandry of these animals we've made our own?

As he knelt next to the grave, he shook off the imponder-ables, and satisfied the cat was adequately covered by a layer of dirt, struggled to his feet, tamped the ground with his shoe, wiped the sole on the grass and stood staring down at the small patch of freshly turned earth. After again considering the situation, but without allowing himself to be drawn into a phrenic theological debate, he bowed his head and recited from memory:

O God, by whose mercy the faithful departed find rest, bless this grave, and send your holy angel to watch over it. As we bury here the body of our brother Tom's Cat

deliver his soul from every bond of sin,
that he may rejoice in you with your saints forever.
We ask this through Christ our Lord.
Amen.

Father Tom reached down and raked mulch over the dirt with his fingertips. He made the sign of the cross over the grave, picked a petal from a Bourbon rose, put it in his mouth and chewed it slowly and deliberately, as he carried the garden trowel back to the garage.

CHAPTER TWO

Once inside the rectory after burying his pet, Father Tom sat at his desk and looked around the room lighted only by the desk lamp. When his sense of well-being wasn't discolored by the stain of loneliness, and now sadness, he found the rectory at St. Michael to be commodious and, despite its age, one of the finest houses he'd lived in as a parish priest. He looked out the window and contemplated Cat's death, how he might have prevented it and, if an unpreventable sign, to what matter of consequence did it point.

He could have kept the cat safe inside; there was plenty of room. Father's house had many rooms, he mused. The rectory building was built in 1892, two years after the church proper was erected. Belle City had a goodly population of hardworking Catholics at the time, and both the church and the rectory were constructed from locally quarried sandstone by parishioner stonemasons, bricklayers, carpenters, and other skilled tradesmen. The building was stark but well-built and utilitarian, comprising two floors and a basement, more accurately described as a cellar. The building had a functional floor plan: the first floor included a priest's study, where he now sat at his desk, with a bank of three double-hung windows opposite his desk overlooking the backyard, the willow tree and the rose garden, and now Cat's grave. There were rows of bookshelves on two walls. The first floor also included a modest kitchen behind the study, a tiny bathroom replete with antiquated porcelain fixtures adjacent the kitchen, and a small housekeeper's bedroom adjoining the bathroom. The house-keeper's room hadn't been occupied for over ten years, and as he sat at his desk in the dim light, Father Tom lamented that he hadn't tried to lure Cat in and locked him in the vacant housekeeper's room when he left the rectory to get his dinner. Hell, he thought, he could have outfitted the room with food and water and a litter box and kept Cat locked in whenever he was away from the rectory, and he may have avoided this heartache. It may have prevented the accident, he reasoned, but it was in neither of their personalities to have done that, and he scuttled the thought as a revisionist lamentation. Cats have free will.

The second floor of the rectory included a full bath with an ornate, claw-foot tub with a jerry-rigged shower, a commode, and a single pedestal sink below a massive gilt-framed mirror that allowed generations of priests to view themselves self-consciously when they stepped naked out of their bath. There also were two spacious bedrooms on the second floor to comfortably house two priests, the second bedroom a vestige from the salad days of the Catholic Church when even a middling parish in a town like Belle City employed a pastor and an assistant pastor. Pleased to again chastise himself for his negligence towards his pet, he reckoned he could have made the assistant pastor's empty room a haven for the cat. Perhaps he could have converted the alley cat into a house cat with a comfortable room and plenty of food, but he hadn't tried, and the words of St. John, chapter 14, taunted him: "There are many rooms in my Father's house, and I am going to prepare a place for you. I would not tell you this if it were not so."

I made no such promises, Father Tom told himself. Cats have free will.

At least he had been comfortable in the rectory, even if he'd not shown Cat proper hospitality or stewardship. Each of the rooms, upstairs and down, was modestly furnished for the comfort of the resident priests. None of the furnishings was extravagant, except the priest's desk in the study. Each bedroom suite was utilitarian, containing a bed, a chest of drawers, a dresser, and a bedside table, all fashioned from modest-grade woods, the varnish finishes darkened by time and neglect. The walls were bare, save for the ornate porcelain crucifix hanging above the headboard of his bed. In the kitchen, an outdated table with a metal frame and Formica surface, and chairs with complementary metal legs and wire backs and vinyl seats were centered on the linoleum floor. The kitchen set was mid-century modern, tacky but useful. However, the dated table and chairs showed remarkably little wear, a testament to the truism that preparing meals and eating at home was anathema to most parish priests.

The priest's study, where he now sat contemplating the death of his pet and what this death may augur, was his favorite room. There was a wingback reading chair with an end table on one side and a floor lamp on the other, in the ell defined by two abutting walls of bookshelves. Father Tom rarely sat in the reading chair, preferring to read at his fancy desk, the centerpiece of the rectory. The desk was old, large and ponderous and fashioned from fine mahogany wood. When he moved into the rectory, the bishop's secretary, who had escorted him on a tour of the rectory, told him the desk had been a gift to the parish from a wealthy farmer made decades earlier. The desk was so old the donor himself couldn't recall where it came from, but he said it had been stashed in his barn as long as he could remember, causing him to curse it on occasion for intruding on space he needed for storing bales of hay and straw. Finally fed up with working around the piece, the farmer and two hired men loaded it up on a mule-drawn dray and delivered it to the local German undertaker, who also worked as a cabinetmaker, and told him to recondition the desk for the priests' house and send him the bill.

The cabinetmaker painstakingly scraped away years of mildew and dirt and bird droppings and livestock dung. He removed and trued the drawers and installed new drawer rails and planed and leveled the base. He stripped the damaged finish from the exterior surfaces, a process both time consuming and laborious and which left him arm weary and coughing in his bed at night from inhaling noxious fumes. He carefully applied several coats of milky mahogany stain to the stripped surface. He lubricated the drawer rails with a fine layer of soap and fastened heavy brass drawer pulls to the drawer faces, installed the drawers, and worked them in and out along the soaped rails until he was satisfied that even the least manly of parish priests could easily work them opened and closed. Finally, he adduced a shiny desk surface that emitted a holy reflective aura by relentlessly applying and buffing the best carnauba wax the farmer's money could buy.

According to the blushing secretary who explained to Father Tom the nativity of the impressive desk, it long was rumored around town that after the desk was completely refurbished and delivered to the rectory and he received his pay from the farmer, the cabinetmaker stood his friends several rounds of beer at the local tavern and bragged in his broken tongue that he'd done sufficient penance, im Voraus, by restoring das wrack of a priests' Schreibtisch that he could commit sins, both venal and mortal, from that day till the day he died, and he'd never have to spend even one minute in purgatory, Gottverdammt!

Father Tom was still sweating from his exertions in burying the cat and from the warmth and humidity inside the room, and had he not known better, he would have thought the heating system was in operation. The rectory was heated by steam generated in a boiler located in the cellar and fed through pipes to iron radiators which hissed and groaned under pressure to the point that at least one skittish priest, years earlier, suspected the radiators would explode, sending him to Kingdom Come in a scalding fog. He demanded the bishop allow him to take other rooms in the winter. Father Tom, however, found the steam-heated building cozy in the wintertime and the hissing steam comforting and the latent humidity good for his lungs and for the grand desk behind which he spent much of his time. However, when the weather warmed, as now, a parish work detail dutifully installed window air conditioners in one of the study windows and his bedroom to cool the air and reduce the humidity that vexed more prissy priests with damp albs, limp soutanes, and soggy Roman collars. Father Tom pulled himself out of his desk chair and walked to the window and turned on the window unit and stood in the rush of cold air to cool himself and dry his shirt, until weak-kneed, he returned to his desk chair.

It was in this weakened and mournful state that the idea for a social club comprised of men like himself, with similar education, experiences, and responsibilities, came to Father Tom. He sat lonely and heartsick, squinting at the lamplight reflected from the polished desktop where he'd intended to write his weekly homily as a means of filling the empty minutes and distracting himself from his loss. But before putting pen to paper, he'd tried a couple of sentences of his homily aloud to see how they sounded, but without Cat to adjudge the strength of his words, he imagined them weak and hollow. Although he'd had Cat as his sounding board for only a few months, he couldn't remember how he'd composed his sermons the many years before the animal arrived.

It was more than writer's block. It was as if in his loneliness he was bereft of the faith which in the past had inspired his sermons and caused the words to flow. He was neither mawkish nor sentimental, so his response to the loss of the cat that curbed his religious zeal at the moment was to curse the homely animal for getting itself killed. And as he sat at his desk, he could feel his temper rise, a temper easily made manifest in his youth and legendary among his classmates at Benedictine College before the Dean of Men suggested he withdraw from school rather than face expulsion for fighting. It had been a lifelong struggle to hold his temper in check, his cross to bear, and now in middle age he felt the heat of that temper at the thought of the driver who killed his pet by speeding recklessly through the alley, unmindful of the harm he caused.

Part of controlling his anger over the years was learning to isolate the source of his anger and then dealing with it. He contemplated the source of his anger, beyond the natural antipathy toward the killer of his cat. As he thought deeper about it, he recognized the true source of his rising anger was not just the animal's death, but also the realization, once again, of the often-suppressed but ever-present solitariness of his vocation. By wandering into his life, Cat had both made him aware of his aloneness and then assuaged it, only to die and leave him to grapple with it, even more alone. Father Tom rose from behind the desk and walked to the window overlooking the rose garden and shouted, "Goddamn you, Cat!" startling himself with the echo of his oath in the room. He immediately crossed himself and silently asked the Lord for understanding and forgiveness for breaking the third commandment of the Decalogue and for losing his temper, a species of murder, he knew, under certain fundamentalist dogma.

His fever cooled by his outburst, Father Tom turned off the air conditioner, went to the kitchen and poured a glass of red wine. Back at his desk sipping wine, he considered ways to address the reawakened recognition of his solitary existence. When he was younger, he had hoarded and prized his solitude like gold. But as he grew older, he wondered if he'd been wrong to squander by remaining aloof the time he could have been among others. And he felt the sense of waste more acutely as the time he'd been allotted, time which at one time seemed endless and expansive, had a defined and seeable horizon.

It was not that he always was alone; he had a parish family, of course, but he was close to no parishioner in particular, and the requirements and responsibilities of his office required it to be that way. He could have a beer or two with the men of the Holy Name Society, but he found them to be distracted by lives so different from his own that they seemed to be from another world which, in reality, they were. The priests of the deanery got together on a regular basis to provide camaraderie and support, but he found their practiced piety and perfunctory pronouncements on problems inherent in the priesthood unsatisfying. The diocese offered interventions for obsessive afflictions such as alcoholism, drugs or pornography, but ignored the underlying cause. The bishop was obtuse and unapproachable on the subject. Besides, Father Tom didn't want to discuss his problems with any of his fellow priests, much less the bishop; he didn't want anyone to get the idea he couldn't handle the job. St. Michael was a plum assignment, and the bishop, with whom he'd had his difficulties, would be all too eager to move him on at the slightest provocation.

Father Tom knew he was heading for a rough patch, and he needed to take steps to keep from slipping into an intractable melancholy. His busiest time of the year had just ended with Easter, and he was now in Ordinary Time and looking at a stretch of solitary days and nights through late spring and summer, with little to occupy his mind but baseball. In autumn, after the World Series, he could look forward to Thanksgiving and prepare for Advent and Christmas, but he needed a diversion now.

He considered getting another cat to keep him company. The local animal shelter always had litters of kittens to pawn off, and it placed appealing mug shots of potential adoptees in the newspaper to tempt the softhearted. But living where he did, with a busy street in front of the rectory and the racetrack of an alley behind, he didn't want to risk getting attached to another animal only to have it indiscriminately slaughtered by some pimply-faced kid driving too fast his old man's car. He could keep a cat locked in the rectory with its accoutrements in the housekeeper's room or the assistant pastor's bedroom, as he'd just considered, but the charm of a cat is its insouciant independence, so keeping the animal penned up in the rectory wouldn't be right. He quickly nixed the idea of another pet.

It was just after he dismissed the idea of getting another cat to leaven his loneliness, and as he poured himself another glass of wine, when he hit upon the idea of organizing a group of clergymen for fun and fellowship. The words "fun and fellowship" actually floated through his mind in that eureka moment, and he chuckled aloud with embarrassment and wondered if it was the wine or his age, or both, that caused him to think of such corny terms. What he envisioned, in that instant, was a poker club like the one he joined at the seminary where similarly situated men could get together in their free time and play cards, have a few drinks, share a few stories and relax.

To that end, he pulled the telephone directory out of the desk drawer and thumbed through the Yellow Pages listings of Belle City churches. He had some familiarity with the other denominations in town and their pastors, primarily institutional knowledge he'd accumulated during his years at St. Michael. On his pad, he wrote down headers for three columns: Church, Pastor's Name, and Church Telephone Number. He listed the United Methodist Church, Grand Hope Nondenominational Family Church, First Baptist Church, Second Presbyterian Church, and St. Paul's Lutheran Church in the first column and their respective pastors, Brian Metzger, Billy Crump, Jim Dunlevy, Donald Northrup, and Theo Swindberg, in the second column. He referred to the Yellow Pages for the church phone numbers, which he printed in the third column. There were dribs and drabs of other churches in town—a liberal United Church of Christ, a fundamentalist Church of Christ, and a mysterious Apostolic Church—but they had tiny congregations, and he didn't even know their ministers' names. He thought he'd start with the bigger churches and, if successful, cast his net farther at a later time.

He considered the roster of names as he doodled along the margins of the pad and sipped wine. In his initial assessment of each man, he drew from his deep well of stereotypical insights, insights he'd often relied on to take the measure of a man; they'd never let him down. Of the clergymen on the list, he knew only one personally—Pastor Brian Metzger. They'd participated in at least two ecumenical services in past Lenten seasons, and Father Tom found him to be affable and pleasant. He had a lovely wife and two college-aged daughters whom Father Tom had met at the services. Metzger was a pillar of the community. He also was a man who seemed to know everyone's business, an attribute Father Tom thought might prove to be both amusing and useful. He placed a checkmark next to Metzger's name.

He knew nothing of Billy Crump, who had moved to Belle City within the last couple of years to start a church, which he did with great success. Father Tom only learned his name when the question was posed to him in the deanery meeting as to who was shepherding the new feel good-church housed in an abandoned grocery store in Belle City. He was embarrassed not to know, but an old retired priest, who made every meeting to feast on the free sandwiches and yellow cake provided at the meetings and who seemed to know everything, mumbled through his crumbs that the little evangelical bastard's name was Billy Crump. Father Tom, knowing nothing of Crump's lineage, shrugged-off the old priest's comment as hyperbole at the time. But now, going down his list, he reckoned from the priest's pejorative and the roguish look on Pastor Billy's face plastered on the billboard at the south end of town that the evangelical might be a sport, and he placed a checkmark next to his name as well.

Tom drew a line through Jim Dunlevy's name. He fancied himself a realist and conceded it would require far too much effort to bring him into the fold, particularly when the Baptist heard his scheme, at least as he now envisioned his scheme, and Father Tom knew from practical experience an activity he himself might consider an innocent amusement likely could strike a hidebound Baptist as frivolous and dissolute or even ungodly.

Father Tom stared at the list. He was on the fence regarding Donald Northrup. He was acquainted with the man: they were fellow Rotarians the first couple of years Father Tom was in Belle City, until the priest, bored, discouraged by the rampant commercialism of the club, withdrew. In his limited view, Northrup was a throwback, a late nineteenth-century man, who held memberships and offices in nearly every organization or club in town. If Northrup participated, it wouldn't be long before he tried to wrest control from Father Tom. And he knew other Presbyterians in other towns where he'd served, and if money was to change hands, his prejudices informed him Presbyterians love money too well, and Northrup might be a problem in a nickel-dime card game where hands could easily be bought, and players could be forced to fold by well-heeled players. Nevertheless, he placed a checkmark next to Northrup's name. He decided to invite him, primarily because Northrup was a stalwart of the Belle City religious and business communities, communities which Presbyterians seemed to view as interchangeable, and might take offense if he wasn't invited. And besides, Father Tom was confident he would withstand Northrup's strong personality. Moreover, he considered himself an accomplished poker player, and he licked his chops at the idea of putting some Presbyterian cash into the St. Michael coffers.

He didn't know what to think of Theo Swindberg. He, like Billy Crump, was relatively new to town, so he'd heard no rumors about the man. He had known Lutherans, including Swindberg's predecessor at St. Paul's, and found them to be steadfast but priggish. None he knew had an ecumenical bone in his body. They tended to be insular and standoffish. In the past, he'd attributed their quirks as much to nature as church policy. Many Lutheran pastors, at least in the old days, came from the Northern Plains, and Tom, snug in his stereotypes, considered perhaps their phlegmatic personalities were the result of childhood exposure to numbing cold winds and bleak vistas and not to any innate defect of mind or spirit. One thing Father Tom appreciated was that the few Lutherans he'd known were not opposed to taking a drink now and then, in severe moderation, and if forced to, they could enjoy themselves, at least in a middling way. He put a checkmark next to his name and concluded he'd just have to see how the mop flopped with Reverend Theo Swindberg.

As he resumed his doodling, he continued to mull over the idea of a poker club for clergymen, and despite his personal enthusiasm, he conceded the men on his list were not really situated the same as he was and could well have different outlooks, much less needs. Each was a married man, he understood, and hence each had the intimate counsel and companionship of a wife. Still, he didn't envy them married, nor had he ever regretted not marrying. He'd spent too much time with altar societies and sodalities and other gatherings of women where he often was called upon to referee disputes over creases in the altar cloths, settle arguments over the choice of chancel flowers (he opted for roses where he could), and be the final arbiter as to the proper meat selections for a funeral luncheon. Hence, he didn't covet spending interminable hours with any woman. Nevertheless, the others had wives, and he'd have to convince them the reason for the gathering was fellowship and not necessarily to relieve the loneliness inherent in their profession, even though he believed most married men were as lonely as he was.

Father Tom decided if he could get the men on the list to hear him out, he could invoke his formidable powers of persuasion to convince them to go along with his plan. He didn't yet know what he would say, but he was confident convincing words would come, as they used to come when he was a young priest and walked to the ambo with only a theme in mind and let a beguiling homily flow with no notes at all. He cautioned himself, however, as he sat at the big mahogany desk in the rectory, that he was older now and made it a practice of writing his homily out in full before the first Mass of the weekend, so he wouldn't make a bumbling fool of himself by walking to the ambo after the Gospel reading with nothing at all to say to his flock. He made a note among the doodles to write down points of persuasion in the event he got the chance to talk to the other clergymen about his idea.

After sitting for a while in near darkness contemplating the singular idea of a poker club for preachers, Father Tom placed a call to each church on his list, other than First Baptist, and as he expected, got no answer that time of night, which allowed him to leave a message on the answering machine, inviting the clergyman to a meeting at the St. Michael rectory. He didn't disclose the nature of his call and said only he wanted to meet regarding a matter of utmost importance to each of them. He left only a date and time but nothing else of substance in the message. He then got up and walked to the window, rested his knuckles on the sill and stared out into the darkness in the direction of the rose garden and Cat's fresh grave and considered what he had just done and why.

Although his idea seemingly was conceived in loss and loneliness, he felt there was something beyond mere forlornness tugging at him. He considered himself a pragmatic priest and not a mystic by any means. Although familiar with the mystical writers—Pseudo Dionysius the Areopagite, de Sales and the Benedictine mystics from St. Aybert of Crespin to

Theobald of Provins—he found mysticism to be amorphous and personal, and he believed mysticism to be the bastard child of obsessive faith, and he was not one to obsess. As a parish priest, he found no need to mine the deeper veins of religious ore; he found plenty of flake on the surface. And as far as religious philology went, he preferred the writings of practical thinkers such as St. Augustine and Thomas Merton who, like himself, had each lived dissolute early lives and later found God.

The closest he came to religious mysticism was his belief that God imbued the universe with an unfathomable harmonic, and through prayer, one might affect its vibration and hence effect desired outcomes. It was the same harmonic, he believed, that caused the walls of Jericho to crumble, aligned the molecules of water in the Sea of Galilee to allow Jesus to walk on water, and caused the earth to tremble and shake and rent the temple curtain when Christ was crucified. It was a conviction he felt most deeply when he finished working in his rose garden at twilight under the influence of his evening wine and he freed his soul from the shackles of theological convention and allowed it to meld with the light of the rising stars. He rationalized this belief not as mysticism but as religious science and as God's intervention in the world through the natural laws of physics and mathematics.

Relatedly, and something he never mentioned to anyone, was his tempered belief in certain aspects of astrology. Beyond the church calendar, he felt an affinity for sidereal time. His fascination with the subject began when he was a young man and recognized that the attributes of his astrological sign, Aries the Ram—headstrong and crass, obstinate and self-seeking—had defined his personality from the time he was a boy. It was his secret belief the Egyptians and the Babylonians had somehow tapped into the eternal harmonic and had devised an elaborate paradigm for charting signs, foretelling events, and defining personality traits. Consequently, each morning after his prayers, he opened the newspaper and read his horoscope to obtain another form of guidance for his day.

He also was a believer in physical signs apart from signs of the Zodiac, another paradox of his personal faith he recognized and accepted after his mother intervened to save his life when he was a young man. He fervently believed God had set signposts for him throughout his life which pointed the way to where he now was in life: a portly, middle-aged parish priest lamenting the death of a stray cat. If the animal's death were a sign, he didn't know yet what it might portend. It did, however, leave him thumbing through the phone book, compiling a list of religious men he intended to cajole into gathering together for forced friendship, an odd idea at best. Yet, there was something about the idea that pulled at him from another realm, and he sat down at his desk and looked over the list of clergymen on his notepad. His eyes were drawn back several times to one name in particular—Theo Swindberg—which he had unconsciously highlighted with a halo of bizarre doodles, and he wondered if there was something about the Lutheran pastor, whom he'd never met, that figured preternaturally into his plan.

CHAPTER THREE

When the rectory doorbell rang the next Thursday evening, Father Tom looked at his watch. It was exactly seven o'clock, the appointed time on the appointed day he'd mentioned in each message left on a church answering machine earlier the prior week. If the visitor ringing his bell was one of the local clergy responding to his telephone invitation, he was punctual. However, when Father Tom opened the front door, he didn't see just one clergyman, he saw a clutch of men at his doorstep, and a rapid survey indicated they all had come but Northrup, the Presbyterian minister. Father Tom smiled, not only in welcome, but also as he imagined the firestorm of forced ecumenism his phone messages had engendered in the form of calls passed among the clergymen now standing on his stoop, two of who were dressed in clerical clothing and the third, the evangelical preacher, wearing a tasteful linen jacket, khaki slacks, dress shirt and tie. Father Tom looked them over and surmised the men had agreed, at least in the interest of professional courtesy, to go to the Papist's lair, all together as a group, prepared for a clerical confab about a subject unknown.

The men generally knew who each other was but they went through a perfunctory round of introductions. In the spirit of collegiality, Father Tom insisted the others simply call him Tom. The Lutheran pastor referred to himself as Theo, and the Methodist and evangelical ministers also insisted on the informality of first names with no ecclesiastical styling. The Methodist extended the Presbyterian's regrets, explaining that Thursday evenings were set aside for the meeting of his Presbytery and he just couldn't miss it.

After the pleasantries, Tom led the group downstairs to

his rathskeller, as he called his basement in a jovial attempt at gentrification. But rathskeller was an inapt word; it wasn't a rathskeller or even a basement, but a crude cellar defined by naked sandstone walls and a low ceiling of exposed floor joists. As the four men clomped down the wooden stairs the treads creaked and the stringers moaned under their weight. At the bottom, the men stood next to an archaic steam boiler. In one corner was an open sump pump and the entire place held the pervasive odor of must and mildew and the dank feeling of damp stone.

Tom had decided against having the meeting in his kitchen or study, thinking the rectory proper too Catholic for their comfort. He'd tried to make the cellar hospitable by setting in the middle of the room a five-foot long, white, plastic table with foldout metal legs and an array of mismatched chairs at the table. There was a porcelain light fixture with a bare bulb over the table. It wasn't the greatest configuration for playing cards, but it was the best he had without wrestling his pristine kitchen table down the stairs. He'd covered the table with an old altar cloth, which none of the Protestants could distinguish from a linen tablecloth, and in anticipation of at least one attendee, set bowls of potato chips and pretzels on the cloth. He told the men there was beer and soda-pop in the ice chest sitting against the wall. He also had two bottles of wine on the ice chest—one white and one red—which were, he assured them, neither tampered with nor blessed but were consubstantial with the wine remaining in the vintner's casks from which they were bottled, a remark that drew a snicker from the Methodist, but the Lutheran merely frowned. Tom noticed the play-on-words went right over the head of the evangelical preacher.

When Tom prodded them to help themselves to a drink, he was pleasantly surprised to see Theo Swindberg fish out a can of Budweiser from the ice chest. Metzger asked for one as well. The evangelical politely asked Theo to hand him a diet cola. Tom helped himself to a can of beer and encouraged the men to take a seat at the table, and to avoid any impression of primacy, he promptly sat down as well. The arrangement was awkward with Father Tom on one side of the long table, Swindberg and Metzger on the opposite side, and Crump at one end. The men watched each other warily. Tom quickly studied the faces around the table, wondered what each man's astrological sign might be and, more importantly, tried to get a quick read on each man as one might any opponent.

Brian Metzger, the Methodist minister who sat directly across from him, was large, about six feet two inches tall, robust and well-muscled and in good physical condition for a man in his fifties. Tom knew Metzger was an avid golfer with a low handicap but an interest in heavy betting on the course, even during a friendly skins game. Metzger had a thick shock of auburn hair with no trace of gray and an open, pink face and just a hint of calumny in his blue eyes. Although he'd moved north from Texas many years earlier, the soft, sophisticated Dallas country club timbre of his voice was still recognizable when he spoke.

Pastor Billy Crump, sitting to Tom's left, appeared to be in his late fifties or early sixties but could have been significantly younger or older. Tom noticed as he followed him down the steps that he was quite short but compact. Tom didn't expect Crump to be so short. He'd only seen the man's head on the billboard and assumed a head that large likely topped a towering frame. Crump was a chucklehead. Tom wondered, as he looked him over in the flesh, if the man had a difficult time finding a hat to fit. His large head was covered with close-cropped black hair liberally sprinkled with grays and whites. He had a tan, weatherworn face, darting brown eyes and a perpetual smile encircling abnormally white teeth. He spoke in a soft, buttery voice, and he struck Tom as a man comfortable in his own skin, whatever skin he chose to wear that day. And he was a different sort of clergyman from the others, Tom knew. His education as an evangelical preacher likely was less formal and more fluid than that of the others. As a result, his behavior would be less predictable, and he presented as a man to keep a close eye on.

Tom finally zeroed in on Theo Swindberg, who was seated to Metzger's left. Swindberg was skinny and angular with thinning brown hair and downcast hazel eyes. His age wasn't readily discernible, but Tom adjudged him to be younger than he looked, perhaps in his mid-forties. He could see that the Lutheran pastor was skittish, fidgeting with his beer can, uneasy in the silence and uncomfortable with the circumstances of the gathering. Had he passed him on the sidewalk wearing no collar, Tom wouldn't have taken him for a clergyman; he looked more like a middle school math teacher or a bank clerk. He struck Tom as something of a mimsy, but he also sensed that if they got into a card game, Pastor Swindberg would be a careful man, a calculator of odds, and not prone to risk taking.

Once he was satisfied with his quick reads of the men at the table, and aware of the awkward silence, Tom set aside his beer and addressed them in his rumbling priest's voice.

"You're probably all wondering why I invited you here this evening. I think it's best to just get to the point and let the chips fall where they may, so to speak. And I'll rely on your professional discretion as to things discussed here this evening." As he spoke, he could feel his pitch of his own voice rise up the scale until it was reedy and harsh. He found it disconcerting. And while he'd prepared an outline of remarks, he left it in his pocket. He was growing so uncomfortable, he just wanted to get the whole thing over with, so he prattled, he realized later, and demeaned himself, but once he spoke, he couldn't take back his words:

"For reasons I won't go into now, I'll confess I've been

suffering from an acute bout of loneliness. No, let me correct that; it's more of a chronic loneliness. And a sense of isolation. I recognize it's an occupational hazard, but it's become uncomfortable all the same. Maybe it's my age. When I was younger, I turned my back on the company of others. At one time, I even considered a monastic life. But I digress," he smiled weakly. He could see the men around the table were as uncomfortable as he was.

"As I'm sure you guys can appreciate, sometimes the cares of this office wear me down, and I have no one to talk to, no one who understands the demands of shepherding a flock."

He tried to stop himself when he saw his confession had little effect on the other clergymen. Nonetheless, he moved onto the main point.

"That said, I realized I spend little or no time in the company of other men of the cloth, others who might understand the demands of the job."

"Don't you have any priest friends?" Crump asked bluntly.

Tom wasn't prepared for the question. He remained silent and mentally inventoried his friends and found the ledger blank. Truth was, he had no real friends, much less any priest friends. He'd always been a solitary man, making only one good friend at the seminary, a little man from southern Illinois nicknamed Shorty. Tom had lost track of Shorty after they left the seminary, and he tried only one time to contact him, when he first started to feel the pangs of isolation, a few years after he was assigned to St. Michael. At the time, he was sitting at the desk in the study, deep in his cups, poisoning his attitude with wine and reminiscences when he recollected his friend Shorty and decided to try and contact him. He wrote a brief note, stuck it in an envelope and addressed it to Shorty's Christian name, c/o St. Meinrad Seminary, thinking the seminary likely kept track of its alumni and would forward the note to his old friend. After several weeks, he received a large envelope from St. Meinrad. He opened it, and inside was the envelope addressed to Shorty, torn open, with UNDELIVERABLE scrawled on the front, the contents misfolded and crammed inside, obviously after being read by someone at the seminary. Tom had been in a fog when he wrote the note, so he took it out of the envelope and read what he'd written in nearly illegible script: *Hey, Shorty, what the hell you been up to, you little fucker?*

He crumbled the letter and the two envelopes in his hands and tossed them into the trash can, cursing himself for his idiocy and cursing the nosey goddamned priests at the seminary who opened his mail.

"It's no secret most of the priests in this diocese are old, Billy," Tom finally answered disingenuously, knowing he was about to place the blame for his lack of fraternity where it didn't belong, "and many of the younger priests are imported from other countries. In either case, my fellow diocesan priests and I have different sets of interests, so to speak. And besides, they don't get my jokes," he added with a wry smile.

Tom started to sweat and itch around his waist, feeling more uncomfortable, wanting to be out of the situation he'd irrationally created. "So, anyway, here's what I have in mind," he hurried on, condensing the entire plan to a few short sentences. "We, that is, the local clergymen, would get together on a regular basis, socialize, enjoy ourselves, swap stories and anecdotes, preserving confidences, of course. Perhaps discuss the scriptures, you know, like a busman's holiday? I also thought it might be fun to spice up our meetings with a few drinks and a friendly game of poker. Say a nickel-dime game, just enough to make it interesting? We can donate any winnings to our respective church coffers or to the poor. I see it as a collegial form of fund raising."

The three Protestants sat unmoved, awkwardly sipping their drinks to avoid speaking, looking back and forth at each other over the tops of their cans, waiting for someone to speak.

"As you know, Father…" Theo Swindberg finally said to the tablecloth after setting down his beer.

"Tom."

"As you know, Father Tom—"

"No, just Tom."

"Okay, Tom," Theo continued, exhibiting slight irritation while looking down at the top of his beer can, "as you know, and with all due respect, our churches take a different view of games of chance than yours."

"Well, Theo," Tom responded somberly, "there's no chance involved in my poker games; I win all the money. You guys have no chance." He took a swig of his beer and laughed coarsely at his own joke, as he was apt to do, and felt better thinking he'd made a good joke to lift the mood. He looked around the table. Metzger had a forced smile on his face, more in response to his boisterous laughter, Tom sensed, than to the joke itself. Theo sat tight-lipped and grim. Only Billy Crump offered a wry chuckle, and Tom made a mental note to keep an eye on the little Bible-thumper if they ever got into a poker game.

"Seriously, though," Tom continued as he warmed to the discussion, "as in all these cases there is scriptural dicta as well as a practical purpose behind any prohibited activity." He could feel the pitch of his voice slide down into its normal octave.

"I won't deign to preach to the choir, as they say, but the Bible doesn't specifically condemn gambling. As you all know, Joshua cast lots to determine the allotment of land to the various tribes of Israel. On the other hand, Christians have had a prejudice against gambling since the Centurions cast lots for Christ's clothing. That's the scriptural dicta, as I understand it, but I'm open to other views."

He paused to take a drink of beer and field comments; however, no one at the table spoke up.

"Despite the absence of an overt prohibition against it in the Bible, I think there's a practical reason for churches to oppose gambling," he went on. "In my opinion, most churches are against gambling because they don't want their congregants to wind up broke and their families ruined. That's not good for anyone, including the church, which counts on congregant offerings to fund its business.

"In any case, we're grown men, not to mention men of God, and I'm certain we won't allow the devil to infiltrate our ranks if we have a beer and play a few hands of poker. And we won't go broke playing a nickel and dime game."

"Can't we just get together to chat, without the gambling and drinking?" Theo asked. Tom noticed that the pastor usually looked down when he spoke and had an aggravating habit of avoiding eye contact when he did look up at him, focusing on the lower part of his face. Theo's misplaced stares made Tom feel discomfited; he thought the man seemed to focus on the long, thin scar that extended from his lower lip to the cleft in his chin.

"No one here belongs to a church that proscribes God's gift of alcohol, does he? As for the card game, I think we need something other than ourselves and our work to focus on. I don't want our little get-togethers to devolve into pity parties or gossip klatches."

"When do you propose to have these meetings, Tom?" Brian Metzger asked after setting down his beer can so he could make air quotation marks around the word "meetings" with his fingers.

"I first thought about once a week, but then I figured if you guys are like me, you're loaded up with meetings and other evening duties. So, I propose the Biblical fortnight."

Tom looked around the table and saw various aspects of diffidence in their faces. He felt as if his timeworn powers of persuasion were proving to be ineffectual with this group of men and he sensed they weren't convinced his plan was a good idea. He began to waver himself.

"Look," he finally said, almost as a pis aller. "I don't want anyone to do anything he's uncomfortable with. Two weeks from tonight I'll be here and ready to host a card game. I'll have snacks and drinks. If you want to join in, I'd love to have you. If not, I certainly understand."

After Father Tom escorted the men upstairs and out the rectory door, he returned to the basement to pick up the empty beer and soda cans and scoop the untouched chips and pretzels back into their bags. As he swept around the table, he weighed every word spoken, every facial expression, every nuanced tone of voice. As he trudged up the steps, he felt his old anger rise, not at the men—they were fine enough fellows—but at himself for proposing such a cockamamie idea. He'd exposed himself to ridicule and chastisement by other clergymen in town, at least behind his back. Moreover, he'd walked dangerously close to the edge, close to admitting as true the underpinnings of some stubbornly held Protestant stereotypes of the priestly celibate life, which was, in the view of critics, one of the great modern-day shortcomings of the Mother Church.

Later that night, long after the men had gone home, he felt the moral weakness of the insomniac as he was kept awake by the bright light of conflicting thoughts flashing about in his head. He finally got out of bed and walked downstairs and stood in the study, in the dark, in his pajamas sipping wine, staring out the window toward the rose garden, indiscernible in the night. A second glass of wine proved to be a soporific and he leaned forward against the window sash, his eyelids drooping, the thoughts in his head reduced to sputtering match heads. He cursed the waning heat of his ire; he cursed the dead cat for getting itself killed; he cursed himself for his weakness, and he cursed the other clergymen for their polite disinterest, and in the middle of his stream of curses, he cursed the whole goddamned idea and hoped no one showed up in a fortnight so the embarrassing affair could, in due time, be forgotten.

Chapter Four

The Reverend Theo Swindberg also had conflicting feelings as he entered the parsonage upon his return from the gathering at the priest's house. His wife Naomi, feeling poorly of late, was in bed reading when he opened the bedroom door to wish her good night. He could tell from her tight-lipped smile she was again feeling the aggravating pain in her belly, but he decided against admonishing her for not seeing a doctor. He told her he'd be in in a bit and if she were still awake, they could recite their bedtime prayers. He gently closed the door and walked to the parlor to sort out his feelings.

He sat in his reading chair and turned on the table light. He silently prayed for guidance and then began consideration of Father Tom's proposal. As the principal pastor of St. Paul's, he was responsible for setting an example of righteousness and adherence to church principles and rules. He was well aware of the Synod's proscriptions against most forms of ecumenism, yet the hard and fast rules offered little guidance in this situation, and consequently, he felt unsettled.

Casting the proposed bi-weekly meeting in a light most favorable to his participation, he acknowledged that Father Tom had not proposed a prayer group; he'd proposed a social group, a men's club, with its intended purpose simply being comradery and fun. The proposal, as it was, was both innocuous and appealing, even when measured against Synodical practices and prohibitions. Moreover, he found the idea of making some friends intriguing. Oddly, of the three other clergymen at the meeting, two were Protestant, yet he found Father Tom, the Roman Catholic, to have the more compelling personality, a straightforward and manful presence unlike the haughty and scheming caricatures of Catholic priests that had been foisted on him by his father, by his father's pastoral friends, and by a few old professors at the Lutheran seminary. He found the priest modest, self-effacing, and open. To Theo, Father Tom Abernathy seemed worldly in a way other clergymen were not, as if he were imbued with a sublunary sense that informed his interactions with other men. And his rugged face was scarred, yet kindly. The priest smiled broadly and laughed loudly, characteristics Theo admired in others but were antipodal to himself.

Theo thought these things about Father Tom and blushed even though he was alone in the parlor. He was glad Naomi was in bed and couldn't discern his thoughts, as she often could, or see the color in his face. In truth, he was embarrassed; he had spent only a brief time in the priest's presence and yet had impetuous imaginings about the man and his makeup. Nevertheless, he sensed at the gathering the priest was a good man, and when he honestly examined his feelings alone in the sanctuary of his parlor, he admitted the priest had a certain charisma he found discomfiting.

Theo went to the kitchen and made himself a cup of Sanka in the microwave. At Naomi's insistence, he only drank Sanka after dinner; she was worried caffeine would keep him awake. He carried the cup on a saucer, with a spoon and small cream pitcher back to the parlor and sat in his chair and stirred cream into the coffee as he again wrestled with the priest's proposal. He'd hoped by getting up and moving about the house he could change his perspective on Father Tom and address his personal concerns with greater objectivity. Based upon his theological and familial background, he couldn't help but consider the priest's motives suspect when he first listened to the message of invitation on St. Paul's answering machine last week and now, as he sat sipping his coffee, he tried to return to that more skeptical and more comfortable frame of mind.

From the time he was young, he'd been tacitly or directly informed that Catholic priests were, in many ways, superficial in their faith and that they engaged in excessive ceremony to cover up a shallow understanding of the true message of the Gospels, such as salvation through faith in Christ's forgiving grace, alone, without works. It was implied the Catholic Church placed inordinate importance on works as a means of salvation in order to hold its members in a form of chattel slavery. He was taught that priests and other Catholic Church hierarchy hawkishly promoted church strictures and Papal Edicts more for pecuniary purposes than for the benefit of parishioner souls.

As he blew into the cup to cool his coffee he gave full rein to this cynicism. He dredged up a convenient anti-Catholic saw—the strict requirement of parishioners to attend Mass every Sunday under the threat of banishment of their souls to a mythical Purgatory for eons. He believed the stricture was not so much a coercive injunction to honor the Sabbath as a disingenuous requirement to keep the sheep in the fold and cash in the coffers. There were other prejudices—the Immaculate Conception and the perpetual virginity of Mary, priestly celibacy, the salutary intervention of dead saints—which rose like fingerprints on the surface of his mind. But as he contemplated the Catholic conceits which stalwart Protestants viewed as hokum, he asked himself, what, in all honesty, does all this malignity have to do with Father Tom Abernathy and his idea for a poker club?

Almost nothing, he had to admit.

So, what was Father Tom's motive in arranging a gathering of clergymen of different traditions to play cards and drink beer? How did it align with Roman Catholic dogma? At least as he understood it. It was hard to tell. It seemed Metzger, Crump and he himself had little to offer the priest except company. And perhaps Father Tom was sincere; perhaps he was, as he confessed, simply lonely in his office with few options for social interaction. That was something Theo could understand, even as a married man.

Over the last few years, he and Naomi had subtly and quietly drifted apart, and he knew between the two of them, he was more to blame. Some of that blame rested with his inability to father a child, he knew, and the acknowledgment of his blame cut him like a knife. He had, he felt, denied her the greatest gift in life. As a result, it was just the two of them and not a family, and in many ways the obsessive weight of two, alone, wearied them both.

On occasion, he thought he could see in her eyes that she was sorely disappointed by her situation, disappointed with him. Yet, they maintained appearances and remained effective collaborators in management of the church. His wife treated him respectfully and kindly, true to her wont, and despite performing all her wifely duties, she was not as warm as she had been in the early years of their marriage. Consequently, he had grown lonely in what he finally admitted was feckless husbandry, and now, sipping hot coffee alone in his parlor, he admitted his awkward relationship with his wife was another reason Father Tom Abernathy's idea for a men's club appealed to him.

But even if Father Tom's motives were pure, and even though the idea of making friends was appealing, he still needed to figure out if joining the group was something he could do and not be in violation of church tenets. Considering his own encyclopedic knowledge of the Bible, he recognized Father Tom was accurate in his assessment of gambling, in light of the scriptures, so Theo leapt over that hurdle easily enough.

His church didn't recognize drinking as a sin *per se*. Even Martin Luther, who had the uncanny ability to find almost any human activity to be a violation of at least one Commandment, waxed philosophically about his good German beer—"Whoever drinks beer, he is quick to sleep; whoever sleeps long, does not sin; whoever does not sin, enters Heaven! Thus, let us drink beer!"—a quote downplayed by the professors at the seminary but tittered about relentlessly by the priggish first year seminarians when downing their first illicit booze, many of whom were away from home for the first time.

Only drunkenness was condemned. The Apostle Paul warned repeatedly against drunkenness and admonished members of the church at Corinth not to keep fellowship with a member who is a drunkard. But Theo believed other letters of Paul indicated he accepted drinkers as brothers and sisters. Paul even spoke favorably of wine for medicine. And occasionally, without pangs of conscience, Theo treated himself to a glass of wine when out to dinner or to a cold beer when he barbecued on the patio, drinks he considered medicaments for his work-worn soul. Although he didn't know the other clergymen involved, he was confident none was a drunkard, and any drinking would be minimal, just enough to demonstrate conviviality and good cheer, and certainly would not lead him or the others down the road to perdition. He concluded, after due thought, that playing cards and indulging in few drinks in the spirit of fraternity and good fun would be fine and acceptable to his church.

With these issues resolved, he came full circle. He was back to the original question which discomfited him, the kernpunkt of his internal debate: could his participation in a group of clergymen be construed as a form of ecumenism proscribed by the rules of his Synod? Before delving into the issue, he got up and went to the kitchen and made himself another cup of Sanka. On his way back to the parlor, he pressed his ear against the bedroom door and heard Naomi softly snoring, and, assured she wouldn't get up and ask why he wasn't in bed, he sat down in his chair, placed his coffee on the table to cool, and picked up his Bible and his Catechism and prayed for guidance.

Theo understood his church's theoretical underpinnings for its refusal to participate in ecumenical activities. The refusal was not just self-righteousness and German stubbornness, although there certainly was some of those; the doctrine arose in the context of his church's understanding of the sanctity of Holy Communion. He knew where to look for scriptural support and turned to The First Epistle of Paul the Apostle to the Corinthians, chapter 10, and read: "We insist that it is the Lord's Table, not ours." Furthermore, according to the Gospel of St. Matthew, Christ alone has the right to say who shall sit at His table. And finally, turning to Psalm 119, he was reminded that no amount of so-called brotherly love, ecumenical spirit, or political pressure should cause us to invite to His table those who have not complied with the requirements laid down plainly in His inspired Word.

Ecumenism, as he understood it, was a form of communion and hence closed to those who are not right believers. Consequently, his church believed in close communion. But so did Father Tom's. In his opinion, Metzger's Methodists were unprincipled in handling the Lord's Supper, and he had no idea how Billy Crump and his church approached the sacrament, or if they even recognized the sacrament at all. If they did, he assumed Crump's approach to the Lord's Supper was the same complacent approach Theo had heard he took to the liturgy itself, a relaxed convenance composed on the fly to make his members feel good about themselves while failing to instill in them the proper dread of the inevitable reckoning over the disposition of their immortal souls.

Recognizing this link between ecumenism and Holy Communion, Theo believed, informed one of the risk in participating in an ecumenical gathering, which was the risk of communing, at least in spirit, with those who do not properly believe to the detriment of one's spiritual health. Theo recognized St. Paul as being outspoken in this belief and so was Martin Luther, an acolyte of St. Paul, so he turned to *Luther's Small Catechism* and read the section under the heading "The Sacrament of the Altar," but it offered little guidance. Nevertheless, he was comfortable with Paul's instructions, and he would follow the teachings of his teacher's teacher.

Theo was clever enough to know his analysis begged the questions: what is a true believer, and who among the men who gathered at Father Tom's rectory is or is not a true believer? He added cream and sipped his coffee, which now was sufficiently cooled to drink, and rationalized that he didn't need to resolve these questions. For the purpose of his instant contemplation, he would assume they all were not. He could not read their hearts.

He set his coffee on the side table and thumbed through the books on his lap. Assuming, as he must, the other three men are not true believers, he needed to resolve in his own mind whether the proposed gathering of clergymen was an ecumenical gathering. If it was not, he could participate. This analysis was clouded by the fact he had immediately liked Father Tom and wanted to trust him. The priest did not intimate in any way that the poker club would be a prayer group. Yet, the teaching of St. Matthew, chapter 18, which was secure in his memory, gnawed at him. Would a group of ministers be considered two or more gathered in Christ's name? He wanted to think not; although Christ is omnipresent, two or more clergymen gathered to play cards and drink beer certainly were not gathered in His name. He concluded, based on the limited information he had, it was quite possible his participation in the group did not violate any covenant with the Synod. But he recognized his analysis was overwrought and likely influenced by his favorable impression of the priest. He decided to give it more thought on the morrow.

Theo glanced at the clock on the parlor wall and saw it was getting late. He needed to go to bed. Tomorrow was Friday, the day he visited the sick and then returned to the church to work on his sermon. However, the tiny amount of residual caffeine in the two cups of Sanka, along with his strenuous intellective debate, left him keyed up and restless. He went to the guest bathroom to rid himself of some coffee, then slipped silently into the bedroom and removed his clerical collar, took off his shoes and clothes, lingering naked only for a moment.

He listened to Naomi's measured breathing as he put on his pajamas. Once dressed in his night clothes, he carefully placed his black trousers on a hanger and hung them in the closet and dutifully dropped his shirt, socks and underwear into the hamper, making sure as he moved about the bedroom that he didn't wake Naomi, who appeared to be sleeping comfortably, swaddled in the sheet and blanket. He lay on his side of the bed without covers—since she had them pulled around herself—and stared at the ceiling in the dark, trying to reconstruct the pattern of the coffering from memory. He tried to occupy his mind with the mundane in an effort to rid it of the faces of the men he'd just met, the priest's proposal, the conflicts of conscience, and the tedious theological arguments, all of which were coursing through his mind like a flume. He bit his fingernails in the dark. Finally, he concentrated on his wife's rhythmic breathing, until exhausted, he fell sleep.

The next morning, Theo awoke early with Father Tom Abernathy and the two other clergymen on his mind. He slipped out of bed, leaving Naomi to sleep, and went into the kitchen and made a pot of coffee and a piece of toast. He picked up the morning paper from the stoop and creamed his coffee and buttered his toast as he did every other morning. But he was nervous and distracted. He looked at the kitchen clock repeatedly. He was waiting for a more reasonable hour to call

Pastor Metzger at the Methodist Church and get his thoughts on the priest's proposal.

After he'd emptied the coffee pot and read the newspaper front to back, it was still early, but he could wait no longer. He called Metzger. If it was too early for the Methodist to be in his office, Theo reasoned, he could at least leave a message urging Metzger to call him back as soon as possible.

Theo was confused for an instant when he heard a woman answer, "Hello." There was a pause before she identified herself as the associate pastor and asked him his business. He asked to speak to Reverend Metzger. The woman demurred, saying only that Reverend Metzger had an appointment and was just leaving. Theo was uncharacteristically assertive, first identifying himself and then insisting Metzger give him a minute or two. There was silence on the other end of the line. Then he heard, "Two more minutes, Theo, and you'd have missed me."

Theo was frustrated over the lost time that unnecessarily jangled his nerves. He should have called earlier.

"What's up?" asked Metzger.

It was as if Metzger's perfunctory question opened a floodgate, damming the outflow from Theo's nervous psyche. He babbled non-stop about the meeting the night before with Father Tom, his concerns about clergy engaging in such activities, his questions regarding Father Tom's motives, his reticence to be involved at all. Metzger stayed quiet and let Theo ramble on until obviously impatient to get going, he interrupted Theo and told him he was making too much of a simple matter. He then informed Theo that, unlike him, he had given the priest's proposal scant thought. As he spoke, it was apparent to Theo that Metzger viewed the matter with a practiced equanimity which was reflected in his genial tone of voice and benign comments regarding Father Tom and his plan. He'd known the priest for a number of years, Metzger said, and he was willing to go along with the idea, which seemed well-intentioned, and see where it goes.

"I've been in Belle City a lot of years," added Metzger. "I was here when Tom Abernathy was assigned to St. Michael. He and I have participated in ecumenical services. As you saw, he can be loud and corny and a bit of a jokester, but his heart's in the right place. And don't misunderstand him; he's much more pious than he'd have you believe."

In response to Theo's implication of possible ulterior motives, Metzger stated flatly that the priest was a good man, what you might refer to as a man's man, a straight shooter. Metzger assured Theo that Father Tom's motives were very likely what he said they were.

"As far as I know, Tom has no family," he added, which to Theo, made dense by concentration on his own self-concerns, seemed apropos of nothing.

He sat silently considering Metzger's comments, but found himself disconcerted by the minister's reference to the priest as a man's man. Metzger tried to politely extricate himself from the conversation, mentioning to Theo that the truth was, he was slipping out early to play golf and had a pending tee time and the other golfers would be waiting. Before he could hang up, Theo asked him, "What about Billy Crump?"

"I don't know much about him. He got into town a year or two before you did. He's building a heck of a congregation, I'll say that for him. I don't really approve of his methods, but if it works, it works. He mostly seems to attract the flotsam and jetsam. But he's also picking up more than the spare change. He snagged a couple of my good members shortly after he got to Belle City, and it still irks me. I wouldn't get too close to him, Theo. He might use friendship as a pretext to visit St. Paul's and try to poach a member or two. Anyway, he strikes me as an odd little fellow. But he might provide comic relief."

Metzger then offered to call Billy Crump later and get his

thoughts and see what he planned to do about Father Tom's proposal.

"I'll let you know what Billy has to say. I've got to get going now."

For the time being, Theo was left to fret over the odd appeal Father Tom Abernathy and his plan held for him, particularly in view of Metzger's comments. He also continued to fret over arcane principles of ecumenism and how Jesus's unambiguous outreach to whores and tax collectors conflicted with the positions of his own Synod. Could socializing with a Catholic priest be worse than socializing with whores and tax collectors? It was a question that finally led him to fret over the paradoxical effect hierarchical edicts of any hidebound church had on the lives of lonely men.

Chapter Five

The weeks after his lame attempt at fellowship dragged for Father Tom. He continually reminded himself his was a pitiful performance and as the days passed his fecklessness was magnified in his mind. He knew he was being harder on himself than he deserved and that the other clergymen, busy men like himself, likely gave him little thought beyond the embarrassed pity they felt for the sad, old priest and his painful effort to make friends. That they gave him or his proposal scant thought was confirmed by the fact he'd heard nothing from any of them since their initial get-together and he assumed they had no interest in the idea, which was just fine with him. The whole matter could die the ignominious death it deserved as far as he was concerned.

He was stretched out in his recliner watching a baseball game when the doorbell rang. He looked at his watch; it was seven p.m. on the nose. He sat up in his chair, slipped on his loafers and went to the door. The three Protestant clergymen were standing on his doorstep, and Tom looked them over head-to-toe as if they were uninvited missionaries who'd stopped by to hand out copies of *The Watchtower,* and he was taking in every detail in the event he had to identify them to the authorities if, chagrined by his abrupt dismissal of their proselytizing, they walked off with his Blessed Virgin lawn ornament or vandalized his mailbox.

Each man was decked out in the most casual of casual clothes: Metzger was wearing plaid golf shorts, a white golf shirt and Birkenstock sandals. Theo was dressed in sharply creased khaki slacks, an ill-fitting blue polo shirt that emphasized the boniness of his boney shoulders, and penny loafers sans socks; Billy Crump had on a pair of faded Levi's jeans, a plaid, short-sleeve western-style shirt, replete with a pointed yoke appliqué across the shoulders and imitation pearl buttons, as well as cowboy boots which bore visible scars across the toe leather and looked to be run down unevenly at the heels. He also was wearing a bright red International Harvester cap with its one-size-fits-all adjustment band stretched to the max. Tom later observed, as he walked down the steps behind him, that the cap covered only the crown of Billy's head, reminding him of the bishop's scarlet zucchetto.

Tom realized he had an incredulous look on his face when Brian Metzger asked, "Is this the wrong night? A fortnight is two weeks, isn't it, Tom?"

"Yes, yes, I sat down and turned on the ballgame and I guess I dozed off. Come in, come in."

Tom followed the men down the steps with cheerful banter and invited them to take a seat at the table as he scurried around the basement dumping potato chips and pretzels into bowls, setting out the bottles of wine and emptying the water out of the ice chest and restocking it. As he fussed, he caught the sidelong glances of the men who seemed to be somewhat abashed by his unpreparedness. Nevertheless, once he got over his initial surprise, Tom was in high good humor readying the snacks and drinks for his guests, and he whistled a spritely version of "Bringing in the Sheaves" in homage to his Protestant brethren.

Once he was satisfied with his offerings, he asked, "How 'bout a glass of wine till the beer chills?" Corkscrew in hand, he asked each man, "Red or white?" and with all three asking for red, he uncorked a cheap bottle of Cabernet Sauvignon and poured four healthy wine glassfuls. He then ceremoniously handed the first glass to Theo Swindberg and said, "Take and drink," which startled Theo, and he spilled some of his wine, leaving a purple blotch on the altar cloth, causing Tom to laugh harder than he had laughed in two weeks. "Gotcha, Theo!"

"Perhaps we should start with a prayer," Tom suggested after he finished handing out the wine and took his seat. "Who wants to lead? Theo?"

Theo declined with a panicked look on his face. "You go ahead. I need to go to the bathroom."

He excused himself from the table and asked where he could find the bathroom. Tom pointed to the stairs, and when Theo was out of earshot, said, "One sin that'll keep a good Lutheran out of Heaven is unrepentant self-righteousness," which garnered a chuckle from Brian Metzger, who was well aware of Lutherans' near pathological streak of anti-ecumenism. "We better say a quick prayer or Theo might sit in the can all night," Tom added.

It was apparent to Tom from the blank look on Billy Crump's face he was uninitiated into the quirks and subtleties of old liturgical churches, and any pointed references to the foibles of dark Lutherans (or to the superficiality of the liberal Methodists or the formal mysteries of his own Roman Catholicism) would be wasted on him. Crump, he figured, would pray earnestly with anybody, any time, any place, as long as the sinner had a dollar in his pocket as thanks for the experience. At that point, Tom wished out loud that Reverend Northrup had attended; everyone, he figured, could enjoy a good-natured poke in the pecuniary ribs of a stalwart Presbyterian. And he could have offered the Presbyterian a sawbuck to lead the prayer, he added, and let them all off the hook.

In mock deference to the historical primacy of the Roman church, and assured by the sworn understanding that no word of their acquiescence would ever be heard outside the group, Metzger encouraged Father Tom to lead the prayer. "It is a Catholic rathskeller," he added in justification. Tom appreciated the Methodist's good humor, stood and recited a short prayer asking for blessings to be bestowed on the gathered men of God, in their vocations and their personal lives, and then hollered up the steps toward Theo in the bathroom to let him know they were done with their formalities, and if he was done with his, he could take his seat at the card table.

When Theo rejoined the group, Tom raised his wine glass and said, "Here's to the first meeting of the St. Michael Poker & Drinking Club." The other men stood up and clinked glasses, each took a deep draught of wine, and Tom felt warm vindication of his idea rise from his belly.

"Since I organized this soiree, I'll make the rules," he said with a grin after sitting down. "Sweet and simple, like the Ecclesiastical Canon of the Holy Roman Church. I suggest five card draw and no wild cards. It's a quick game and amenable to figuring odds. I propose a nickel ante, a dime on the first round of betting and up to a dime raise, with a three-raise limit. How about a quarter on the last raise? We'll take turns dealing, and keep a close eye out to make sure Theo doesn't deal from the bottom of the deck."

He glanced at Theo and watched him blush, both at the suggestion of chicanery and in pleasure at being singled out for attention by their host.

"Any objections to the rules?" Tom looked around the table. "Hearing none, the rules are unanimously adopted."

"You always this formal, Tom?" Crump asked through the same rascally grin Tom recognized from the billboard on the south end of town. "I shoulda dressed up."

"Rules are like fences, Billy," Tom responded as he opened a fresh deck of Bicycle playing cards. "Remember what Robert Frost said about fences? 'Good fences make good neighbors'? Good rules make good games. Every game has its rules. Like golf, right, Brian? Can't play golf without rules. If you didn't have rules, you wouldn't be able to cheat."

Tom had some loose change in his trouser pocket and took a few coins out and laid them on the table. Crump carried his coins in a blue Crown Royal sack, which impressed Tom with its practicality and indicated to him the little evangelical was neither a novice card player nor a teetotaler. Metzger had his money in a ziplock bag, and Theo rested an old-fashioned leather coin purse on the table. Tom took a nickel from his pile and placed it as his ante in the middle of the table. The other three did the same, but it was a reach for the short-armed Crump who was sitting at the end of the table.

"Yes, Billy, I like rules," Tom added as he counted the pot to make sure everyone was in, "but according to the bishop, I just don't like *following* rules. Pot's right; let's deal."

Tom picked up the deck of cards and shuffled and bridged, shuffled and bridged, all the while keeping up a constant stream of chatter. Theo was fascinated by Tom's deft handling of the cards, and he watched his movements closely. When Tom tossed Theo his last card he said, "Here's an ace for the good Parson Swindberg," and Theo's eyes widened when he picked it up. He looked as if he suspected the priest might be dealing from a marked deck or engaging in some sort of sleight of hand or other shenanigans. Tom chuckled, not because of the surprised look on Theo's face, but at the way the man was holding his cards: in a loose, splayed array, like a small-handed kid might hold Old Maid cards. His amusement was short-lived, however, as he focused on Theo's hands. His were the fingers of an anxious man, Tom observed, with fingernails gnawed down to the quick.

Tom dealt himself a pathetic hand. Crump, sitting to his left, discarded one card and asked for one. Metzger drew three, and Theo stopped chewing his thumbnail long enough to ask for three cards as well. As soon as he picked up his cards, which he held in his hand in his exaggerated array, Theo began a low hum that sounded melodic and familiar to Tom.

Metzger glanced sideways at Theo and smiled. Tom discarded three and took three. Crump, at the dealer's left, opened the betting with a dime. Metzger folded. Theo saw Crump's dime and raised a dime. Tom tossed in his cards. At that point, Theo reasoned if Tom was working from a crooked deck he likely would have dealt himself a better hand. Crump met Theo's raise and raised again, this time a quarter, and Theo called and laid down his hand. It was a good hand—three threes with an ace kicker. Crump tossed his hand onto the discard pile without showing what he had, and Tom made a mental note that the little Bible-thumper had just showed himself to be a four flusher. With a doleful smile, Theo raked in the pot and began to stack the coins next to his purse.

Tom passed the deal to Crump, who took off his cap and hung it on the back of his chair, popped his knuckles in an exaggerated way, and shuffled the cards. He was masterful in handling the cards, exhibiting amazing dexterity with his pudgy fingers as he shuffled and as he dealt the cards, with each man's successive card landing aligned on top of the previously dealt card as gently as a butterfly on a daisy. The second hand was uninspired, with each man drawing three new cards. Theo checked the bet, Metzger opened for a dime and Tom and Crump folded. Theo pondered his position with his left thumb nail at his teeth. It would cost him a dime to stay, so he tossed his cards on the discard pile, and Metzger swept the pot of thirty cents.

So the rounds of cards progressed with little money lost or gained. The deal was passed around the table, so each man could have a turn at dealing the cards. Tom enjoyed watching the men shuffle and deal as much as he enjoyed the competition. Crump continued to be masterful at handling the cards. Theo, who dealt after Crump, suffered by comparison. He was awkward and bumbling and his mishandling of the cards resulted in at least one misdeal, although the other three men assessed no penalty for the error. Metzger was an adequate dealer but maddeningly slow.

As they played cards, the men helped themselves to chips and pretzels and beer, which was now cold. Metzger and Crump and their host clearly were enjoying the conviviality. Crump showed himself to be something of a raconteur, regaling the other ministers with stories of his travails as a boy when his Pap, an itinerant preacher, dragged him around the mid-South where his old man preached at tent revivals on Saturday nights and operated a floating card game in the tent other evenings of the week. His father put young Billy to work as a beer runner, he told them, who walked to the nearest tavern to bring back buckets of beer for the card players. In those days, the tavern operators would sell buckets of beer to a kid if they knew it was going down the road to old Preacher Crump's card game. When he got older, his Pap would stake him in the games, where his ability to turn a card often let them turn a good profit. Or get run out of town. Nevertheless, to this very day, Crump told the other men, there's something about the smell of beer and the smooth feel of a hand of cards that dredges up old memories, some delightful, some not so much so.

"I worked up a powerful thirst fetching beer," he added as he raised a dime after drawing one card, "and even as a boy the Devil gave me a powerful taste for the stuff. I've been battling the Devil ever since…I'll see your dime and raise you another dime…and that's one reason I have a beer now and then, like this one here," he said lifting up his can, "with you boys, just to show the Devil I can have a drink or two but still resist his temptations to give myself over completely to the juice."

Tom and Metzger were still in the hand and waiting for Crump to stop prattling before seeing the bet. Theo had folded before the first raise. After the final raise of twenty-five cents Crump turned over his cards, one by one, showing a five, four, trey and deuce, all clubs, and when he turned over the last card, the ace of clubs, he hollered, "Up jumped that Devil!" Neither Tom nor Metzger could top a straight flush, and as Crump raked the change off the table into his velvety bag, he chanted, "Looky here, looky here, looky here, praise Jesus!"

Tom laughed about Billy filling his straight flush on the last card and told Crump he embodied the old adage that 'It's better to be lucky than good,' to which Crump replied, "'Luck is not chance, it's toil; fortune's expensive smile is earned.'"

Theo, who had been watching absentmindedly as the other men finished the hand, perked up at Crump's last comment, which, due to his vexing memory (for him something once learned was never forgotten), he recognized as a line from an Emily Dickinson poem, and he wondered if Crump had a hidden vein of erudition, or if he had cynically committed poetry to memory so he could spout it out in his stump speech sermons, to add rhyme and meter to his fire and brimstone. Theo considered that; but what did he know? He'd never heard Crump deliver a sermon; he barely knew the man. He chastised himself for being uncharitable and presumptive. Perhaps Billy Crump just liked poems and found a serendipitous opportunity to fit a line from Dickinson into the conversation.

As Crump cleaned up the pot and Metzger shuffled for the next deal, Tom sipped his beer and focused his attention on Theo, who appeared to be deep in thought. It was difficult to tell whether the man was enjoying himself or not. He barely smiled at Crump's jibber. It appeared to Tom the man just couldn't relax. His hands were always aflutter and he shifted in his seat until Tom asked him if he wanted a cushion to sit on so he could be more comfortable. Theo declined, and as they played, Tom noticed he was trying to control his restless body by nibbling on his fingernails. And other than humming melodically, he showed little satisfaction when he won a hand. But he'd only won a couple small pots early on. When he raised a bet, ostensibly on a good hand, he did so with a loud, melodic hum, and the other players folded, leaving little money in the pot beyond the antes.

Because Metzger was a methodical dealer, maddeningly slow at shuffling the deck and precise when doling out the cards, either absentmindedly or to show his impatience with the Methodist, Tom began to whistle the old Irish reel "Drowsy Molly" as Metzger shuffled another time. The priest had an accurate ear for the melody and his whistle was clear and on key. Suddenly, Billy Crump leaped out of his chair and, as Tom whistled, danced around the table, performing an admirable impression of an Irish reel. Metzger laughed so hard, he could barely deal. Theo watched Crump in wide-eyed wonderment and laughed out loud, mostly in bewildered embarrassment at the preacher's unabashed display of impulsiveness. Tom started laughing as well, which brought an end to his whistling, and Crump stopped dancing, took his place at the table, huffing and puffing, and picked up his cards without saying a word.

"Where'd you learn to dance like that, Billy?" asked Tom.

"When I was a boy, my Pap thought it'd be a good draw if me and my brother could dance and sing old time spirituals out in front of his tent. He had ideas like that all the time, my Pap did. Anyway, he had an old Negro down in Tuscaloosa teach us the steps to lots of dances—jigs, two-steps, reels—all that. Me and my brother would come out before the revival started and dance in front of the tent to lure in the gawkers. Then we'd go inside and dance across the stage and recite the Lord's Prayer. Then Pap would go to preachin'. It was a sight."

Tom shook his head and wondered if there was anything at all that wouldn't come out of Billy's mouth over time and considered the little man great good fun and was glad to have him in the group. The other men, recovered from Crump's surprising display of nimble audacity, picked up their cards and continued play. Theo took three cards, Tom took two, Crump two and the dealer, Metzger, took three himself. Theo was first to bet and he checked. Tom bet a nickel. Crump called the bet and then raised a nickel, Metzger folded, as did Theo. Tom called Crump's raise, unsure as to whether he was bluffing or raising on a good hand but raised a dime to smoke him out. Crump saw Tom's dime and raised a quarter. The priest folded his hand and Crump raked in the money with his obligatory "Looky here, looky here, looky here. Praise Jesus. More for the poor."

Tom looked at his watch and announced the next hand would be the last hand of the evening. It was Theo's deal, and after the ante, he shuffled and dealt each man five cards. Theo stroked his chin nervously after he picked up his hand and began to hum loudly. Metzger shot him a sidelong glance and winked at Tom across the table. Tom listened intently until he recognized the tune Theo had been humming all evening. Metzger drew three cards. Tom took two cards and Crump drew three card as well. Theo stayed with a pat hand. Metzger bet a nickel, Tom raised a dime, and Crump raised another dime, and Theo called the thirty-five cents. Metzger checked the bet and so did Tom and Crump, but Theo raised a quarter. Since it was the last hand, the other three players called Theo's bet, and with great delight, he laid down a full house—three deuces and two jacks. Metzger and Crump tossed their hands facedown onto the discard pile. Tom looked at his hand one last time—he also held a full house: three fours and two queens. He tossed his cards face down on the discard pile and pronounced Theo the winner.

As if he'd sensed what Tom had done, Crump picked up his Crown Royal bag and softly recited, "Though I have all faith, so that I could remove mountains, and have not charity, I am nothing."

Metzger and Crump saw themselves upstairs to the rectory door with promises to return in a fortnight. Theo was dropping his last winnings into his coin purse as Tom collected the empty beer cans and brushed the crumbs off the altar cloth. Theo offered to stay and help Tom clean up and also offered to have the tablecloth laundered to remove the wine stain, but Tom assured him neither was necessary. The two men trudged up the steps one after another and Tom saw him to the door.

Standing at the open door, Theo summoned his nerve and asked Tom, "How'd you know you were dealing me an ace in the first hand?"

"I didn't; it was just a happy coincidence."

Theo wasn't sure what to make of the comment but took the priest at his word and said nothing more. As Theo was walking down the porch steps, Tom called after him, "Hey, Theo, I have the same feeling about 'A Mighty Fortress is Our God' that Lincoln had about 'Dixie'; it's a fine tune as far as rebel anthems go, but I don't think you should hum it every time you're dealt a good hand. It's a tell, and you're never going to win any decent pots if you keep it up."

CHAPTER SIX

Over the ensuing months, the biweekly card games resulted in little money changing hands among the clergymen. The men had studied each other well enough to know when each held a formidable hand or merely was bluffing. As expected, Tom and Billy Crump proved to be the best card players; Theo tried but seemed to lack a certain acumen for the subtleties of the game. Metzger was, for the most part, disinterested or distracted. He had difficulty concentrating on the game.

Tom noticed other, more subtle changes in the players as they became more comfortable with, or perhaps contemptible of, each other. Although disengaged when playing, before the games and between hands, Metzger labored to be more affable and gregarious and, correspondingly, irritating to Tom. His good humor, which set a light tone for earlier card games, lately had become tedious and stale. Of late, during the first hand of the evening, he made a point to tell a joke, usually applicable to the clergy and with the butt of the joke usually being a Catholic priest, which prompted Tom to ask him if the Methodist publishing house sold joke books written just for Protestant preachers who wanted to roast a Catholic priest. It seemed to Tom the Methodist was over-compensating for some deficiency he couldn't identify in a man who appeared to have everything. And though he outwardly appeared light-hearted and disinterested in the outcome of the card games, he remained a cautious card player, never overreaching or chancing a bluff when engaged, throwing in his hand when his ability to concentrate was overmatched by his thoughts.

After the first few meetings, Billy Crump began to display an irritating side as well. His long-winded tales took a darker turn as he babbled between hands about his struggles growing up and his herculean efforts at overcoming adversity in his life to become a preacher of the Word. And he shamelessly bragged about his successes, particularly in establishing congregations throughout the mid-South. Metzger, who was well-aware of Crump's church-building methods, was tight-lipped and silent through his soliloquies. Theo was indifferent, finding Crump to be a coarse but harmless bumpkin who told wild, unbelievable tales around the card table and likely told them from the pulpit as well. Tom wasn't sure if Crump's posture was an affectation he assumed around classically educated clergy or his natural bent. He leaned toward the former; he suspected Crump was self-aware and cultivated his image to fall in line with expectations. He was, at least superficially as Tom recognized, a self-drawn caricature of a southern Bible-thumper. But who's not a caricature, a stereotype? Tom even questioned whether Billy Crump was his real name.

Tom looked around the card table at the embodiment of his long-held belief in the factual underpinnings of stereotypes. He recognized that the reliance on received ideas when assessing a man's character can lead to prejudice and malignant small-mindedness, yet he'd long been a believer in the generally accurate and illustrative function of stereotypes all of his life. Like it or not, stereotypes have root in facts, he conceded, and are a good place to start if one doing the assessment had the ability to discard the prejudicial aspects of the accepted stereotype found in the subject. He believed he had that ability. And the group of men at the table, himself included, comprised the epitome of clerical stereotypes: the portly, affable Irish priest, the dour Lutheran prig, the vapid Methodist, and the Bible-thumping rube.

But it was Crump's behavior as a rube with feigned naïveté that irritated Father Tom most this particular evening. The man alternated between arrogance and practiced obsequiousness.

He continued the noisome habit of repeating, "Looky here, looky here, praise Jesus" in his nasally twang when he won a poker hand. "Praise Jesus, more money for the poor," he'd added to his refrain as he dropped coins into the Crown Royal bag, one at a time, sometimes repeating, "Come to Papa, come to Papa" with a smarmy smile. After one such display, Metzger observed that if Billy kept winning nice pots he'd soon have enough ready cash to erect a second billboard on the north end of town.

"Perhaps," Crump said to Metzger without looking up as he counted his coins, "if your membership tanks you might consider placing your own billboard. Perhaps with a picture of your new associate minister? They say she's a looker."

Father Tom noticed Metzger blanch and fold forward at the comment, a pained look in his eyes, as if his groin were on fire, as if he'd been kicked soundly in the nuts. Tom sensed some relationship between his reaction to Crump's rib and his disengagement during the card games.

"Is that what they say?" Metzger asked with a hard edge to his voice once he recovered. He shifted in his chair and pulled himself up to his considerable height and glared down at Crump. "Was that remark merely sexist, or was it commentary on the Methodist practice of ordaining women, or did it have some other nasty intent?"

Tom spoke up to defuse the tension. "Okay, boys, let's play cards. Leave it alone."

"I meant no offense," Crump said flatly, a tense smile on his face as he set his bag to the side. "But I will say one last thing: every one of us has his own way of finding souls to save. You guys got it easy. You get most of your members when they're babies, before they understand the underpinnings of your pomp and circumstance. By the time they figure out what's really going on, they're invested and you keep most of them for life. On the other hand, I have to go after the disenchanted and unchurched. It's a constant labor, and expensive, and I use all means at my disposal."

Theo thought Crump's comments about old line churches, which obviously included his own, opprobrious and could see that Metzger also was quietly fuming. Theo remembered what the Methodist had mentioned about Crump's tactics for seeking souls during their telephone conversation, and he figured Brian likely was biting his tongue in deference to Tom's intervention. In any event, it seemed to him that Crump had crossed a line, yet no one spoke up to disabuse him of the notion held by many preachers of his ilk. Theo looked to Tom, who had to realize Crump's characterization applied most pointedly to him and his parishioners, and saw that the scar on the priest's chin had reddened considerably in response to the remarks until it looked like a pulsating, external artery ready to burst. Nevertheless, Tom remained tight-lipped and grim until he finally spoke up in measured tones.

"You're right about the labor, Billy. I sometimes think all this life consists of is placing one foot in front of the other, trying to do good, day in and day out, until one day you just step right into your grave."

"And they say we're dark," remarked Theo, disclosing more self-awareness than Tom thought him capable of, causing the priest to smile at the pastor's insight.

However, Father Tom's uncharacteristic and saturnine comment caught the men off guard. Theo thought Tom should have taken Billy to the woodshed for his obnoxious blathering, and he was disappointed when Tom turned the other cheek, and in such a resigned and cheerless manner at that. In the wake of the exchange, no one spoke, and the only thing that could be heard was the riffle of the cards as Tom prepared for his deal.

"Tell me, Tom," Brian Metzger finally asked, more to ease the tension around the table than to delve into spiritual esoterica, "as a man, and not as a priest, are you afraid of dying? Despite all my faith and all my training, I'll admit there are times I am, to be perfectly honest."

Tom didn't find Metzger's admission odd. From his years of pastoring the sick and dying, he'd learned of the many who feared death, most had too great an opinion of themselves or too much worldly matters to live for. In regard to his own fear of death, he at first was tempted to respond flippantly, offering the affirmative aphorisms rough boys at the seminary, like himself, often spouted in response to a question whose answer was so obvious: is a bear Catholic? Does the Pope shit in the woods? But he held his tongue and gave the question due consideration. The answer he arrived at was not so obvious.

"It's not fear I feel when I consider my own inevitable death, Brian," Tom answered as he doled out the cards. "It's more a feeling of embarrassment. You know, it's like that self-consciousness you feel in one of those dreams where you show up at some formal shindig, uninvited, naked, or barefooted? Since I've not died before, I don't know the etiquette of it, and I feel a bit embarrassed that I might not do it well. And I don't think I'm alone in that regard. How many times have we heard about a family member or hospice worker leaving the moribund person's bedside, just for a minute, to go the restroom or have a smoke or get a cup of coffee, only to come back and find the sufferer dead?

"I think it is the indignities the dead suffer that bother me," Tom went on. "The disregard for the former life, the gawking curiosity, the rough handling of the body, the tossing and turning on the embalmer's steel table, the draining of the lifeblood, the cork up the ass—"

"Indignities are personal torts," Metzger offered. "Why worry about it if you're dead? There's no indignity if you are immune to the insult. I don't worry about that; I have greater fears."

"Well, I look forward to it," Crump volunteered, undeterred by the silent reproof of his last comments. "I want to meet Jesus face-to-face. I've got a few questions for Him."

"I'll bet you do," Metzger replied.

"He's got some explaining to do."

Not wanting to allow an opportunity for Crump to elaborate on his blasphemy, Theo asked if they could drop such a morbid subject and get back to the card game. Since he'd lost the earworm and no longer hummed when he had a good hand, his luck had started to change, and although he had a long way to go to master the game of poker, for the first time in his life he felt he could master a secular skill.

Tom agreed with Theo. He just wanted to have Crump shut up and play cards.

He wasn't aggravated by Crump's poor grammar or hokey mannerisms or even his crass invocation of Christ's name every time he won a poker hand, nor was it Crump's theology, which Tom grudgingly acknowledged was not fundamentally different from his own, differing mostly in procedural matters and fine print, that offended him. Unlike himself and Theo, who believed formality best arranged man's relationship with God, Crump was not anchored to any conventional dogma, and he could position himself to be the arbiter of the Bible on any subject, recognizing no learned intermediary or schooled interpreter, such as the Pope or even Martin Luther, necessary for an adequate understanding of the sacred texts. Tom saw Crump as a madding interpreter of his own truth, ungrounded and unprincipled, and he resented the preacher's unconstrained freedom just to be. So it was for that, to an extent, Tom felt some jealousy when thinking about Crump's freedom to navigate spiritual waters, but he also was certain the preacher's position was like a rudderless ship, destined to be splintered against the rocks and shoals of hard times at the first rush of evil winds.

When he searched his soul, Tom had to admit there was another, and related, rudiment of the evangelical's personality which irked him: it was the man's innate recklessness. He sensed a maverick streak of unpredictability when the man played his hand, rarely folding a bad one, raising and re-raising and calling the bet, while holding questionable cards with an aggravating cocksureness that remained even when he was shown to be wrong. Tom figured this audaciousness likely imbued all aspects of the man's life, and sitting next to him at the card table was akin to sitting next to a ticking bomb, and it made the old-line priest a little nervous.

At the moment, however, Tom didn't feel additional antipathy toward Crump because he'd offended Brian Metzger. He'd become weary of the Methodist, and not because of what he was, but because of what he wasn't: there was so little to him, yet he was large and moved ponderously, crossing and uncrossing his heavy legs, lifting his right hand with great effort when reaching for his cards, seeming to struggle to raise the heavy signet ring that looked to have grown into the flesh of his finger, a gold ring with Southern Methodist University, Dedman College circumscribing a Greek Revival relief on the face, the Greek letters ΠΚΛ on one shoulder and a pair of crossed golf clubs on the other shoulder. A country club chaplain, insouciant and bored. Tom heard other Texans describe a man like Metzger in their own unique idiom: he was all hat and no cattle.

Tom admitted his assessment of both Crump and Metzger were unchristian, but over time he'd come to trust his instincts. And he could pray for forgiveness.

Although he fancied himself a pretty good judge of character, he still was having trouble adjudging Theo's. For reasons that were not yet clear to him, he'd not grown bored with or contemptuous of Pastor Swindberg or his oddities, and he felt compelled to study him more closely during a recent card game. He didn't do so to discover another tell among the man's fidgets and twitches and fingernail biting, but to discover what substance there was to the man who, unlike Metzger, likely had unsounded depth. During their card game, Tom studied Swindberg so closely he was distracted by his quirks to the point he himself played sloppy poker, made a misdeal, and absentmindedly threw at least one winning hand onto the discard pile.

The Lutheran seemed to have character, but it was always hidden behind a doleful facade. So to Tom, Theo's principal oddity was his state of perpetual gloom, and out of that gloom arose the twitches and fidgets and nail biting and lesser peculiarities. He seldom smiled and rarely made small talk, even about issues within his religious ambit. There were times, however, when they were playing cards and Theo was immersed in the game, Tom could see a glint in the man's eye, but whether it was a fleeting spark of enjoyment or a lambent expression of momentary insight, Tom couldn't tell. It was as if any brief light of joy retreated behind a meddlesome cloud that floated across Theo's mood along with the next card dealt to him, blocking any revelatory light, leaving the man in gloomy resignation. At those moments, Tom wondered if Theo was in fact a Virgo who'd never had an entire day of fun in his life. Yet, Pastor Swindberg never missed a gathering of the club, played a pretty good hand of cards, drank a beer or two, and was always pleasant. He spoke when he was spoken to, and although he was glum even when winning, he was the only player who offered after each game to stay behind with Tom to clean up.

Unbeknownst to Tom, Theo did have fun and did enjoy the card games and even more so enjoyed the time alone with Tom after the card game. And although Theo seldom offered a word, he listened attentively while the priest rattled on about one mundane subject or another as they straightened up the rathskeller. Theo had two self-assigned tasks. The first was to shake the crumbs and motes off the tablecloth. Tom took mischievous delight in watching Theo handle the tablecloth. He'd carefully remove it from the table, shake it, place it back on the table and methodically press out the wrinkles and folds with the palm of his hand. Tom considered telling Theo the origin of the cloth, but instead took a jokester's delight in watching the venerable Lutheran pastor take painstaking care of the Catholic altar cloth. He would wait to tell him when the timing was right, he decided, and when he did it would be a great good joke.

Once the altar cloth was rid of every little particle and neatly placed on the table, Theo, with broom and dustpan in hand, swept clean the floor around the table. The first time he took on the job Tom covertly watched as Theo deftly worked the broom around and under the table and chairs, showing himself to be a man unsurprisingly adept at keeping things tidy. And as he watched him working the broom to whisk the rough concrete floor, Tom couldn't help thinking the skinny clergyman could have stood sideways and hid himself behind the broomstick to avoid being seen performing what another might consider a demeaning task. But Theo appeared uncharacteristically animated, almost gay, as he worked, as if cleaning the floor was a spiritual task which permitted him to dump the dark cloud that loomed over him in perpetuity into the trash can along with the dirt and crumbs he'd swept from the floor.

As they tidied up after the card games, Tom made small talk while Theo politely listened and offered a diffident response or two while diligently sweeping. The priest enjoyed talking about baseball, of which Theo knew only a little. Not wishing to betray his ignorance of the subject, he didn't join in the conversation, other than to offer a polite yes or no or a shrug of the shoulders, and he let Tom monopolize the conversations. Tom was a great fan of all baseball and particularly the local professional team, the St. Louis Cardinals. He watched as many games as he could on television and listened to games on the radio if he was driving or piddling in his rose garden. He had insight into the players and the plays, which he was always happy to share with Theo with an air of authority. He wasn't rude or tiresome about it; it was just that Theo was a polite listener, which allowed Tom to babble on, unchallenged, as long as he cared to, making observations and pronouncements and predictions, citing statistics and numbers and other supporting trivia.

Late at night after the most recent card game, after the cellar was tidied up and Theo had gone home, Father Tom sat at his big desk in the study in contemplation and prayer. Yet, despite his attempts at deep concentration, thoughts of Theo Swindberg intruded on his meditation. He conjured up the image of the man folding the altar cloth, but it didn't seem as funny as it had before. He thought about him moving about nearly noiselessly with the broom, trying to get the last specks from a relentlessly filthy cellar floor, his eyes downcast, his shoulders slumped, but with a purposeful calm around him. Tom got up and poured himself a nightcap, a healthy glassful of cabernet, and gave himself over to the intruding thoughts. He would, once and for all, try to figure out what it was that had attracted his attention to the Lutheran pastor since the inception of his plan for the poker club.

As he sat at his desk sipping wine, looking at Theo from every conceivable angle, he eliminated objectionable traits such as vainglory and arrogance out of hand. Theo, although very bright, had neither of these characteristics. He considered that the man might simply be taciturn or shy. But even quiet or bashful men aren't necessarily devoid of joy. With that thought, he homed in on Theo's seeming lack of joy. After another glass of wine and considerable thought, he believed he'd isolated in the man's character an essence of anxious sadness. Or perhaps it was unhappiness. Two sides of the same coin. With that, his pastoral spirit took over and he wondered if there was something he might do to lift the man's gloom. Perhaps that was where the signs were pointing all along.

But before he could be of help to Theo, he needed to know the genesis of the man's melancholy. He figured there must be something causative in the man's life. He must certainly be a Scorpio, Tom reasoned, and would tactfully ask him his birthdate at his first opportunity. He then wondered if Theo's predilection for gloom was caused by his biochemistry or his upbringing, or if it was a product of his education, his training, or his theology. His physical makeup was beyond his ken; his background and private life were beyond his reach. He'd heard stories about the Lutherans' dark theology, but he wasn't convinced Theo's temperamental traits were a result of his internalization of church doctrine. Still, he would have to start his inquiry where he had access, so he decided his first step was to find out if Theo's disposition might be, at least in part, caused by a long-term exposure to an occupational hazard.

The following Sunday, after hurrying through his homily and rushing through each of the Rites at eight a.m. Mass, Father Tom excused himself from the queue of parishioners outside St. Michael and walked briskly to the rectory where he changed clothes. He got into his car and drove across town to St. Paul's Lutheran Church. He stepped through the church doors just in time to see Theo and a raft of altar boys ("servers," the Lutherans called them, he learned from the church bulletin he was handed by an usher) walk up the center aisle.

Father Tom had always thought St. Paul's was a magnificent church structure, at least from the outside. He'd driven by it many times and admired its external design. It was constructed from gray stone and had an impressive spire topped with a large concrete cross. The entry was guarded by heavy wooden doors which granted entry to the narthex. Once inside the narthex, he found the interior of the church to be just as grand.

The church had a spacious nave, which he entered quietly once Theo and the servers processed forward far enough up the aisle to divert attention from an obtruder. The nave was furnished with two rows of stout, hardwood pews separated by a parqueted center aisle. He slipped into a back pew just inside the nave and stood respectfully as Theo slowly completed his procession, and the congregation sang all five verses of "Open Now Thy Gates of Beauty," accompanied by an impressive pipe organ that Tom could only hear, but not see, since the organ loft was somewhere over his head and out of his line of sight.

Once the congregation sat down, Tom leaned into the aisle to get a better view of the front of the church. There was a communion rail separating the nave from the chancel, an altar centrally positioned in the chancel, an ornate baptismal font on the right side of the altar, as one observed the altar from the nave, and a complementary ambo on the left side. The altar, font, and ambo were all fashioned from matching wood. There was a massive crucifix, also constructed from matching wood, suspended at the rear of the chancel by thin cables which were, as Tom noticed, barely discernible in the low-level light, giving the impression the cross was levitating over the altar and the officiant.

Theo was decked out in complete vestments, and Father Tom wondered if he followed the same vestment rubric that he followed. The Lutheran was wearing a white alb and a chasuble of the same shade of green as the one he had worn at eight a.m. Mass. There was a cloth runner atop the altar cloth that matched the chasuble. Not only were the vestments similar to his, as the service proceeded, Tom found the order of the liturgy very close to the Catholic liturgy. However, he found the interposed Lutheran hymns ponderous and slow, dark and phlegmatic like Theo himself, and Tom, being a believer in the transformative power of music, made a mental note that perhaps Theo's personality was shaped, in no little part, by his lifelong exposure to melancholy church music.

Theo recited the same Gospel passage Tom had read at Mass. Although the minister was holding an impressive Bible, it was obvious he recited the Gospel from memory, without looking down at the text. Tom found that to be no mean feat since it was a long reading. As in his own liturgy, the sermon followed Theo's recitation of the Gospel, and Tom listened intently for substance, even though he was distracted by Theo's flat and passionless voice. Nevertheless, the sermon was well-delivered but heavy, liberally interlaced with the theme of death. More specifically, the sermon focused on the inevitability of death, the deservedness of death, and the tortuous result of death. As he sat in the pew listening to Theo drone on about each man's inevitable extinction, Tom started to get a better feel for the man's morose psyche. Theo attempted to leaven his dense message toward the end of the sermon by suggesting a sinner could avoid his just desserts by absolute faith in the redemptive death of Christ Jesus. Faith, Theo preached, and not good works, was the key that unlocked the door to Heaven. Tom listened for more uplifting substance, but when it was not forthcoming, he suspected Theo ascribed to the axiom that only a little leavening is needed to leaven the whole loaf.

Tom had looked around the nave as Theo preached, and from the stoic faces of the congregants, he assumed they were inured to Theo's bleak worldview. He concluded the pastor's sermons must follow the same thematic outline, week in and week out, since no one appeared to react to his discomfiting words. He was amazed Theo could get butts in the pews with his message of sin, death, and punishment, all recited to a dismal soundtrack of hymns that resembled funeral dirges. But he admitted he was being uncharitable in his silent critique, and it wasn't until much later that Tom learned Theo's sermons employed the standard "law and gospel" whipsaw which

Lutheran dogma required in every sermon, changing only in costume and cloth. In any event, by the time the liturgy reached the Lord's Supper, Tom recognized the liturgy, as a whole, was based on conventional logia and saw little in the service to that point that could resolve the question as to whether Theo arrived at his ministry with a glum disposition or whether his ministry itself induced in him his glum disposition.

Father Tom was impressed, however, by the orderliness of the Lutheran's exercise of the Rite of Holy Communion. He appreciated how the usher released the communicants pew-by-pew, allowing a small group to approach the communion rail, bow in unison, kneel, take the bread and wine, rise, bow again, and walk solemnly back to their pew. He thought in some ways their ritual compared favorably to his own Eucharist in which parishioners pushed forward in a disorganized queue, took the Body and sometimes the Blood of Christ in a perfunctory or insincere manner, and, in many cases, slipped out the narthex or side entrance rather than go back to their pews for the remainder of Mass.

When the service concluded, Theo and the servers processed down the main aisle as the congregation sang "Lord Dismiss Us with Your Blessing." Pastor Swindberg didn't see Father Tom as he passed the last pew; he was solemnly staring at his shoe tops as he processed out. The congregants were released by the ushers beginning with the front pews. As he watched the congregants in the front pews stand to walk out, Tom noticed a tall, blonde woman step into the aisle. He watched her walk down the aisle toward him with long, assured strides, an agreeable smile on her face, and a glint of cheerful good humor in her eyes. Although he knew his stare was unseemly, he couldn't look away. He continued to watch her as she passed his pew, appreciating the natural sway of her hips, which cast the hem of her skirt against his knee. He felt a catch in his breath as he turned at the waist to watch her walk out the narthex.

Father Tom's was the last pew released, and he stood impatiently in line with the congregants as they passed through the narthex in Pastor Swindberg's receiving line. He checked his watch incessantly, calculating the length of time it would take to drive back to St. Michael for 10:30 a.m. Mass. When he finally moved out of the building and down the front steps, he found it a lovely morning, warm but not humid, a pleasant breeze rustling the leaves of the mammoth sweetgum trees in the churchyard. The fine weather was salutary, and he relaxed, figuring he had only a few paces to go to say hello to Theo and head back to his church.

Father Tom was the last person in line, and when he approached Theo and reached out to shake his hand, he thought he saw a brief flash of panic in the pastor's eyes. Yet, he couldn't be certain of what he saw because he was nearly face-to-face with the lovely blonde woman he'd watched walk down the aisle. She was standing at Theo's left elbow, and her complete lightness of aspect, which was antipodal to Theo's overall darkness, nearly blinded him. He stood dumbly in front of Theo, blinking, until Theo finally said, "Naomi, this is a friend of mine, Tom Abernathy. Tom, this is my wife, Naomi."

When Father Tom offered Naomi his hand, she pressed it warmly, and he looked down at her long, pale fingers and felt an uncharacteristic self-consciousness at the sight of his knit shirt stretched tautly across his belly. He wanted to say something, a greeting of some sort, but his hampered breath wouldn't let him speak. He just nodded politely and looked up and saw a good-humored twinkle in her eye that was consubstantial with the light of her being, and later, when he thought of little else other than her, he wondered if the little Lutheran pastor had ever experienced the full power of her beautiful light.

As he walked away from the church, he turned to catch one

more glimpse of the woman standing next to Theo. He was fascinated. She was not beautiful in the conventional sense; the totality of her being made her lovely beyond words. He could hear her chattering with the ladies who had walked ahead of him in the receiving line but who now were gathered in a giggling clutch around the pastor's wife. He could hear her peals of laughter above theirs. He took an involuntary inventory of her features from afar to commit to memory, but it was unsatisfying because he already had stood within arm's reach of her and saw up close how striking her features were. Nevertheless, he noted she was robust, at least as tall as her husband, with strawberry blonde hair brushed back from her forehead and tucked behind her ears. Her skin was fair and flawless and complementary to her hair color. She was shapely, with fine shoulders, womanly hips, and lean muscular legs. She stood erect, her chin elevated, not in haughtiness but with an air of easy self-assurance. He also committed her clothing to memory; she was wearing a common white blouse and a cotton skirt, mid-calf length, fashioned from mint green fabric with a yellow flower print. He didn't readily recognize the flowers from a distance, but he knew they weren't yellow roses. Perhaps they were Heliopsis.

At the curb, he turned to listen one more time to her laugh, to see her broad smile, to watch the soft folds of her cotton skirt circumscribe the curves and crevices of her form in the morning breeze until he could barely breathe. As he stared at the couple, it struck him that Naomi's laugh and cheerful manner were in stark contrast to Theo's dour disposition and whatever it was that sustained her husband's doleful world-view, it did not originate with her. He lingered a bit longer, enjoying her laugh, finding it both charming and uplifting, and decided a man could not be in a bad mood hearing that laugh. A normal man, that is.

It wasn't until he was in his car driving back to St. Michael that Father Tom could freely breathe again. He was so flummoxed by his array of feelings and by the mental image of Theo's wife standing splay-footed and relaxed, chin up, the morning breeze blowing softly around and between her sturdy legs, that he drove past the crosstown boulevard, which was the most direct route between St. Paul's and St. Michael. He found himself on the south edge of town, and when he craned his neck to read the street signs, he was startled to see Billy Crump's smiling face overhead on a billboard, smug and condescending, his sharp eyes cutting straight into him. It immediately occurred to him the billboard was placed right where it was just for this moment, positioned so he would look up and see Crump's accusatory smile.

Was it a godsend, that little bastard's face on the billboard? A sign? Although he didn't have the memory for scripture Theo possessed, he had committed a few verses to memory he felt were particularly useful and pragmatic, and Crump's face caused him to recall Galatians, Chapter Five: "This I say then, walk in the Spirit, and ye shall not fulfill the lust of the flesh." Walk in the spirit, he told himself; occupy your mind with good. He began to recite the rosary, focusing on the routine exercise, leaving no room in his thoughts for the comely Naomi Swindberg. By the time he'd finished the first decade, he was pulling into the rectory garage. He parked and hurried into the house to change into his vestments for 10:30 a.m. Mass.

CHAPTER SEVEN

That Sunday night as he tossed and turned in his bed, Father Tom couldn't rid Naomi Swindberg from his thoughts. He found it a wicked trick of the mind, as he lay in the dark, that he could see her standing at the foot of his bed, laughing, the yellow flowers on her skirt glowing eerily in the dark. And despite covering his head with his pillow and reciting the rosary out loud, he could hear her voice, hear her laughter, and in her words and laughter was disclosed everything he wanted to know about her, significant and insignificant, yet he couldn't comprehend it. It was as if he perceived all things about her from the apparition, not in a form that could be expressed in words, but as an ethereal essence embodying his long-suppressed salacity in a form that defied words. Even though she spilled out more of her essence with every peal of laughter, he didn't recognize her impletion; it was as if her soul was speaking to him in tongues in girlish mockery of the fat, old priest whom she'd rendered speechless just by pressing his hand outside St. Paul's that morning.

He knew Naomi wasn't in his room, but her image and voice were so real, so lifelike, he could barely breathe, and he sweated heavily as he labored for air. He tossed his pillow, damp with sweat, on the floor and lay flat on the mattress. He turned to prayer to rid himself of thoughts of Theo's wife, and as he lay on his back in the dark, he prayed and prayed evermore fervently. He prayed that God would show him one flaw in her, just one flaw, so he could see she was not in reality perfect, but only perfect in her apparitional state. But in the dark, God disclosed to him no blemish or defect. And as he again visualized her standing in front of the church in the morning breeze, her loose skirt fluttering around and between her legs, he was disconcerted by the despicable sensation of a watery mouth and swallowed repeatedly to rid himself of saliva.

He tried praying again, and as he prayed, Father Tom's thoughts wandered from Naomi to Theo until he finally gave up on the prayers and concentrated on Theo, reasoning that by concentrating on the husband, he could temper his improper fascination with the wife. Soon, however, his thoughts circled back around and circumscribed both of them with wonderment. He wondered how Theo could be such a dour old prig with Naomi in his life. He wondered if Theo knew what he had in the woman, or if he appreciated her as a mate. He wondered if Theo had a prurient bone in his body. He wondered if Theo ever slipped into the bathroom after Naomi bathed to smell the sweet confection of her soaps and powders as he had done as a boy after his mother's bath. In his wonderment, he imagined Naomi sitting on the edge of the tub wrapped only in a towel, slowly working lotion into the soles of her feet, and with that, he realized his wonderings had gone too far but he was at a loss as to how to stop them.

"Cleanse me from secret faults, Lord, and spare your servant from sins to which I am tempted by another," Tom spoke out loud, reciting a favorite psalm of St. Augustine who, through his writings, was a spiritual mentor and moral conscience for men like him consumed by sins of the flesh. But images of Naomi at her bath intruded on his Augustinian prayer. Old priests had a cure for thoughts like these, he reminded himself, and those cures went beyond mere prayer. He considered getting out of bed and going into the back yard and cutting a stout willow switch from the tree overhanging Cat's grave, but he was exhausted and admitted that he could beat himself bloody and raw and she still would invade his thoughts. He lay there for hours until he finally rid himself of all thoughts of

Naomi by slipping into a hypnopompic state wherein he was haunted by another female voice:

"Tommy!"

"Yes, Mama?" he whined in his stupefaction.

"Get up and get ready for school."

"I'm tired, Mama; I want to sleep a while longer."

"No, Tommy, get up now. I'm leaving for work. I don't want to worry about you falling back to sleep and being late for school."

"I'll get up, Mama. I promise."

"Now?"

"I'm awake, Mama."

"That's my sweet lamb, my sweet boy. Your lunch is on the sideboard; when I get home from work, I'll make you a good supper, you hear?"

"Yes, Mama."

"And no fighting today."

"No, Mama."

"I don't want any more notes from the Sisters, you understand?"

"Yes, ma'am."

"And do your chores when you get home."

"I will."

"I know you will, Tommy, my sweet boy, my sweet little lamb."

Father Tom awoke Monday morning, tired and dispirited from the lack of restful sleep. He'd slept, but restlessly and only in brief fits, as eidolic laughter and womanly voices insinuated themselves into his smattery dreams. But he forced himself to get out of bed to begin the week. He looked at the clock and realized he had to hurry to get cleaned up and ready for morning Mass. He had no time for coffee and struggled across the churchyard, slipped unseen into the sacristy, and donned a cassock and alb. He stepped out into the chancel and appreciated that Monday morning Mass was always poorly attended, which suited him just fine. He recited the opening words of the liturgy either staring down at the text or casting his words aimlessly over the heads of the calculable elderly who peopled weekday Mass. He conducted the liturgy half-heartedly, and in his fatigue, repeated much of Sunday's homily. He relied on routine to muddle through his priestly duties, both during Mass and during the rest of the day. Monday evening he sat at the edge of his rose garden and sipped wine until the combination of wine and fatigue rendered him enervated and he trudged up to his bedroom and collapsed on his bed and slept.

And all that week, Father Tom struggled to get up in the mornings. During the day, he tried to keep busy, to keep his mind off Theo and Naomi and focus on his duties to his parish. He said morning Mass, attended obligatory meetings of the Parish Council and Finance Committee on Tuesday evening, and made visits to the sick. The evenings he had no meeting, he tried to occupy his mind by piddling in the rose garden, weeding, pruning, and mulching until darkness forced him inside. Once inside, he spent the rest of the evening and into the night reading scripture, praying, and preparing his homily. When he met his spiritual obligations, he treated himself to a glass or two of wine and watched the last few innings of the baseball game on television. He was in luck that week because the Cardinals were playing games on the West Coast and the telecast lasted late into the night. He watched television until he nodded off, and hopeful of a decent night's sleep, roused himself, turned off the set and made his way up to his bed.

This he did a couple of nights, and consequently Wednesday and Thursday nights he had near-restful nights' sleep. But by Friday, as the weekend drew near, thoughts of Naomi nearly overwhelmed him. Beginning Friday night, her specter breached his dreams, and he awakened with a start, angry that he couldn't shake his infatuation. And infatuation is how he finally justified his feelings. An innocuous, childish infatuation which should be easily overcome by a grown man, particularly a middle-aged priest. He admitted to himself that his fiery infatuation with Naomi Swindberg was kindled by the brief and unexpected encounter he had with her the previous Sunday outside St. Paul's as she stood next to Theo in the receiving line. And he reasoned that because he'd only seen her one time, and very briefly at that, she'd become enlarged in his mind, an outsized darling of his thoughts.

Perhaps she was an icon to which he endowed more appealing attributes than she deserved, he told himself. It may well be, he then reasoned, that her allure was potent only because of the weakness of his character precipitated by the loneliness he felt more acutely since he lost his pet. Moreover, she made such an impression because he'd not expected to find anyone like her married to Theo Swindberg. He finally convinced himself that if he steeled himself and saw her again, just one more time, he'd be prepared to see her in a different light, and she would assume more realistic proportions in his imagination, and he would rid himself of his infatuation. Another furtive look at Naomi would desensitize him like an allergy shot, he concluded, and allow his natural defenses to alleviate the irritant.

Father Tom figured Sunday morning Theo, being a punctilious little bastard, would adhere to his rigid liturgical schedule and start processing down the center aisle of his church toward the exit at a minute or two after ten o'clock, with Naomi in his wake, and he decided to drive past St. Paul's at just the right time to see her standing out front next to her husband. So, after eight a.m. Mass, he changed into a plaid shirt and a baseball cap and sunglasses. He chuckled at his reflection as he walked past the study window and wondered if old Cat would recognize the shifty old priest if he were to suddenly come back from the dead like Lazarus. He sat down at his desk and stared at the clock on the wall. He started having misgivings about the plan, but he knew of no other remedy. Contemplation and prayer were failing him. He had no one to talk to about his feelings. Once he saw her, and realized she was a mere woman, he could move on.

He waited in his car at the end of the block just past St. Paul's. When Theo stepped out of the narthex and headed down the church steps, Tom put his car in gear and moved slowly down the street toward him. Theo took his position and stood stalwartly and glumly, a Lutheran hymnal in hand, waiting to meet his congregants. As Tom rolled nearer Theo, he lowered his car window and heard the exit hymn echoing from within St. Paul's nave—"Abide, O faithful Savior, among us with Thy love; Grant steadfastness and help us…" as the congregants began their exodus. However, he went deaf as Naomi stepped through the church doors and walked toward Theo. There she was, just as Tom had imagined her for a week, bright and attractive and perfectly formed, wearing a blue sheath skirt, white, buttoned blouse and stylish ecru heels, which made her stand almost a head taller than her husband. Although he couldn't hear a thing, Tom kept the car window open as he moved slowly toward Theo and her. He could see she was engaged in a lively conversation with another woman, and just when he was parallel to her, she threw her head back and laughed the merriest, most charming laugh he'd ever heard, and he reflexively praised God for restoring his hearing at just that moment.

He felt his heart pounding, looked away, and being careful to avoid bowling over a group of congregants crossing the street, pulled away quickly from the curb and headed back to the rectory. When he got home, he went upstairs to his bedroom to change clothes for 10:30 a.m. Mass. He threw the ball cap and shirt on the floor in disgust. He was lightheaded. He paced back and forth, barely able to lift a foot, stumbling and swaying, but not stopping. He could feel his old rage rise in his chest, and when he stopped near the head of his bed, he drew back his right hand and drove his fist through the papered wall, just under the porcelain crucifix, which was left swinging ominously like a pendulum on its hanging nail as he stared mutely at the damage done.

CHAPTER EIGHT

After a recent meeting, Father Tom admitted to himself the St. Michael Poker & Drinking Club was a failure, at least from his point of view. He sat at his desk in the study and considered dissolving the club. He no longer looked forward to the company of the men as he had in the weeks immediately after convening the club. In truth, the group had done little to assuage his pervasive loneliness which, sitting at his desk, he felt more acutely than ever before. His loneliness was aggravated by his chance encounter with Naomi Swindberg.

The only aspect of the meetings he really enjoyed and lifted his spirits, if he was honest, was the time he spent alone with Theo straightening the basement. But this time also exacerbated his feelings of guilt. An unintended consequence of forming the club was that he was burdened by an intense and sinful infatuation with another man's wife, which was reason enough to disband the group. Each time he sat across the card table from Theo or worked quietly alongside him tidying the cellar, he was tempted to blurt out his feelings for Naomi to relieve the awful pressure that had built up in his soul. Theo's quiet decency flummoxed him; familiarity had caused him to be even more bewildered by Reverend Swindberg. During the poker games, Theo remained punctilious and dour but unwaveringly polite, playing each hand in an estimable way, never overplaying and never relying on the bluff, and this caused Tom added consternation. He wanted to dislike Naomi's husband.

He wanted to place the blame for his disappointment in the club on the other two players. As he sat at his desk he tried to resist dwelling on the off-putting idiosyncrasies of these men that inspired his animus. He'd obsessed over them enough, he knew, and it was petty and uncharitable. Yet, three months of meetings had confirmed his earlier assessments of the other two men. Billy Crump proved himself to be an impulsive gadfly. He refused to fold bad hands, bet recklessly, and if he lucked into a pot, he was loud and aggravating and sometimes profane in his casual invocation of Christ's name. During the game the prior evening, Crump took Tom to the raise limit on an ace high, and when he called, Tom laid down three jacks, causing Crump to cackle and crow, "Looky there, looky there, praise Jesus," as Tom raked in the pot. What galled Tom even more was his supposition Billy's character traits indicated the man may well be an Aries, like himself. And Billy's stories continued to wear thin. He'd told his funniest anecdotes at the early meetings, then moved on to dark and humorless stories. And when these failed to get the reaction he wanted, he resorted to repeating plot lines of earlier tales with variations only in the operative details, which caused Tom to dismiss all of Billy's stories as so much bullshit. Except, that is, the story about Billy dancing across the revival stage. Tom acknowledged the little man could dance.

Metzger, over time, continued to overplay his affability and confirmed Tom's assessment the appealing trait was superficial and transitory. Tom couldn't put his finger on precisely why Metzger declined in his estimation, but he thought it might be related to an emerging hauteur which Metzger earlier had concealed. His disinterest and obvious distraction implied he was there only in his big body; his thoughts were elsewhere, and Tom was suspect. Had Metzger taken the measure of the other men, as he was prone to do, and found himself to be a cut above? Did he have a competing interest outside the group? Tom began to lose the good feelings he'd had for the man when he knew him only as a co-presider at Lenten ecumenical services.

Giving into temptation, Father Tom grudgingly admitted there was another aspect of the man's personality that added to his devaluation in his estimation. It was Metzger's excruciatingly noncommittal, tippy-toeing approach to each hand of poker. It was a petty consideration, but Tom considered it all the same. During recent games, his bets and raises were equivocal; his decisions to stay in or fold were chary and time-consuming. The Methodist demonstrated pernicious inaction which disclosed an aggravating timidity and indecisiveness or distraction, traits which were off-putting to a man like Tom Abernathy. For a big man, there wasn't much there, is how Tom summed up his estimation of Brian Metzger, and he imagined him to be a Libra.

Father Tom wasn't proud of his tendency to evaluate the worth of other men like one would grade livestock or vegetables. He thought it unchristian. And since he'd met Theo and Naomi, his heart was filled with the most grievous of sins, and he took pains to order his thoughts and behavior to counterbalance the weight of transgression on his soul. As he sat quietly in his study, he considered perhaps it were his own character flaws which caused him to devalue the Methodist and the evangelical preacher, and he tried to be more charitable in his consideration of the men. He prayed for both men; prayed for strength to love both men. But he still considered folding the club.

It wasn't altruism or Christian charity that moved him to cast the two in a more benevolent light; he knew it was selfishness and fear which prompted him to do so. Lately, he took to worrying about the disposition of his own immortal soul, which until recently he took for granted was safe in the arms of the angels. He considered seeing a fellow priest for the Rite of Reconciliation. He'd not been so discouraged about the arc of his life since the lost days after he left Benedictine College and abandoned his mother, and although she'd forgiven him many years before her death, he still grieved for the pain he'd caused her, particularly when he was melancholy and lonely, as he was now, staring at his mother's picture placed on his desk.

As he had done many times over the years, rather than seeking formal Reconciliation, he relived his lost days as a form of punishment or penance, he wasn't sure which. He was just a kid, barely twenty years old and recently booted out of college, when he packed a few changes of clothes, underwear, and toiletries in an old valise and walked from his mother's house to the bus station. He looked at the schedule on the wall and bought a ticket on a bus headed to St. Louis with the money he'd taken from his mother's pocketbook. He had no particular reason for heading to St. Louis, other than the next bus leaving the station was bound for St. Louis.

He got off the bus in a small town along the route when the driver made a stop to pick up more passengers. He went into the dingy station and used the men's room and bought a sandwich, but when the other passengers climbed on the bus he didn't re-board. He heard the driver sound the horn and dodged out a back door when the driver came in to account for his passenger. He loped away from the bus station, turned and watched the bus pull out. He walked up and down the streets near the bus station until he found furnished rooms for rent, immediate occupancy. He walked back to the bus station and called the landlord from the phone booth, met him within the hour, and paid two weeks rent in advance from the stash in his pants pocket. He bummed some bedclothes—two sheets, a blanket, and a pillow—off his landlord. He made the bed and unpacked his suitcase.

His rooms were of the quality one would expect to be rented to a young man with poor prospects for weekly rent. They were one half of a shabby clapboard duplex, but they accommodated his meager needs. He had a tiny living room, a kitchen, a bath, and a bedroom. A skinny dope dealer and his woman occupied the other half of the duplex. Tom figured out the couple's business by watching the parade of scraggly visitors going in and out at all hours of the day and night. At first, he thought the girl was whoring. And perhaps she was, but he later discovered their primary business was selling drugs. He didn't pass judgment. He didn't have a taste for the stuff himself, but what others did was their business. He preferred alcohol in those days, and he frequented several seedy bars within walking distance of the duplex.

The day after he moved in, he began looking for work. He bought the daily paper and walked to the bus station to call prospective employers. He was just about broke when he found a job as an unskilled laborer on a construction crew. He'd been walking around town knocking on doors when he saw a sign on a chain link fence: HIRING. Inside the fence, Tom saw a couple backhoes, a skid loader, stacks of concrete forms, a couple cement mixers and piles of sand and gravel. Moving around among the implements of work were a couple young men about his age. He went inside the office and told the man sitting at a desk he was looking for a job. The man looked him over pretty good and remarked that he seemed to be well-muscled, stout enough to handle a laborer's job. When he asked Tom if he had any experience, Tom told him the only experience he had was a week's worth of looking for work. The boss remarked it didn't take a goddamned Einstein to shovel rock and sand and carry hod, and if he wasn't a goddamned troublemaker, he'd hire him on and make good use of him, if he was willing to work hard.

Tom worked hard on the job, and the boss was happy with him, and he put away some money to send to his mother. He bought a small television and had a telephone installed. But he rarely watched television and never called anyone. He was a loner who usually left the job site right after work. Most evenings he would go home, take a quick shower, and go back out for the evening. Some nights, he'd eat; some nights, he didn't bother to eat. One night a week, he played softball on the company team. Most nights, he'd stagger home drunk, weave around the cars parked in front of the duplex, fiddle with the front door key, and plop down on his bed, sometimes too drunk to undress. There were times, if the alcohol had not rendered him insentient, he'd lay on the bed and think about his mother, vowing to call her first thing the next morning, tell her where he was, apologize for taking her money and swear he was going to pay her back, but he never did. As time went by, the thought of calling her made him edgy and self-conscious to the point he quit considering it at all.

Sometimes, his evening spent in a bar ended with him and another patron rolling around on the barroom floor or the parking lot gravel to settle some real or imagined grievance. The hard work made his body lean and tough and he fancied himself a pretty good scrapper. He loved to fight. When he drank, he got obnoxious and feisty, and there always was someone at the bar ready to take up the challenge. Most times, he came out on top, but he found himself banned from a couple of his favorite watering holes. He always was embarrassed when he sobered up, but the embarrassment didn't dissuade him from looking for trouble when he drank, and he often drank.

As he sat in his study, a middle-aged priest, he could feel his face flush as he thought about those lost days and the singular event that caused him to bring those days to an abrupt end. He considered the memory of whom he once was to be his most valuable moral asset. He made himself think about the young man he once was as a form of self-flagellation, particularly when he was overwhelmed by the burden of his own sin. Sitting at his desk, he recognized the seminal event of his lost days was apposite to his inappropriate thoughts about Naomi, and he forced himself to visit that event once again.

It was a Sunday morning when he woke up on the living room floor in his duplex. He tried to open his eyes, but he could do no more than squint. He touched his eyes and found them swollen, with only slits to see through. He rolled over and felt a searing pain in the ribs on his left side. The pain was so sharp he wanted to vomit, but he hurt too much to stand, so he crawled across the floor into the bathroom. He held onto the sink and pulled himself up, but when he looked in the mirror his face was so grotesquely disfigured he was nearly unrecognizable to himself. His eyes were purple and swollen. The bridge of his nose had a grape-sized lump and appeared to be broken. He had a gash through his lower lip down to his chin. His shirt was covered in dried blood. He leaned over the toilet and retched, but the pain in his ribs was so intense he couldn't bring himself to vomit.

He lowered himself to the floor and crawled back into the living room. He lay on the floor and tried to breathe slowly through his mouth. His foray into the bathroom had caused his mouth and chin to start bleeding, and he swallowed repeatedly to keep from choking on fresh blood. He calmed himself to keep from panicking. As he lay there, he desperately tried to piece together the events from the night before, as if doing so would piece together his damaged body.

He remembered standing at the end of the bar drinking beer, holding onto the bar to keep from falling down. He was woefully drunk and felt rancorous and low, his feelings aggravated by loneliness and by the abject disdain he believed others in the bar were showing him. No one spoke, he remembered, but he imagined their thoughts, and he stared ominously at one guy until the man cursed him and asked what the fuck he was staring at. That much he remembered. But the confrontation didn't go anywhere when he challenged him; the guy just laughed and said he didn't want to fight the town drunk.

Tom remembered picking up his coins from the bar and

staggering to the jukebox. He dropped some coins in the slot and pushed the buttons. The music started to blare, and he was too drunk to stand still, so he tried to dance around the room to keep from falling down. At first, he danced alone, banging into barstools and drinkers and tables until he headed for a cute little blonde sitting at a table with her man. He grabbed her roughly by the arm and pulled her up and tried to spin her around. Lying on the floor of his duplex bleeding, he recalled the frightened and disgusted look on her face when he pulled her close and tried to kiss her. As he swallowed his blood, it all came flooding back: he'd made a play for another man's wife. He recalled her husband was big and brutish and grabbed him by the shirt and pulled him away from his woman and punched him in the face. Tom swung wildly and fell on the floor, and the man pounced on him, rolled him over, and sitting on his chest, punched his eyes and nose and mouth with both hands. Finally, when Tom's eyes were swollen shut and he was choking on blood, a couple of guys pulled the man off, but as Tom was dragged away, the man came back at him, kicking him two or three times in the ribs with the toe of his work boot.

Tom lay on the floor of his duplex, battered and bleeding and trying to recall how he got home. He tried to reconstruct the minutes after his beating. He remembered the bartender giving him a bar towel to stanch the blood flowing from a gash that ran from his lower lip to his chin before he told him to get out and never come back. He recalled that he couldn't see to walk home, so one of the other barflies led him home like a horse in blinders. The guy opened the front door and pushed him in, and he staggered forward and passed out on the floor, where he still lay after his aborted foray into the bathroom. He rested his head on the floor, stared at the ceiling, and contemplated his situation. He knew he was damaged but wasn't sure how badly. He didn't know what to do. He needed help but didn't know where to turn. He grabbed the telephone cord and pulled the telephone off the end table. He dialed his mother's number. She answered only with his name:

"Tommy?"

"Mama, can you come and get me?"

"I knew you'd call, Tommy. I went to Mass this morning and prayed to the Holy Mother that today you'd call. I knew you would call."

"Mama, can you come and get me?"

"Of course, Tommy. I'll come and get you."

He told his mother where he'd been hiding out, the name of the little town and the street address of his shabby duplex. He hung up the phone and lay on the floor and wept. And it hurt terribly to cry.

Now, as he sat at his fancy desk in the study of the St. Michael rectory looking at his mother's picture and having wicked thoughts about another man's wife, he was disgraced by thoughts of his beating. Yet, he didn't feel sufficiently chastened, so he rubbed his finger along the vertical scar that trailed from his lower lip to the cleft in his chin, and as he did so, he felt the tempering heat of ignominy, and it was good.

CHAPTER NINE

The most recent evening they cleaned up after the poker game, Theo had amazed Father Tom with his knowledge of the current baseball standings, as well as the team records and statistics that put the teams in their places. Without looking up from his broom and dustpan, Theo began discussing baseball, in general, and the St. Louis Cardinals in particular, supporting his comments with an array of arcane numbers and percentages, which informed Tom that Theo had done considerable homework on the subject. The comments he made as he swept the cellar floor seemed incongruous coming with such assurance and force from the usually deferential pastor.

From the first gathering of the club, Tom had taken Theo for a bright man, so his grasp of this minutia was not all that surprising; what Tom did find surprising, however, was how Theo had invested himself in the subject and was eager to cash in on his investment. It was apparent to Tom that Pastor Swindberg had watched the ball game on television the previous evening when he made pointed comments about the team's inability to move runners along. In the course of the game, the Cardinals had stranded at least eight runners on base, Theo said. And it was a chronic problem, he pointed out, supporting his remarks with the team's anemic batting average with runners in scoring position. Theo also pointed to the team's lack of stolen bases, citing the number of attempts, the low number of successful steals, and the corresponding high percentage of men thrown out due to stealing. As he listened, Tom found Theo's comments and opinions not only interesting and well supported in fact but also consonant with his own thoughts. Tom tossed in his own observations regarding the team's shortcomings, such as its overall lack of team speed and paucity of good throwing arms in the outfield. He countered Theo with his opinions as to ways to improve the roster. The two clerics finally agreed, as they fussed with their domestic chores, that the local big-league team's manager had to go.

"Did you ever play baseball, Tom?" Theo asked, as he stored the broom and dustpan in the corner, reluctant to have the conversation end.

"I played when I was a kid. Everybody played baseball in those days. I played in high school, too. Played some intramural at college," he added, then stopped abruptly when he realized where even a casual comment might lead. He did not want to provide Theo with a segue into his lost days. He didn't want Theo to ask him anything about his college days and he certainly didn't want Theo to pry into the life he'd led after he dropped out of college. He didn't want to tell Theo the truth, which he would have been required by his conscience to do, if he asked.

The truth was, he had continued to play ball after he left Benedictine, but he didn't care to share the details with Theo or anyone else. Tom slowly dried the inside of the ice chest with a rag, while Theo quietly puttered around the table, making sure the bags of chips were closed, smoothing the tablecloth, and arranging the chairs in an orderly alignment, deferential to Tom's silence.

Still, by the time he finished wiping out the ice chest, Tom was so thoroughly immersed in reverie prompted by Theo's question, he stood silently staring at the empty cooler as if it secreted memories from his youth. What Theo's question about playing ball caused Tom to conjure up was a suppressed memory of a specific incident related to ball playing, an unseemly and embarrassing event from his lost days, and the details he recalled weren't pretty and caused him to blush with shame thinking about them with Theo in the room.

During the time he was hiding out, after he'd been on the job with the construction gang about a week, one of his co-workers asked him if he wanted to play on the company softball team. They needed players, the fellow said, and Tom looked like a guy who could hold his own on a ball diamond. The company team, his workmate explained, was one of eight teams in a men's slow-pitch softball league, and the team rosters for the most part comprised tradesmen and laborers and construction workers and farm hands. They played Wednesday evenings in the city park on a poorly lit diamond that was functional, but rough. The field suited their style of play, the guy added with a laugh. Wear a cup, he was warned, and a mouthguard might be a good idea, too. It wasn't baseball, Tom understood, but close enough, and he jumped at the chance to play. He saw it as a way to get out of his room and hang around with other men and do something other than hang in the bars and get drunk, at least on Wednesday nights.

When he showed up for his first game, the first thing Tom realized was he likely had wasted the money he'd spent on new sneakers; several of his teammates were ready to play in high top work boots. His team was a motley collection of good old boys, some of whom had a gift for the game and others not. His buddy from the job who managed the team was sitting on a bench along the third base line making out the lineup and told Tom he'd be playing third base and batting last in the order, at least until he got an idea how he could hit, which Tom thought was fair and suited him just fine.

The second thing Tom realized was the guy stuck him at third base because no one else wanted to play the position. In slow-pitch softball, as Tom soon learned, the ball is pitched underhanded and loops down toward home plate from a slow, high arc, which provoked aggressive batters and one-night-a-week wonders to swing the bat with all their might. There were generally two outcomes: the hitter would pop up or hit the ball viciously. Also, most hitters tended to pull the ball and since most batters were right-handed, Tom, in his first inning at third, got plenty of action. Fielding chances at third were not without risk. The infield was rough and ill-kept, with clods of dirt and exposed rocks that caused the ball to take random bounces or wacky caroms if it struck a chunk of crap just right. In his first inning in the field, Tom took a few glancing blows off his chest and thighs, but he kept the ball in front of him and made the plays, which caused his teammates to hoot and holler and laugh. Between innings he'd rearrange the bulk in his crotch, repositioning the jock and cup he wore under his jeans. After the first inning, as he sat on the bench drinking a can of beer, the guy next to him showed him a chipped front tooth and a bruised jaw he'd earned playing third the week before Tom joined the team.

Now, as Tom stood in the rectory cellar, ice chest in hand, his memory gravitated to one particular softball game on one particular Wednesday night late in that particular softball season of his lost days. His team was tied for first place in the league, and the two teams were scheduled to play a playoff game. After getting clobbered in the gut and chest and legs by unpredictable balls in the first few games he played, Tom made it his business to carry a rake home from the job and he'd spend about a half hour before each game raking out the dirt around third base, which he did again before the playoff game. When he took the field, he was able to concentrate on the play, rather than on self-defense, and in the playoff game, he made several stellar plays at third, robbing batters of sure hits down the line. The game was tied in the late innings and tempers were short. The volatile atmosphere was inflamed by the beer the men drank on the bench between innings. Tom had been hectored relentlessly by the opposing players for several innings when he was in the field. They tried to rattle him, hoping he'd make an error at third, hoping they could cop a run on a misplay and win the game. But for seven innings, he hadn't flinched at any ball hit to him.

Now, as an old priest in the rectory cellar with Theo staring at him blankly, he stood stock still, immobilized by his memory of the game and recalled exactly how he felt when he came up to bat in the bottom of the seventh, with two outs and the game still tied. He gripped the handles of the ice chest with the same intensity as he'd gripped the bat that night. In the quiet, interrupted only by the whisking of Theo's broom against the concrete floor, he could hear the opposing players shouting, calling him foul names, whistling, booing, and cursing as he stepped into the batter's box. His teammates were just as raucous, on their feet, shouting obscenities and threats at the players across the infield. In those days, he had a volatile temper, but he tried to shut out the voices, tried to calm himself, tried to concentrate only on his turn at bat. He stood motionless on home plate, leaned the knob of the bat against his left knee and slowly turned to the opponents' bench, the middle finger of each hand raised in salute.

The umpire grabbed his bat, stuck it in his face, and told him to get in the box and bat, or he'd throw him out of the goddamned game. The umpire then told the players on both benches to pipe down, or he'd call the goddamned game right there and then, and no one would win. Tom dug in and watched the first pitch as it arced up into the yellow lights and floated down towards the plate like a big white balloon. He leaned back and timed his swing, hitting the ball as hard as he'd ever hit a ball, sending it over the chain-link fence in left field. As he rounded the bases feeling pretty damn good about himself, his teammates crowded around home plate cheering, waiting to mob him, but before he could get to them, the third baseman threw a hard elbow into his ribs and doubled him over. He paused on the third base line to catch his breath, straightened up and jogged home to score the winning run. Once he tagged home plate, he raced back toward third and tackled the third baseman from behind as he walked off the field. He rolled him over and bashed him in the face two or three times with each fist and it took four or five of his teammates to pull him off the guy. A melee broke out until cooler heads prevailed. Then he and his teammates repaired to a local bar to celebrate, and he never paid for a drink all night. But now, as a middle-aged priest standing dumbly in his cellar, holding an empty ice chest as if it were the Ark of the Covenant, he remembered with embarrassment how good it felt to win, but more so, how good it felt to punch the guy in the face. And he recalled how, after he was ordained, the realization hit him he likely would never again engage in a good fistfight, and, at the time, the realization, in an odd way, disheartened him.

"I wasn't good at baseball," Theo finally said, ending the awkward silence. While Tom remained speechless, Theo walked over to store the broom and dustpan in the corner. "But I like the game, especially the cerebral aspects."

"Cerebral? I doubt anyone ever called Ty Cobb cerebral," Tom chuckled, breaking his long silence.

Theo blushed and turned his back to Tom and rearranged the broom in the corner. He was upset with himself. During the two-week hiatus between recent meetings of the St. Michael Poker & Drinking Club, he had immersed himself in the study of baseball, so he wouldn't be either mute or ignorant if Tom wanted to discuss baseball as they straightened the cellar after the game. He'd put a lot of work into studying baseball, and although he'd learned a lot through his studies and had already impressed Tom with his grasp of statistics, he realized his last comment was a goofy cliché, making him sound callow and inexperienced about the game, and he felt as if his studies had been for naught.

He hadn't started out his analysis totally ignorant about the game. As Tom said, everybody played organized baseball when they were kids, and he was no exception. However, after a few seasons, he was bored by the pace of the game, particularly as viewed from the bench, and when he noticed the talents of the boys around him blossoming as they got older, he accepted that his own ability to play, as well as his physical maturity, was stunted by comparison, and he promptly quit, rather than further embarrass himself.

Listening to Tom talk about baseball kindled interest in the game. The way Tom talked about the game made him think he'd done himself a disservice by dismissing the sport at an early age. Tom described the plays and statistics and other minutia in rich and tasty tones, as if each baseball fact was a choice morsel he first rolled around in his mouth and savored before spitting it out. As a result, Theo hungered for more knowledge about the game. So, each morning after he read the news, he'd spread open the sports section on the kitchen table and go through the division standings to see how they were affected by the games of the day before. He then would look at the box scores. He focused on the local team, but to keep their accomplishments in context, he reviewed all the scores. The first morning he sat and memorized baseball statistics, his head ached, but it was a sweet sensation, like the ache one gets in his muscles when he strenuously works his body. He couldn't remember the last time he'd applied his formidable memory to such intense exercise, much less an exercise involving information from the secular world, but he enjoyed the challenge.

Each day thereafter, he memorized the lineups listed in the box scores. He committed team and individual batting averages to memory. He accumulated a good working knowledge of pitchers' ERAs, noting which pitchers were starters and which were relievers. He faithfully watched the team standings and, as the regular season was coming to an end, had familiarized himself with the plethora of possibilities that could result in the Cardinals making the playoffs. The bottomless well of statistics fascinated him. To keep them in historical perspective, he visited the public library and had the librarian order in *The Baseball Encyclopedia: The Complete and Definitive Record of Major League Baseball* through interlibrary loan. He kept the book, innocuous enough, on a shelf in his office at home. There was almost nothing in the game that couldn't be reduced to a numerical expression, he reasoned, much like physics or geometry. He watched as many games on television as he could, discreetly, so as to not make Naomi curious about his behavior. He particularly enjoyed watching games played in stadiums he wasn't familiar with. He'd researched all the big-league ballparks and compared their geometries and the distances from home plate to the outfield walls. He had a pretty good idea which parks favored right-handed batters and which favored left-handed batters. He accumulated all of this data in a scant two weeks. Yes, baseball is a cerebral game, he said to himself as he fiddled with the broom, but he recognized his awkward attempt to impress Tom turned out to be rubbish.

Theo enjoyed the mental stimulation of studying baseball so much that he decided to master the subtleties of poker, a game he knew had its own applications of arithmetic and arcana. He again visited the public library and researched the subject and ordered *The Theory of Poker: A Professional Poker Player Teaches You How to Think Like One* by David Slansky. When this book came in, he hid it along with a deck of cards under an outdated copy of *The Lutheran Hymnal* inside a bottom drawer in his desk in the church office. He began by studying the book when Naomi thought he was at church working on his sermon. He quickly understood that by comparison, learning baseball was a walk in the park and chuckled at his droll play on words, thinking Father Tom himself might find it clever. Mastering baseball as an aficionado was pure memorization; to master poker, he would have to learn poker theory, as well as more subjective concepts such as deception, bluffing, when to raise, when to fold. He would need to memorize the estimated numerical odds of winning implied by each hand he was dealt.

His study of poker was both practical and esoteric in form. He would lock the office door and deal four hands, face-up on his desktop, to himself and to imaginary players. He then would consider his hand, quickly calculate the odds, decide whether to fold or take cards. He would do the same for each imaginary player, and then assess his decisions based upon the outcome. He'd then consult Slansky's book for tips or to confirm the soundness of his play. He had fun with the game, even assigning names—Tom, Brian, and Billy—to each imaginary player. And when he dealt, he practiced a good-natured patter as Tom did when he dealt, speaking quietly, however, in the event someone with church business might be lurking outside his office door.

As he studied baseball each morning at the kitchen table and poker in the privacy of his church office in the afternoons, Theo found himself enthused about subjects well outside the realm of theology for the first time in a very long time. He recognized by the stupid comment he'd made to Tom, however, that he may have mastered the numerical underpinnings of baseball but not the spirit of the game. Still, he was heartened by the fact he'd learned his poker lessons well, to the point where Tom complimented him on his finely played hands as they walked to the front door of the rectory after cleaning up after the last game. Theo accepted the compliment, despite the leaden tone in which it was offered. He'd noticed all evening Tom seemed to be in an irritable mood. The priest glowered at Metzger's opening joke and was testy and impatient with the deals. And when he dealt, Tom himself skipped the good-natured jabber and shuffled and divvied cards in an abrupt and businesslike manner.

Theo dismissed Tom's mood. Men such as Tom and himself often had matters of great consequence on their minds, he knew, and it wasn't uncommon for such matters to weigh heavily and affect the spirit. So, despite Tom's demeanor, Theo considered the compliment about his poker playing high praise and looked forward to the next card game. He concluded, on his way back to the parsonage, that it was a grand idea Father Tom had to bring the men together for a few drinks and a few hands of poker. He knew at the next meeting of the St. Michael Poker & Drinking Club, he'd be able to hold his own with Father Tom and the other men around the poker table and afterward, while the two of them tidied up the cellar alone.

CHAPTER TEN

After watching Naomi grimace in pain and occasionally hearing her vomit in the bathroom for over a month, Theo had gently insisted she call the doctor. Uncharacteristic of her stubborn independence, she readily placed the call and then asked him to go along to the appointment, making him concerned she was concerned.

When the nausea first presented, Theo secretly prayed it was a sign of pregnancy. However, as the weeks went by, other signs indicated she wasn't pregnant. Nevertheless, as they sat in the doctor's waiting room, he suggested she ask the doctor to run a definitive pregnancy test, just to be sure. Theo stayed in the waiting room when Naomi was called into the inner office. He busied himself by making notes for his sermon, and he was reading the designated Gospel from Luke when the receptionist summoned him. He met Naomi in the doctor's private office, where she sat in front of the desk while the doctor sat going over her chart. She gave Theo a wan smile when he walked in.

The doctor mouthed a greeting, but Theo, distracted by Naomi's paleness, merely mumbled a pleasantry. The doctor proceeded to tell them in a perfunctory manner that he would order a battery of tests to rule out any serious problems. It was his preliminary opinion Naomi was suffering from cholecystitis, or inflammation of the gallbladder, perhaps the result of stones, he explained, which could be confirmed by an ultrasound. Because of her age and her generally good physical condition, and also because of Theo's station in life, he tip-toed around the classic description of one prone to gallbladder disease as "fat, fair, forty, and flatulent."

"Once we confirm gallbladder disease, I'll send her to see a surgeon. Nowadays, the procedure is quick and simple. The surgeon goes in with a laparoscope," he went on to say, "and removes the diseased organ, and she'll be laid up only a short time, not like the old days when they cut you open neck to navel." Naomi smiled at Theo's audible sigh of relief and patted his knee.

Theo was so relieved by the doctor's dispassionate recitation of his wife's preliminary diagnosis, he suggested he and Naomi stop for lunch on their way home, a frivolity they didn't often allow themselves. And as they lunched, Theo was unusually talkative. He told Naomi details about the poker club. She knew he'd joined a men's club of some sort, but she knew nothing of the card games or of the men who played. He mentioned Brian Metzger, the Methodist minister, but could think of nothing particularly interesting about the man to share with his wife, other than he wasn't into poker and he golfed a lot. He tried to describe Billy Crump, whom he referred to as the oddest man of God he'd ever met, because other words failed him. He mostly talked about Father Tom, about his banter and his jokes, how he laughed at his own jokes, and how his gregariousness set the tone for each gathering. He even told her how Tom tipped him off to his "tell" after the first card game so he could win a few hands.

Naomi smiled as Theo babbled on; she'd not seen him so animated in a long time. It was, to her, a charming trait he'd mostly kept hidden throughout their years of marriage. "So your priest friend is a big joker?" she said, picking at her food. She had little appetite, but feigned enjoyment so as to not spoil Theo's mood.

"Oh, no, no, no," Theo replied through a mouthful of salad. "Brian Metzger, you know, the Methodist pastor I just mentioned? He knows Father Tom pretty well, says he's more pious than he lets on. He likes to laugh; and it's not a prayer group anyway, Naomi."

Naomi moved the food around on her plate and smiled at Theo's strict adherence to protocol and dogma, an adherence that for her had become tiring of late. There would be no illicit prayer group for the right Reverend Theo Swindberg. Nevertheless, she was happy Theo had found something to keep his mind off her, something to avert his attention and constant worry about her, her health, and their relationship.

For some time, she'd been thinking Theo needed something else in his life other than her and his duties as principal pastor at St. Paul's. Despite her recent ailments, she'd always been the stronger one in their relationship. Theo, she realized shortly after they were married, was physically and emotionally frail, and he relied on her too much for support. Sometimes he exhibited debilitating bouts of anxiety during which he'd sit in the parlor and tremble, holding her hand like it was a lifeline to his sanity. He was too intense, too studious, too prim for his own good, she tried to tell him. Or for the good of their marriage, she told herself.

She never doubted the depth of her husband's love for her; she only lamented he knew no good way to express it. Relatedly, he didn't seem to enjoy their life together, although she knew the stolid clergyman would say married life was not meant to be enjoyed, as much as endured, and as properly as possible. So, she was left to repent and pray fervently for forgiveness each time she'd considered shucking her role as the dutiful parson's wife and hitting the road.

"He likes baseball?" she asked, hoping to dispel the gray brume that had settled over her side of the table.

"How'd you know?"

"I see the newspaper on the kitchen table some mornings. You leave it open to the baseball scores. Did you know that? I've also seen some of your notes and squiggles and underlines. And that big book on the bookshelf? I know when you're studying, Theo."

Theo blushed and looked down at his plate.

"I'm happy you've found a friend, Theo. I think it's cute."

She herself felt a sharp pang of jealousy immingle with the chronic pain in her gut. Not of Father Tom, but of Theo's new situation. Although she was cordial with the ladies of the congregation, she had no real friend among them. The times she'd thought about running away from Theo and the church were the times the loneliness was oppressive. But at those times, she reminded herself there was always a loneliness associated with being a pastor's wife, and she had known it when she married Theo. She'd seen the loneliness in her own mother's life. But her mother had her children. So each night of her married life, Naomi prayed for the strength to stay in her marriage and for the companionship of a child. So far, having a child was not to be. Yet, she couldn't help but hope and pray.

As she watched Theo finish his sandwich, she counted the twinges of pain in her belly and was silently conflicted. She'd not wanted gallbladder problems to be the genesis of her recent sickness. She was, of course, relieved the doctor thought her problem was not serious, but she was also bitter about the latest disappointment when she determined she could not be pregnant. Still, she was not one to wallow in self-pity, and she pulled herself out of her reverie and stared across the table at her husband who, by now, had finished his lunch and was summoning the server for the check. She looked him over from the motes of food on his chin to the fresh spot of mustard on his shirt. She concluded, at that point, that God really did work his plans in mysterious ways. God may well have decided, in his infinite wisdom, that she could never raise children and still be the wife that Theo needed to take care of him.

CHAPTER ELEVEN

Father Tom was right. He was not the only player eyeing up the other men at the meetings of the St. Michael Poker & Drinking Club. Behind his hokey exterior, Billy Crump was quietly taking the measure of each man for his own purposes.

Crump had found Belle City clergy to be naïve and complacent when he arrived to scope out the town as a possible site for a missionary church. Although the other clergymen around the card table had no reason to remember, Crump had attended services at each of their churches, several times. He'd also attended services at the Baptist and Presbyterian churches. He'd seen the other men at the card table do their jobs. With the exception of Father Tom, he was unimpressed. Still, he'd jumped at the chance to meet the men close up and divine what hold each might have over the members of his congregation.

Crump was initiated into his brand of religion while still sucking at his mama's teat, he liked to say in coarse company, listening to his pap preach at tent meetings in villages and hamlets throughout the mid-South. He himself had been born in Kentucky during a stopover on his father's circuit. Hence, he was born and bred in Kentucky and considered himself a Kentuckian and at one time referred to himself as Colonel Crump, Colonel of the Kentucky Christian Soldiers at camp meetings, until he got a cease and desist letter from the Commonwealth of Kentucky that demanded he stop implying he held a commission from the governor. In any event, he was a Kentuckian by birth but wasn't from the Bluegrass regions of the state, with their verdant pastures, miles of white board fences, thoroughbred racehorses and columned homes populated by folks with refined manners and money. He was from the hard, rocky Pennyroyal Plateau, an area replete with poor prospects dictated by its karst topography, numerous caves and deadly sinkholes.

His father's revivals drew the mean and low, folks who subsisted as scab coal miners or hired hands or laborers to earn meager wages, or took welfare money and supplemented their fare with truck garden greens, fatty meats, fish, and game. And his father was a man of his people. As a youngster, Billy's life was hard. Pap made little money preaching, and although the visitors to the tent gave what they could, his father still had to run a floating card game and drag from the pot to make ends meet, a fact that bedeviled Billy when he was a younger man but served as a source of pride and inspiration in his middle years. His old man would send him down the road to the local tavern to get two pails of beer for the card players, with the cost of the beer chalked up to a tab at the bar, which the barkeeps always knew old Preacher Crump would pay in full before he left town. It was then Billy developed a fondness for the taste of cold beer in the summer sun, and up to the present, he still recalled no beer tasted as good as the swallows he stole as his wage for making the beer run for his old man.

His pap was always puzzling over ways to increase the draw to his tent rallies and thereby increase his take. So, Billy and his little brother were taught to dance, an exercise for which Billy seemed to have a natural affinity, and the boys would dance and sing at their father's command, and when they were youngsters, they thought it good fun. Yet, despite his father's shenanigans for making money, the Crumps were constantly living hand-to-mouth. But growing up poor where everyone around him was poor confirmed in Billy the lifelong belief God really did prefer the poor; there were so many.

As Billy entered his teens, he balked at his father's buffoonery and would catch a cuff or two on his ear or the back of his head for his stubbornness or for a cheeky response. Although he was small in stature, other than his head, and looked younger than his years, he found singing and dancing at tent revivals an affront to his burgeoning dignity. Moreover, as he approached manhood, his father assumed a different posture toward him, as if the older man sensed he had an adult son who displayed a winsome talent for showmanship and who may try to usurp his primacy in the shadowy, perfervid world of itinerant soul-saving. They would fight, sometimes physically, and when Billy reached eighteen years of age, he ran off and joined the Marines.

Billy's years in the Marine Corp were life-changing. In April 1970, South Vietnamese troops moved into Cambodia, pushing toward Viet Cong bases. Later in April, a U.S. force of thirty thousand troops, including three U.S. divisions and a young Billy Crump, mounted a second attack. He remained in Cambodia for about sixty days, fighting for his life. During one intense battle, Billy, in complete disregard for his own safety, rescued two wounded members of his platoon, likely saving their lives. Under normal circumstances, Billy would have received a commendation, but in the haze of battle, his actions were overlooked. Moreover, the U.S. wasn't supposed to have troops in Cambodia, so the battle officially never happened. Later, Billy thought it was just fine that no one singled him out for saving his buddies; he likened it to Christ's admonition to not let the right hand know what the left hand was doing.

In any event, the rescue of his buddies was transformational, not because he considered himself a hero, but because he learned his life calling was to save others. He understood he wasn't bright enough or wealthy enough to go to school and embark on a career in medicine or the like, so he decided to enter the family business. He would do more important work—he would save souls. And in doing so, Billy would be a good Marine and charge ever forward, regardless of the odds or the intensity of the battle at his front.

Hence, Billy Crump grated on traditional pastors when he went after members of their flocks, but he didn't care. He figured the ends justified the means. Furthermore, his years in the Marines instilled in him a healthy abhorrence of monolithic, rule-bound institutions, such as old-line, traditional churches, and he took great delight in tweaking the noses of the Catholic priests, the Methodist ministers, the Lutheran pastors, and the Presbyterian clergy in the towns where he established his churches.

Early in his career as a preacher, Crump didn't stay in one place very long; he started out preaching in a tent, like his father. After a few years of traveling about, he sought a wife. And he had plenty of women to choose from, despite his physical shortcomings. Women, he learned, flocked around a man who exuded a sweet scent of illicitness. Still, he chose Maggie, a slip of a girl whose portentous full name was Mary Magdalene and whose approach to men was quite the opposite of that alleged of her namesake, at least by Pope Gregory the Great. She played hard to get, and he was forced to pursue her properly until she finally agreed to marry him. They were wed in a quiet service conducted by a pal from the tent revival circuit. The next day, the newlyweds hit the road.

Naturally, children came along. His firstborn was a son whom they named Billy Junior Crump. On the night of the child's birth, he sat on the edge of the stage in his empty tent and contemplated the future. He didn't want to drag his wife and son around the countryside like his father had done him. Moreover, he recognized that canvas and poles and rope didn't make for a lasting legacy. He decided he wanted a brick-and-mortar church where he could put down roots. To that end, he saved and borrowed and begged enough money to buy an abandoned storefront in Corbin, Kentucky, and opened his first real church, the first Grand Hope Nondenominational Family Church. The first Grand Hope Nondenominational Family Church was successful. The rolls expanded to the point the congregation outgrew the old storefront, and Billy initiated a capital campaign until they had enough money through tithes and pledges to build a new church.

His marriage was successful as well. He soon had three more children—two daughters and another son—all born one year apart. When the youngest girl, Hannah Mae, was old enough to learn the scales, he taught the kids to sing in four-part harmony, as well as dance, and employed them in his services. They were a huge draw and continued to be a huge draw until Billy Junior reached thirteen, and his father, wanting to spare him the humiliation he had felt as a teenaged sideshow geek, released his son from the group, leaving a disharmonic trio to carry on. The trio devolved into a duet, and finally his youngest daughter, Hannah Mae, sang as a sweet-voiced soloist into her twenties.

Since he'd learned early on his particular gift was conversion of the unchurched and the disenchanted, he began to feel, after nearly fifteen years in one spot, like a miner who'd played out his claim. Also, he couldn't completely rid himself of his inbred peripatetic habits. With Maggie and the kids well settled, and with a large church family in Corbin for their support, he struck out on his own, time and time again. And after twenty years of work, he'd founded at least five missionary churches—all called Grand Hope Nondenominational Family Church—throughout Tennessee and Kentucky. Belle City was his first foray north of Dixie, but not so far from Corbin that he couldn't go back and visit his wife on occasion.

Billy's *modus operandi* was to find a promising town and live there for a while, getting the lay of the land, as he would say, and once he did, he became a fisher of men. In every town, there were the unchurched, the downtrodden, the homeless, the drunks, and the mentally ill to whom his special brand of salvation was appealing. They comprised his core of disciples around whom he'd build a new church. His greater gift, however, was to go after the disenchanted churched, those believers who'd grown tired of the impractical teachings of their hidebound churches, the stubborn and repetitive liturgies, the tired music, and the passionless preaching chock-full of esoteric interpretations of scripture that seemed to belie the plain meaning of the words on the page.

Proselytizing the disenchanted churched took time and patience and a good understanding of the disenchantments. To gather the information he needed, Crump attended services at each of the traditional churches in Belle City. He didn't need to study the liturgies; he'd heard them all many times before. He studied the pastor and his flock. If the pastor was personable and engaging and offered a hopeful and useful message, Crump figured there would be slim pickings from that congregation. He found it particularly useful to see how the pastor interacted with the church members as they passed through the post-service receiving line.

It was rare to find unassailable relationships in traditional churches, although he'd decided that Father Tom Abernathy's at St. Michael Catholic Church were about as good as he'd seen. His parishioners seemed engaged, attentive, and genuinely receptive to his homilies. Father Abernathy, he noticed, was personable and friendly after Mass, fun-loving to the point of playfulness, particularly with the children. The priest was, it seemed, well-liked by his flock, and Crump later saw nothing in Father Tom during their poker games to disabuse him of the notion that St. Michael would be a hard nut to crack. And since he genuinely liked the man, he'd settle for the normal offal and not actively seek any of the priest's parishioners.

Pastor Swindberg was a horse of a different color. Crump had attended St. Paul's several times, trying to get a feel for the man. He sat in the back of St. Paul's and studied the pastor and the congregation. He found Swindberg's conduct of the liturgy uninspired. He seemed to sleepwalk through the formalities. His sermons were pedestrian and boring, and Crump made a mental note of the restlessness of some congregants and the slumberous faces of others, mannerisms which were obvious to Crump's trained eye. After church, the pastor was stiff and formal in his receiving line, reticent to engage, lacking in warmth and charm. In fact, Crump noted the only item of interest about St. Paul's, its pastor or its congregation, other than possible vulnerability to his methods, was the pastor's comely wife who stood next to him in the line and offered the only relief from the morose atmosphere indigenous to Lutheran church services.

Meetings of the poker and drinking club confirmed Crump's opinion that Swindberg's congregation was accessible, primarily because the principal pastor was so unlikable. He showed himself to be punctilious and shy, averting eye contact at all costs. Yet, Crump knew it would be difficult to dislodge any lifelong Lutherans, with their old-fashioned Teutonic stubbornness and resistance to change, but figured it worth his while to try, and he made a mental note to do so.

In Crump's estimation, first formed after visiting the Methodist church, Reverend Brian Metzger was, despite his imposing physique, a lightweight. His estimation was confirmed by observations during the card games. But he had a preformed prejudice against the Methodists. He found their services insipid and noncommittal, lacking the doctrinal and dogmatic convictions and constancy of the Catholics or the Lutherans. After only one visit to the Methodist church, he was convinced he could seed his new church in Belle City with more than a few disenchanted Methodists, and it didn't take him long thereafter to strike a major coup.

When he arrived in town, he'd familiarized himself with

Belle City's movers and shakers, and he was delighted to see the Chief of Police at the Methodist Church service. Within a week, he'd found a reason to visit the chief in his office. Crump proposed holding a tent revival, and, as he explained to the chief obsequiously, he wanted to make sure the city was okay with the idea, to find out if overflow street parking would be a problem for the police, and to see if there were any permits or licenses he needed to obtain. He wanted to do everything according to the book, he explained. He was charming and solicitous, and by the end of their conversation, Crump had garnered the chief's support for the project and his commitment to attend the revival. Crump knew at that point he had the man hooked and only needed to reel him in, which he later did. In Billy's world, no matter what the undertaking, the ends always justified the means.

CHAPTER TWELVE

Because Theo and Naomi were never far from his thoughts, Father Tom was abashed when he answered his telephone and heard Theo's voice. The pastor wanted to meet in the morning for coffee at a coffee shop in a small town about fifteen miles from Belle City. Tom thought his choice of meeting place overly cautious, but due to the nervous tension he detected in Theo's voice, he told Theo he'd meet him there.

When Tom arrived, Theo was sitting in a booth by a front window chewing his thumbnail, a cup of coffee and a small plate sitting in front of him. Tom could see by the coffee slopped down the side of the mug and the flakes of sugar glaze on the plate, Theo had been there awhile, although he was punctual in arriving. Tom slid into the booth and asked the server, who startled him by appearing silently next to his shoulder, for a cup of black coffee.

"You want something to eat, Tom? A donut or something? My treat."

Tom thanked him but declined, admitting he'd eaten a hefty bowl of raisin bran earlier. "Good for the bowels," he added, patting his stomach with a smile.

The remark about the bran seemed to pass through Theo without effect. Tom had sensed when he walked up to the table that Theo was in a glum mood, glummer than usual, and thought he'd test his disposition with the silly comment on the salutary effect of dietary fiber. Theo didn't even smile. He appeared to be deep in thought to the point of nervous distraction, perhaps reconsidering his invitation to meet, perhaps considering the words he wanted to say. So Tom took his coffee from the waitress, added a splat of cream and stirred slowly and deliberately and said nothing, waiting for Theo to get to the point of the meeting in his own good time. After an awkward silence broken only by the by the rat-a-tat-tat of the spoon in the coffee mug, Theo blurted out, "I didn't want to join your group for obvious reasons, but other than Naomi, I have no friends."

Theo stared down at his plate, gathering his thoughts and continued, "We never socialize, Naomi and me. Other than church functions, we're never invited anywhere."

Once the words were out of his mouth, Theo returned to his thumb, which Tom could see was red and inflamed around the cuticle. As Tom considered Theo's brief but powerful unburdening and observed his anxious manner, he felt a profound sense of sorrow, although in his mind any sorrow he felt for Theo was tempered by the fact that Theo had Naomi, and in Tom's view, there was little more a man should want or need to be happy.

"I see the looks on the other guys' faces when we play cards. I'm not obtuse; I'm actually self-aware, if you can believe that." He looked up and dried his thumb with his napkin. "I know I'm a difficult man to like. I know people think I'm a self-righteous prig, and perhaps I am. I'm not proud of it. I'm not sure what to do about it. But I'm human; I'd like a friend or two like anyone else."

Tom recognized how difficult it had to be for Theo to call him and ask to meet and then to say the self-abasing things he'd just said. It was a soul-baring Tom never would have expected from the seemingly stoic pastor. He searched for a proper response, something meaningful but not maudlin, but all he could say was, "We're like engineers, Theo; we've made ourselves necessary to society, but who the hell wants to spend social time with us?"

Theo remained long-faced and responded only with a

resigned shrug of his shoulder. Then he offered a wan smile at Tom's insight. "I know what you mean," he offered. "I have several engineers in my congregation. Insufferable know-it-alls, they are," which drew a chuckle of agreement from Father Tom. But before Tom could offer a confirmatory anecdote on the maddening habits of engineers, Theo blurted out, "It's always been that way with me. When I was young, the other boys teased me about being the parson's perfect little boy. And I was. I was well-behaved, mannerly, never gave my folks a minute's worry growing up. I was so aloof and strait-laced in college, my acquaintances called me Iceberg. But my moderation in life cost me, Tom. I'm bland. I lack a certain seasoning others seem to like in a man."

Tom appreciated Theo's metaphor. Seasoning. Yes, seasoning. He himself had been so well-seasoned, he was nearly eaten alive by the world when he was young and tender. But he'd survived. For what? To be sitting in a coffee shop listening to a dispirited Lutheran pastor lament his lack of seasoning, and all he wanted to think about was the man's wife? And himself. Always himself. The sin of self-centeredness. Think about others, he told himself, and not about her. Or yourself. Others are seasoned, as well. He couldn't control the coarse thoughts that cascaded through his head. Seasoning. Season to taste. Yes, taste. The taste of Theo's wife. He closed his eyes and silently recited a prayer to St. Augustine, perhaps the only saint who could understand his feelings, asking him to intervene on behalf of his damaged soul.

As he sat there, both nauseated and aroused by his thoughts, Father Tom began to wonder if recent signs had pointed him in this direction, made his path straight so he would be here, at this time and this place, to either commit the unpardonable sin of covetousness or to offer succor to the man whose wife he covets. Then, as if St. Augustine heard his thoughts and prayers, he had an epiphany—he was exactly where he was meant to be, and he was subliminally informed of what he should say to help relieve Theo's discomfort:

"Well, Theo, I'd be pleased if you'd consider me your friend."

Tom's comment elicited no immediate response from Theo, and he wondered if the man had even heard him.

Theo continued to look blankly at him and then away to stare out the window and uttered a weak, "Thanks, Tom. I knew you would." Theo turned his face back to Tom and said, "Naomi's not well."

It was a comment the priest found to be perfunctory and inappropriate in response to an offer of friendship. But wasn't listening to such things the essence of friendship? Nevertheless, he wasn't able to focus on Theo or his response. It was his turn to avert his face from the man sitting across from him as he felt his face flush warm with the blood of sin and contrition. The familiar catch in his breath at the mention of her name hampered his ability to speak. As he looked out the window, he hoped Theo hadn't seen his reaction, and he considered whether the man chose to ignore as insincere or compensatory his offer of friendship because he had earlier read his filthy mind and decided to mention his wife's health to shame him.

"We don't think it's anything serious," he added. Tom exhaled slowly. "They think it's her gallbladder. She's going in for tests next week."

"I'll keep her in my prayers."

"But not at Mass."

"No, my bedtime prayers."

"I appreciate that, Tom."

The two men drank their coffee, which the waitress had quietly topped off, and didn't speak. Tom hoped the moment would pass without further mention of Naomi; he wasn't sure how he would react if Theo again said her name. Theo licked his fingertip and dabbed up the sweet remnants on his plate, sucking them off his finger with an audible smack. Between swallows of coffee, they finally made tedious small talk about baseball, the vagaries of Midwest weather, and the sweet relief of being near the end of summer and free from the intense heat and humidity.

However, having heard thousands of confessions over his years as a priest, Father Tom knew there was something else on Theo's mind he wanted to say. If it was another confession Theo was harboring, Tom hoped this time it was the confession of a venal sin for which he felt equipped to dole out a dollop of absolution and move on. He did not want to hear another painful soul baring. But whatever else was on Theo's mind must be of great importance, he reasoned, for the pastor to risk meeting with a Catholic priest in public, even if it was just to enjoy coffee and a donut fifteen miles from his church.

"When Naomi first took sick, we got our hopes up," he finally said. "We thought she might be pregnant. We hoped and prayed she was pregnant. But she isn't. I must tell you, Tom, not being able to have a child has been a terrible disappointment for us, particularly for her. She never complains; she views it as God's will. But I can see a look in her eyes when she's around children."

Tom was taken aback by the frankness and intimacy of Theo's comments. Moreover, he was discomfited by such talk. He remained quiet and tried to clear his mind of images of Naomi and Theo in that way. Although he'd been celibate since he decided on his plan in life, as a young man, particularly in the lost days between Benedictine College and when his mother saved him, while he was working on the construction crew and living a profligate life, Tom was initiated into the mysteries of the carnal act that could result in creation of life, and he didn't want to think about Theo and Naomi in a heated clench, both with eyes pinched closed to spare themselves the lasciviousness of seeing a look of enjoyment on the other's face.

Still, as skeptical as one reading his heart might be, Father Tom was well aware of and sympathetic to the burdens of womanhood, from their minor monthly anguishes to the major events of pain and suffering. He also was aware of Thoreau's aphorism, "Most men lead lives of quiet desperation," but he thought more so women. He knew from many years of Pre-Cana counseling most women longed to be married but knew little of what marriage required of them, both emotionally and physically. He later learned through his awkward attempts at marriage counseling that often, shortly after the wedding ceremony, a woman would find the man she married to be both distant and needy at the same time. And in some instances, she soon found him repulsive when he forced himself on her. The revulsion didn't necessarily arise only when the man was brutish or coarse, but the revulsion could occur even with a timid or solicitous man if the man was no longer the man she originally thought him to be. He wondered if Naomi ever felt this way. On the other hand, in the case of Naomi and Theo, he wondered if she ever found herself repulsed by his touch when Theo turned out to be exactly the man she thought him to be.

"It's my fault. Something's wrong with me," said Theo, which didn't surprise Tom since he couldn't consider Naomi to be anything less than perfect.

Perhaps, in actuality it is no one's fault; perhaps it is God's will, Tom considered as he looked across the table at Theo. He wondered if the anxious little pastor would make a good father. He certainly was no one to judge. He knew nothing of fatherhood. The possibility of him being a father even in the days before he was ordained was as remote as him now being named Pope. The way the needle on his moral compass spun, he never would have taken the chance, never would have sired a child outside of marriage, much less outside love. And he'd never been in love. But he'd never before met a woman to love.

Nonetheless, he knew he wouldn't have been a good father had he taken another direction in life. He had had no one to learn from. His own father abandoned his mother and him when he was only nine years old, leaving him with a distrust of fathers in general and with scant sympathy for men in Theo's situation. Yet being human and mortal, he couldn't help but think about it. What would a child of his have looked like? What personality would the child have exhibited? He knew looks and personality would have depended upon, at least in part, the woman he mated with.

For Tom such woolgathering was pointless, and he turned his attention to Theo, who was sitting across from him with a pained look on his face. He looked at the pastor's fingertips and saw they were chewed down so far that several had dark remnants of dried blood at the quick. Tom silently castigated himself for thinking of himself and not taking the man's problem more seriously. Theo surely must be distressed, he thought, to so painfully maim his hands. Just because he didn't identify with Theo's unhappiness, it didn't mean he couldn't be empathetic.

"Have you considered adopting a child?"

"We've not discussed it. It's all so difficult for me to discuss. But I know she wants to be a real mother." Theo paused then looked up at Tom sheepishly. "Not to say adoptive mothers aren't real mothers. I know they are wonderful mothers. That was insensitive of me. What I mean is, she wants to carry a child."

Tom sat staring straight ahead, rotating his coffee cup on the tabletop. Theo turned to look out the window, trying to avoid Tom's eyes. Tom was trying to put his finger on an odd feeling he had about Theo's comments.

As if he were attuned to Tom's thinking, Theo started

fidgeting, uncomfortable with the import of his words: "This is what I wanted to talk to you about, Tom; confidentially, of course: there are times, like now, I've seriously thought about setting her free, before it's too late for her, let her start over with a new life. She's considerably younger than me—"

"Surely she loves you," Tom interrupted, hoping the release of words would lessen the tightness in his chest, to quell the rapid heartbeat immediately engendered by Theo's words about setting Naomi free.

"There are many types of love, as you know."

"I need time to give this some thought, Theo. You know our church doesn't countenance divorce, either. Seems like a drastic step."

"I need advice, Tom, and I don't know where to turn. And the clock is ticking, as they say."

Theo stirred his coffee, which by this time was cold and unpalatable when he sipped it; he'd waved away the server when she offered to warm his cup, and he was in the midst of his divulgence. Even in view of the profundity of his comments, Tom could feel there still was more Theo wanted to say, more on his mind. For his part, Tom was still wrestling with the untoward sensation he felt when Theo mentioned setting Naomi free to start over. To start over...

"The Synod doesn't embrace the idea of divorced pastors," said Theo. "That's the problem." He paused. "Protestant clergy think they can have it all," he added with a mordant edge to his voice.

"Surely she loves you," Tom said irresolutely, not being able to think of anything else to say. In truth, he didn't know if Naomi loved her husband or not. He had no way of knowing, although the night he saw her in his room at the foot of his bed, he had sensed everything there was about her, including what was in her heart, and he didn't sense in it a place for Theo. But that was only chimera, and selfish, wishful chimera at that, he reminded himself. But isn't the substance of love just as illusory? Surely she loves him, he told himself, again irresolutely. Surely.

"Naomi's father was a Lutheran pastor. So was mine, and my mother's father, as well. These are marriages arranged by expectation. Daughters of pastors understand the job and make good pastors' wives. The pastor gets a spouse and a helpmate—a Sunday school teacher or a music or choir director. Naomi runs our Christian Education Department. Anyway, our marriages can be fine arrangements. And respectable relationships."

"I assume they evolve into loving relationships."

"As I said, there are many types of love."

Tom agreed with a short nod of his head. Theo was right, he reminded himself. He recollected a bit of Greek philosophy he'd studied describing six types of love, in the classical sense: eros, philia, ludus, agape, pragma, and philautia. He assumed these marriages of expectation were not based on eros and certainly not ludus, but more likely involved philia which over time evolved into pragma. He knew the erudite little Lutheran had to be cognizant of the types of classical love but sensed they were not what he meant when he said there are many types of love. Even Tom understood the six Greek classifications didn't allow for all the subtleties involved in marriage.

On occasion in his ministerial capacity, Tom had puzzled over the most powerful and compelling type of love he'd ever witnessed—the irrational, overwhelming and frightening, rarified love certain couples had for each other. This type of love was, in his experience, most uncommon but could, where it resided, provoke lovers to turn their backs on reason, religion, or on life itself to satisfy the demands of their love. He felt he might be in the one-sided throes of this species of love. He often wondered why, when God had commanded His creatures to love Him above everything else, He allowed a love of that magnitude, a love that contravenes God's express command to love Him above all things, to enter the world. Such a love places in peril the souls of the lovers. Perhaps, as some fundamentalists are wont to believe, Satan is indeed the architect of love. On the other hand, Tom reasoned, people sin all the time and hence the need for Confession and Absolution. And how is sharing a love which is greater than the love for God a greater sin than others, other than the violation of the admonition to love God above everything else memorialized as the first and perhaps most important Commandment?

In any case, such musings over the existence of condemning love were for another day. He knew from Theo's posture and his repeated allusion to many types of love that it was not the relentless, soul-searing type of love he was looking at between himself and Naomi, nor perhaps in any of the marriages of expectation, which Theo alluded to and quietly confirmed.

Theo told Tom his secrets without looking up from his tepid coffee. As he finally raised his head he said, "You know the parsonage where Naomi and I live? That house is nearly ninety years old. For ninety years, it's been continuously occupied by a Lutheran pastor and his wife. I can tell you for sure there've been many babies conceived in that house over ninety years, but I can also tell you with a fair amount of certainty, most resulted from dutiful copulation, and in ninety years, those walls have witnessed few, if any, conceived as a result of passionate lovemaking."

Father Tom could only imagine.

Chapter Thirteen

What Theo didn't tell Father Tom over coffee was, from the beginning of their relationship, he hadn't wanted to marry Naomi. He believed had he possessed the emotional strength to refuse the arrangement, it was almost certain she now would be happily married to another man, raising a brood of his children, and the thought that he'd denied her a chance at happiness made him heartsick.

He arrived at the parsonage unmindful of the fifteen-mile drive from the coffee shop. He'd spent the entire trip castigating himself for his emotional weaknesses: first, for his pitiful display of self-debasement before the priest, and, more so, as he'd done hundreds of times before, for failing to have the strength to walk away from marriage early on when he didn't feel the marriage right for either Naomi or himself. But the damnable thing about the entire situation, the one stumbling block to setting her free to live, was that despite the tepid feelings he had for Naomi at the outset of their marriage, his love for her was now almost overwhelming. Even though he loved her with little demonstration and much reserve, he could not imagine life without her. Yet, he wanted to do what was best for her, whatever that might be. That agonizing dilemma, which at times was nearly unbearable, caused him to bare his soul to Father Tom.

When he beat himself up, as he often did, he looked back at his relationship with Naomi, its genesis and progression, and tried to figure out if there had been a point at which he could have gallantly extricated himself from the arrangement. It was a moot point, he knew, but the upbraiding bloated his well-deserved Weltschmerz, the world of pain he deserved to live in, the apt term taught him by an old German philosophy professor at the seminary. The truth was, there was no point at which he could have avoided his marriage. It was inevitable. As the single daughter of the principal pastor, Naomi was seen by others as a natural match for young Reverend Theo Swindberg when he was called to be associate pastor at St. John's Lutheran Church. And after a respectable amount of time, he found himself the object of others' machinations.

Naomi was the Christian Education Director, and her father, the principle pastor, firmly encouraged him to serve as youth minister. The position placed him in her ceaseless orbit, and after a while he was caught up in the vortex and couldn't escape. That ceaseless orbit was an attribute he'd found disconcerting when they were younger. She exhibited a restless energy that made him feel nervous and unsettled. She never sat when she could stand, never walked if she could run. She was pretty, if not beautiful, strong, and robust. Her physical gifts intimidated him. And she added to her striking appearance by acting older than her years. She was self-assured and commanding.

Alongside her, he felt puerile and small. He had always been slight in stature, but in those days he was spare and gangly. His albs hung limply from his narrow shoulders and he seemed hidden behind his stole. The chasuble he wore to administer the Lord's Supper made him appear diminutive and immaterial to the cloth that covered him, and the first time he saw himself in the mirror with it on, he questioned whether he would accept Communion from such an inconsequential little man.

Naomi may have overawed him physically, but intellectually she was not his match, at least in the beginning of their relationship. He had a facile mind and a remarkable gift of memory and would, when engaged in informal conversation or when preaching to the congregation, recite Bible passages by chapter and verse from memory. Early on, he'd impressed her with an encyclopedic knowledge of Reformation history. He had, he boasted, committed *Luther's Small Catechism* to memory by the time he was six years old. He was a purveyor of Christian trivia, and when they started to formally date and were out to dinner or sitting in the living room of her father's parsonage, she would sit in glassy-eyed silence as he rattled off countless banal anecdotes about the early church, the Reformation, and Martin Luther. He finally realized he'd gone too far when once, over dinner in a nice restaurant, he related the myriad ways saints and martyrs had been tortured and murdered until Naomi made mock vomiting sounds. He took great pains to limit his comments, both in number and content, thereafter.

Naomi, on the other hand, was a young woman more interested in getting things done than in learning arcane facts. Church history may be of academic interest to an intellectual such as Theo, she'd reasoned, but it had little practical application. Her side of a conversation generally centered on prosaic topics, such as which study materials they should purchase for the Sunday School or the logistics of decorating the gathering hall for the next holiday season. She relished hectoring her father and the church counsel to designate more parking places adjacent the church as handicapped parking for the benefit of old or feeble congregants. She coached a girls' basketball team in the YMCA league, teaching the kids a rugged and relentless style of play. Her teams dominated their division three years in a row, causing parents of opposing players to petition the Y to ban her team from the league lest someone get hurt.

Although Theo enjoyed Naomi's company, he got panicky when rumors of their inevitable joining reached him. He inventoried his emotions and found a woefully short supply of deep feelings for her. He was a practical man and he knew they were very different people and he was concerned a contrived marriage might be miserable for both of them. So, for a while, he stopped asking her out on dates, hoping to shut down the rumor mill. Still, as the two of them were thrown together more and more in their respective jobs, the inevitability of the match was apparent. There were forces at work beyond his ken.

He had never imagined being married to anyone, much less a woman like Naomi. He held the quaint notion that if he ever married, he would marry for love. His had been a bleak childhood. It was not bleak in the sense that he was abused or suffered in any way—his parents were exceedingly civil and respectful to him and to each other—but he couldn't recall any overt displays of love or affection between the two of them or between them and him. How he had ever developed such a romantic notion as marrying for love puzzled him until worldly experience taught him men often fantasize about romantic notions until the world disabuses them of their fantasies. Nevertheless, when he was young, he concealed in his heart the silly notion that a man and woman should marry for love, and children should be the natural result of that love.

As momentum grew for a match between Naomi and Theo, he considered his future and the impact the marriage might have on his career. Bachelor Protestant ministers were viewed with suspicious eyes, he knew, and their motives or their proclivities sometimes questioned. Moreover, every pastor he'd ever known had a wife who served as a workmate. His intellectualization of the prospective marriage showed it to be a prudent one. Yet, he was still troubled by his secret heart's desire. In the end he surrendered to expectations and to the practical aspects of a marriage well made. He adopted as his guiding principle the philosophic construct that there are many types of love. He and Naomi were married, and he assumed, for her part, she felt little more for him than he felt for her, but he'd hoped that together perhaps they would find their type of love.

Naomi proved to be an estimable wife. She grew lovelier over time. Her muscular form rounded out; she wore her hair stylishly and dressed tastefully and as well as could be expected on a pastor's pay. But more than her looks, he appreciated the quality of her character. She was consistently cheerful and good humored. She worked at her assignments diligently. She also showed herself to be much brighter than she'd earlier let on, and Theo soon adopted a great respect for her mind. At each church he served she was by his side, hardworking and thorough, and she made him proud.

Yet, as time went by and they were unable to conceive a child, Theo began to regret his decision to marry her and loathed the practical effect of the marriage on his wife's life. His regret and loathing were complicated, moreover, by another, unexpected feeling: it dawned on him one morning as he watched her shuffle around the kitchen in her bathrobe and slippers fetching his coffee and eggs and buttering his toast that he loved her more than he loved life itself. Regrettably, as their marriage receded into formality, he found it too awkward tell her what he held in his heart.

So it was that their marriage settled into a comfortable routine. Naomi attended to mundane wifely tasks with competency and without complaint. She was a tidy housekeeper and good cook. She made sure his clothes, including his vestments, were cleaned and pressed. As far as her intimate wifely duties were concerned, she never balked at, and even welcomed, his attentions, even though he knew he was barely competent in that regard. But incompetency in technique was not his greatest deficiency, and as time went by, the prospects for Naomi being a mother grew less and less. Their inability to have a child tortured him, not for his sake, but for hers. Yet, she never complained and accepted her fate with quiet resignation.

Theo, on the other hand, refused to resign her to such a

fate. She was still young enough to bear a child, if she didn't wait much longer. He mined the profound depths of his love for her, and it yielded a nugget so repugnant, yet so practical, he needed to discuss it with someone. That was when he called Father Tom to meet him for coffee. He wanted to run past the priest the idea of divorcing Naomi, so she had time to find a man who could make her a mother.

CHAPTER FOURTEEN

Had Father Tom's eyes been able to peer into the place where his imagination dwelled during his conversation with Theo at the coffee shop, he would have seen Naomi sitting at her kitchen table, sipping tea, with an array of newspaper clippings and photographs and assorted papers spread out on the table. She'd been a prolific chronicler of events of her life beginning in fifth grade until she abruptly quit during her second year of college. The collection in front of her was from one of the scrapbooks dedicated to her days in high school. Over the last couple of years, she'd developed a ritual of paging through scrapbooks when Theo was out and she was feeling melancholy and alone, and the scraps in front of her had been loosed from the binder by frequent handling.

Since there had been no Lutheran high school near the small town in rural Nebraska where her father pastored St. John's Lutheran Church, Naomi had attended the public high school. Those days were her first exposure to the unvarnished, secular world and its inhabitants, and she loved every minute she spent there. She picked up a newspaper clipping that featured a picture of her, her head nearly to the net, elbows flared, pulling down a rebound in a regional playoff basketball game. She lingered over the picture for several minutes and recalled the game and sweet sensation of play. Her recent bout of illness caused her to covet the days when her body was an asset. The photo reminded her of when she was strong and tough and a star forward with a ferocious rebounding technique. But now, looking at the picture of her threatening posture and the grimacing smile on her face, she felt self-conscious and mean

126

as she recalled the untampered glee she took in throwing an elbow under the basket or putting a knee into an opposing player's thigh. Nevertheless, as she held the clipping between thumb and forefinger, she still felt there was something good in unbridled aggression when one was a girl. But she was no longer a girl.

She flipped the scrapbook to the last page and unfolded the program from her high school graduation ceremony. There was her name. She, as a preacher's kid, had been selected to give the invocation, and now, as she sat quietly at the kitchen table, she recalled how awkward and ungainly she felt standing in front of the crowd, reading the words she had worked through with her father's help. As she gently rubbed the smooth, dry cover of the program with the palm of her hand, she tried to recall what she had said that evening, but could remember none of it and uncharacteristically, she had not saved a copy of the prayer with the program.

On the inside pages of the program was an alphabetical listing of her classmates. She slowly went through the list A to W and then Y, running her finger under each name, noticing for the first time she had no classmate with a surname beginning with an X or a Z. She tried to conjure up a face for each name. For some she could, particularly her basketball teammates, but for many others she could not. Oddly, not one name aroused a sense of curiosity in her. She'd taken little interest in their lives when she was in school and had even less of an interest after graduation. Even the modicum of curiosity about their lives she had felt at the time dissipated into stubborn indifference. Sitting snugly at the table in a comfortable parsonage and sipping warm tea, she felt perhaps she was cold and deficient because reading the names did not arouse in her any curiosity as to how their lives evolved: where they went to college, who they married, where they were living, what they were doing for work. When she earnestly questioned herself, she conceded her disinterest may have been engendered by a malignant form of jealousy.

No doubt none of them, even if they had been interested, would have to wonder how her life unfolded. Everyone knew the pastor's daughter was destined for a quiescent life. Even as a little girl, Naomi knew she would someday marry a pastor and nurture him and their children in the insular cocoon of the church. It was preordained for her as the daughter and granddaughter of Lutheran pastors. Yet, as a young woman, she was not bereft of other, more worldly, dreams. After high school, she enrolled in Concordia College, a small Lutheran college located in Seward, Nebraska, a town of about 7,000 located three hours away from her home. Her plan was to major in Christian Education Leadership, training she felt would be valuable in her role as a pastor's wife.

Somewhere in a box in the basement of the parsonage was a scrapbook containing mementos from her first year of college. She'd not looked at it since she made the last entry, and even in her recent doldrums, she had no interest in doing so. Yet, she never had been able to bring herself to throw it away and moved the scrapbook along with her other belongings each time she changed residences. Now, as she sat at the table sipping her tea, the pain in her belly provoked her, and she thought perhaps it might be salutary to revisit her college days as a form of expiation. She had no need to retrieve the scrapbook from the basement to revisit those days; the most important events were indelibly etched on her soul.

The Concordia College campus was small, having around 2,000 students when she arrived on campus. The school was a close-knit, religious community. From the first day, she found the other students to be warm in their acceptance of her. They were helpful and supportive. She had planned to give up sports and concentrate on her classwork, but she carried with her a reputation as a top-notch basketball player, and it wasn't long before the women's basketball coach sought her out. He offered her a starting position on the team as a freshman. As the semester progressed, she excelled in the classroom, finding her Introduction to Director of Christian Ministries class promising. She particularly enjoyed her Old Testament as Literature class. She found the Intro to Psychology a bit amorphous and unsatisfying, a chopped salad of common-sense concepts dressed with jargon, but she needed the class for her major and stuck with it. The only disappointment she suffered during her first semester of college was the scarcity of young men. There was a goodly number of young men in the college preparing for the seminary; however, there were none in her classes that piqued her interest.

Second semester was more hectic than the first. She enrolled in another required psychology class but counterbalanced the boredom with a New Testament as Literature class. Basketball consumed much of her time, with the season in full swing after the semester break. After sitting through classes, she looked forward to the sweet freedom of basketball practice, where she could channel her pent-up aggression into useful movement. The team was mediocre, but the physical exertion and allure of competition kept her interested. In her secreted scrapbook were pages filled with articles from the *Seward County Independent* and the campus newspaper, highlighting her exploits on the court. As she sat thinking about her days playing basketball at Concordia, she decided to go to the basement to find the scrapbook after all. However, when she tried to lift herself from her chair, she felt a sharp, stabbing pain under her rib, and plopped back down in her chair to indulge in unverified reverie.

During her second semester, she sat next to a young man in her New Testament class whom she thought to be the prettiest boy she'd ever seen. She learned from chatting with him before class that he was a theology major with grand plans to attend a Lutheran seminary after he earned his bachelor's degree. He didn't want to tie himself to a church after he was ordained, he told her, but envisioned himself organizing youth ministries in inner cities or going overseas as a missionary. His plans seemed grand and exotic to her at the time. But thinking about him now, in the security of her warm kitchen, and remembering how he'd slouch across the aisle toward her desk, leaning his face precipitously close to hers to earnestly relay his grandiose plans for do-gooding, Naomi shuddered because the features of the face she'd thought so beautiful then were too late recognized by her as formed from candle wax and easily manipulated by her in her need.

This boy, and she could not bring herself to even think his name, was like her, tall and athletic. He played both tight end and linebacker on the college football team. And while Naomi was fair and pale, he was swarthy and dark, and when they began dating, she liked to walk with him across the campus and glance at their reflections in the large pane-glass windows of the academic buildings to assure herself he really was there with her and to get the full effect of their physical dichotomy. When they walked together, she felt she both absorbed and reflected some of his dark beauty, making her feel beautiful for the first time in her life.

Naomi went home after her freshman year of college and took a paid position as the Summer Bible School Coordinator at her father's church. Most churches had vacation bible school for a week or two during the summer, usually in the evening, but her father's vision was to have a faith-based summer school for grammar school kids in lieu of daycare. The church counsel allotted a stipend for the coordinator, and with her one year of related classes, the counsel deemed Naomi perfect for the summer job. She took to the job like a natural, at least in the beginning. As the weeks went by, however, she became disinterested and a tad lazy. She realized now, as a grown woman and married to a pastor herself, that her poor performance must have been difficult and embarrassing for her father to witness and tolerate.

As the summer passed, she became petulant and uncommunicative when her communication with the boy from college broke down. He had stayed in Seward and worked for a caterer and spent his free time in the gym working out with the football team. At first, when the academic year ended and Naomi moved home, he would call her a couple times a week. It wasn't uncommon for her to get a cute greeting card or brief note written in his stilted hand every week. But after the first month, all communication ended. She considered driving up to Seward to confront him but lost her nerve. She was dispirited, and her mood affected her job with the church.

Mercifully, the summer drew to a close, and she moved back to Seward to begin her second year at Concordia College. When she finally confronted the boy at the gym, he was sheepish, even contrite. He rattled off what she later learned to be stock excuses for this type of behavior in a man—he was confused; he was scared because he cared too much; he needed time—the disingenuous litany every bastard recites to the scorned woman. But as he told her of his shortcomings and pled for forgiveness, she saw him only as more beautiful, and they picked up their relationship where they'd left off.

Naomi was smitten. She wanted to spend all her waking hours with the boy. She considered quitting basketball. Her grades suffered. She had a ravenous appetite through which she stoked her self-esteem, and she began to gain weight. For his part, the boy became coy and circumspect. He would toy with her feelings—when they were together he would vacillate between being cold and distant and warm and affectionate. He was aggressive, physically, but she had drawn a clear line in that regard and rebuffed his every advance. Finally, he implored her to understand his needs and, for the first time confessed he was in love with her. Her head was spinning and, at his insistence, she reciprocated with an admission of her love. At that point, she knew what the inevitable outcome would be. He, as his type always does, insinuated there was a way she could prove she really loved him. And she recognized that because of the circles she turned in, and the expectations others had for her life, she would never again meet a boy as beautiful as he. Finally, alone in her dorm room, she gave herself to him, and he was crude and rough and everything a man should be.

Afterwards, she was so stricken with shame and guilt she told the boy she never wanted to see him again. She avoided the places on campus where she might run into him. She, of course, didn't tell anyone what she had done. She had no one to tell in any event. For a month, she couldn't look at herself in the mirror without cursing the image for being a dissolute whore. There were days she actually thought she no longer wanted to live, but she finally recognized that no matter how badly she had sinned, killing herself would be a greater sin.

She plodded through the subsequent years of college, focusing on her studies and basketball. She stayed in Seward between semesters and got a job stocking shelves at the Hy-Vee grocery store. She worked out rigorously at the gym, lost weight, and toned her body. She was strong and ruthless on the court, finding the game an outlet for her festering remorse. At the end of four years, she took her degree and moved back home. She was working as the temporary Christian Education Director at her father's church when Theo Swindberg was installed as assistant to her father.

Sitting alone in her kitchen thinking about her days in college, Naomi steeled herself and admitted that one of her most profane and abominable acts came after she moved home and met Theo, and as she silently confessed, she was sick with shame and regret over it. She had recognized right away that Theo Swindberg, the assistant pastor, was naïve and vulnerable. He was a kind man, bright but awkward, almost backward in his manner. He was not beautiful; he wasn't even handsome. But he was unmarried. And he knew nothing of her past. No one but she and that boy knew about her past. Once she decided she should marry Theo, it took little effort to guide him to the same conclusion.

Her father and mother were elated. They planned a beautiful wedding at St. John's with her father presiding, her sisters as bridesmaids, and a gala reception in the church hall with the entire congregation invited. As her mother helped her dress the day of the ceremony, she looked at herself in her wedding gown in the mirror and scampered to the bathroom to vomit. Nevertheless, the wedding went off without a hitch and was a great social event for the St. John's congregation. Theo and Naomi remained in town a couple more years until Theo was called to pastor a church of his own.

As Naomi sat at the table with scraps of paper and photographs spread out before her, evidencing the happiest days of her life as a schoolgirl, she again read through the names listed on the graduation program. Kids, she thought: all of them were kids then. And now they were no longer kids, and it was very likely many of them had kids of their own. She slumped back in her chair and breathed slowly to control the pain in her gut. At these times, when Theo was gone and she was alone, she allowed herself to admit that not having a child was a great disappointment in life, an even greater disappointment than thoughtlessly giving herself to a pretty young man. She did not allow herself to think of such things when Theo was in the house, because after their years of marriage, they could sometimes read each other's thoughts. She was certain as to the cause of her barrenness and didn't want Theo to find out.

First as a small child and then as a young woman, she had sat in the church pew and listened to her father preach, and her father always preached on the same relentless theme—the wages of sin are death. Theo was fond of saying there are many types of love, but she was certain there were many types of death, too. And the death she was enduring in the form of barrenness was a result of her particular sin. As much as she wanted to believe in God's grace and forgiveness, she was convinced she was barren as God's punishment for giving into temptation.

Not only was she laboring under the yoke of her sin, she compounded that sin monthly. Theo thought he was the reason they could not conceive a child, and she did nothing to disabuse him of the notion. He had, if she were honest about it, a fumbling approach to lovemaking. It was never like her first time with the boy in college, never that good. That's how she knew what she had done as a college girl was a damnable sin. She didn't believe Theo was physically deficient in regards to fathering a child. While he was awkward and at times incompetent, and in no way did he engender pleasure in her, he did what a man needs to do to impregnate a woman. Her body simply was not receptive, and although Theo didn't know the irony of his comment, it was true their childlessness was an act of God.

Now she was sick. She could barely keep down the tea. She'd had nothing to eat all day but a wedge of buttered toast. She felt cramped and gassy. So, the doctor thinks he knows the cause of my complaint, she thought to herself as she put the scraps of paper and photos back into the book. And he's ordered tests to validate his diagnosis and recommend a remedy. He knows nothing, she silently contended. She had little use for tests or surgery or any other corporal intervention. She was sanguine when she considered the possible outcome. It was clear to her this recent affliction was another punishment from God, this time for the years of sin, the years of deceiving poor Theo and letting him think he was at fault for her barrenness. There was nothing any medical man could do to cure her sickness, she conceded. As her father always preached, the wages of sin are death.

CHAPTER FIFTEEN

Father Tom sat at the desk in his study working on his homily. His contemplation of chapter 9 of The Gospel According to St. John, which related how Jesus healed the blind man, was intruded upon several times, however, by snippets of his conversation with Theo at the coffee shop, the interruptions perhaps provoked by the Gospel itself, particularly verse 2 when the disciples asked Jesus if it was the man or his parents who sinned, causing him to be born blind.

He lay down his pen and eased back in his chair. He would, he decided, give himself up to the interruptions and recall the conversation with Theo, word-by-word, as best he could remember, and perhaps by doing so, rid his mind of the constant intrusions. He could then get back to the task at hand. As he mulled over their conversation, there was one aspect which perplexed him: he'd noticed when they were together at the diner, not once did Theo say anything that would indicate he wanted to have a child, wanted to be a father. All his references were to Naomi's feelings, and Tom couldn't figure out if Theo's attitude was ennobling or if the man realized, and admitted through omission, that he wouldn't be a good father or had no interest in having a baby. But when Tom thought about Theo's mauled fingernails, his anxious brow, and his doleful aura, he concluded Theo wouldn't be the best of men to raise a child.

From that conclusion, Tom's thoughts naturally wandered to thoughts of himself, whether he would have been a good father. No, he quickly conceded. This thought prompted him to board another train of reverie taking him back in time to the point where his father abandoned his mother and him, and he felt the old anger in his belly. He'd been so hurt and dejected when his father left that he refused to look at a photograph of him from that time on, even though his mother kept a few in an old picture album. And when his mother died, he salvaged all photos of her and of himself but burned the photos of his father, after giving them a passing glance just to confirm it was him in the snapshots he was destroying.

Still, the images of the man at the time he left, both physical and temperamental, were fixed like an image on a wet plate in his mind, and he could see everything there was about the man as if he were standing right in front of him in his study in the rectory. His old man had been bandy-legged and wiry, but wickedly handsome, with an allure women could barely resist, and his comeliness had certainly contributed to his problems. He was dissolute, a gambler, and a drinker. When he drank, he caused trouble. Tom recalled at least two times his mother had to get out of bed in the middle of the night and bail his father out of the county jail where he was being held on misdemeanor charges of public drunkenness and disturbing the peace as the result of a bar fight or other such mayhem.

Tom also knew his father to be incorrigible in other aspects of his life. Shortly before he left them, his mother woke up and found his father on the living room sofa with a strange woman. Tom had cracked his bedroom door to witness the commotion about the time his mother was beating his father mercilessly with a heavy candlestick. In the meantime, the woman scurried out the front door wrapped only in one of his mother's sofa slipcovers. After his father escaped his beating and rushed out the door, Tom continued to peek as his mother unceremoniously picked up the woman's abandoned clothing and shoes with a broomstick, dropping them like dung in a brown grocery bag. At daybreak she took the bag to the rubbish barrel in the backyard and burned it. It was shortly after this indiscretion that his father packed his bag and took off to

Texas, ostensibly to look for work but in reality just to look. He never came back.

The morning his father left, Tom lay in bed feigning sleep. "Tell Little Shithead I'll be back," he heard the man say, and for a while he missed his father. Mercifully, he remembered his father as neither brutish nor affectionate, merely indifferent, often referring to his son as Little Shithead, a sobriquet young Tom had transmuted into to a term of affection. As he aged, he considered perhaps his father had been prescient and envisioned his son's years as a troublesome teenager and young man and hence nicknamed him. On the other hand, perhaps he, the father, considered himself a shithead and, consequently, referred to his son as Little Shithead.

Tom thought himself a motley amalgam of both his father and mother. His hair and eyes and skin tone were dark like his father's. He inherited certain of his personality traits from his old man, too. As a teenager and young man, he was dissolute and vexatious with a bad temper, fueled by a streak of unreasonable anger. On the other hand, he got his size and physical strength from his mother, who was a plain woman, but not unattractive, fair, tall, with broad shoulders and wide hips. She was a stubborn Catholic Irishwoman, nee Kelly, and his old man often said he'd made an honest woman of her, in more ways than one, when he, a fallen-away Presbyterian Scot, took her as his wife.

As a priest, Tom tried to be like his mother, who displayed the wondrous dichotomy of womanhood: she was both tough and tender at the same time, and he believed those aspects of her personality served him well in the priesthood. And where he suspected his father was an atheist or at least agnostic, if the man even knew the meaning of the terms, she was stubbornly devout but not showy in her Catholicism. She lived the parable of not allowing one hand to know what the other was doing. And without allowing anyone to know, she saved him from the devils his father vested in him, and in doing so, saved his life.

For most of his life, he hated his father, or at least the memory of the man. When he was a young priest, he prayed for forgiveness, recognizing hate as a species of murder. But looking back on his circumstances as he neared middle-age, he recognized the pejorative Little Shithead, laid bare, was nothing but a crude reference to a kid his father never really wanted. He accepted, as an older man, that he really did hate the man and would confess as much when he saw another priest for confession.

So it had been that Tom long accepted his experience with his own father, albeit limited, likely rendered him unfit to be a father. Perhaps, then, it was his father, he reasoned, even more than his mother, who had directed him to the priesthood. He could be Father with no emotional entanglements, enjoy paternity in a nominal sense only, and if he simply did his job and followed the precepts of the Mother Church, he could avoid damaging anyone else for their lifetime.

CHAPTER SIXTEEN

Thoughts of his parentage invariably led him back to his lost days. When his mother arrived at the duplex to take him home after he was severely beaten, Tom could barely hobble to the door to answer her knock. When he opened the door, his mother issued a loud gasp, and hesitant to touch his damaged face, let her hands fall limply at her side and wept. Tom enveloped her shoulders in his arms and gingerly lay his head on her shoulders and cried with her.

When she had no more tears to cry, she helped her son into the house and set him on a kitchen chair. She proceeded to clean his wounds with soap and water. She shuddered at the gash in his lip and chin and told him he likely needed stitches to close the wound. He sat there mutely and accepted her painful ministrations, thinking it rightfully earned pain. Once he was cleaned up and salved, she told him to stay on the chair, and she moved quickly through the rooms of his warren, collecting and packing his belongings in the valise. As she worked, Tom could hear her sniff back tears, and he hung his head and wept bitterly, but silently, over the things she surely must be seeing: half-filled cocktail glasses with doused cigarette butts, tattooed around the rim with ruby red lip prints; mounds of dirty laundry on his bedroom floor; plates with congealed and moldering food scraps in the kitchen sink; and his foul bathroom with its filthy sink and shower and overflowing trash can where he had, several nights before in a drunken stupor, indiscriminately flung a used condom.

Once outside the duplex, she helped him into her car, where he rested his head on the back of the seat and said nothing. As they drove, the only sound he made was the occasional groan or gasp if she hit a bump or took a corner too sharply. His mother said nothing either as she drove. Once they arrived in their home town, she drove to the hospital and helped him out of the car and into the emergency room. He sat stoically on a gurney as the doctor manipulated and taped his fractured nose. The x-rays showed two cracked ribs on his left side which, the doctor explained, would just have to heal on their own. The doctor irrigated the slits that were his eyes with a warm salt solution and then examined them as best he could with an ophthalmoscope. His preliminary impression was there was no structural damage to the eyeballs, but he recommended Tom see an eye doctor when the swelling went down. Finally, the doctor sutured the gash on his lip and chin, a painful procedure even with anesthetic that caused tears to leak from his eyes and trickle down his cheeks.

After the hospital visit, his mother drove him to their house. She helped him out of the car, but before they went inside, he told her he wanted to see her rose garden, and she walked him over to the flower bed, and barely able to see, he bent over and sniffed the Rugosa and Wichurania and Mister Lincoln roses, finding the sweet scent palliative and reassuring.

Once in the house, she helped him undress and tucked him into his bed. His face ached and throbbed, and he didn't feel like sleeping. She insisted he rest, left the room, and closed the door behind her. He lay in bed listening to her walk around the house with purposeful steps. He knew she was trying to make the house comfortable for him. He heard her unpack the valise and start the laundry. As she moved about, Tom, who hadn't attended Mass in years, was amazed when an earworm from his youth crept into his head:

> Gentle woman, quiet light,
> Morning star so strong and bright
> Gentle Mother, peaceful dove
> Teach us wisdom, teach us love…

As the hymn coursed through his mind, he lay in bed, the edge of his quilt between his teeth to muffle the sound, sobbing, allowing tears to flow from his damaged eyes until they pooled in his ears. He was both embarrassed and relieved by the crying.

As the days went by, he knew he was a burden being bedridden, but his mother was unfailingly cheerful and attentive to his needs and brought him everything he needed. She was still working, so she would make him breakfast and serve it to him in bed and set a wrapped sandwich on the chair beside his bed for his lunch. When his ribs healed sufficiently to allow him to roll over in bed, he reached for his glass of water on the nightstand and felt a strange object. He picked it up and held it close to his face and saw that it was her old Bible. He rolled on his back and lay the Bible on his chest and vowed when his eye problems resolved, he'd read the book, cover to cover.

With her help, he progressed from bedridden to chairbound to ambulatory in a few short weeks. He would spend the time she was at work reading the Bible or doing the crossword puzzle in the newspaper. When he could move about, he washed the dishes, swept, tidied his room, and sometimes cooked a rudimentary meal for their supper.

Once his body was healed and he felt strong enough to be useful, he went out and looked for work. He'd acquired marketable skills as a construction laborer and found a local contractor willing to hire him. As he worked during the day, he rarely interacted with the other employees, preferring to keep company with his own thoughts and to avoid the temptations offered by after-work drinks in the company of rough men. He spent his evenings at home with his mother, often outside on his hands and knees, weeding and pruning in her rose garden when the weather was good and her roses were in bloom. After supper, he'd often repair to the living room to read the Bible, surrounded by her quiet solicitude. His mother knitted or crocheted and avoided the television so as not to disturb him. One evening as he was reading, his mother approached him quietly with an unrequested cup of fresh coffee. He took it from her hands and looked down and reread the scripture passage from St. John he'd just finished reading: *Then saith he to the disciple, Behold thy mother!* and he was both amazed and terrified and his hands trembled, spilling coffee on his knee. He felt for sure it was not an instance of mere happenstance.

It was during his silent hours of hard labor on the construction job when he arrived at a plan of redemption. He'd contemplated the recent signs in his life: he'd survived a savage beating that could have killed him; his mother had prayed for his call and he had called her that very day and she had nursed him back to health; and finally, the correspondence between her appearance in the living room with a cup of coffee and the verse from St. John. He was not sure where the signs were pointing, but he was convinced he had a purpose in life, and if he cleared his head and listened only to his heart, his path would become clear. And it did.

As much as he wanted to, he didn't share his plan with his mother. He was concerned he'd fail and disappoint her once again. She never questioned him, and she let him be. His first step was to enroll in night classes at the local community college to complete his general requirements. He looked forward to class and found he enjoyed school for the first time in his life. Although he was physically weary at the end of the workday, he was emotionally and intellectually fresh and participated in class discussions, made sure his assignments were complete, and studied diligently for examinations. He was amazed to discover the breadth of his own intelligence when matched against that of others in class, an attribute he'd always obfuscated with self-loathing and anger. He took as many classes as he could fit in his schedule and in three semesters, he had his prerequisites completed.

His next step was to apply to and be accepted into a four-year college about twenty miles from home. He'd saved money living at home with his mother, and after contributing to household expenses, there was enough to buy a used car to commute to class. He finally quit his job to concentrate on his studies. He'd done some research and determined that for him to remain on the path he'd set for himself, he would major in philosophy. It was in college where he first was introduced to the Greek philosophers and the classical categorization of various types of love: eros, philia, ludus, agape, pragma, philautia.

Although he appreciated classical philosophers, he gravitated to the quasi-philosophical writings of Christian apologists such as C.S. Lewis. He relished Thomas Merton's *The Seven Storey Mountain* and was particularly drawn to the tortured *Confessions of Saint Augustine*, for whom he felt an affinity. He kept an Augustinian quote as his lodestar as he traveled forward on his path: "My sin consisted in this, that I sought pleasure, sublimity, and truth not in God but in his creatures, in myself and other created beings. So it was that I plunged into miseries, confusions, and error." Saint Augustine distilled into few words what Tom himself was feeling and provided further impetus for cleansing remorse and a quest for redemption.

As college graduation neared, Tom took a bold step, one he knew could result in a significant setback if not successful. He placed a call to the Diocesan Vocation Director and asked for a meeting. At the meeting, Tom confessed his sketchy history as a practicing Catholic, but he also confessed his heartfelt desire to become a priest. He tried to explain, to the director's obvious amusement, what he felt were signs from God. He told him the signs were his calling. The vocation director was skeptical. Tom needed his support to be admitted to St. Meinrad Seminary, the only seminary he'd researched thoroughly and was determined to attend. When the vocation director balked, Tom felt his face flush with anger but held his tongue, didn't get sarcastic, didn't make a challenge, though he felt challenged, even disrespected. He internalized the director's skepticism and sarcasm and felt it was God's test.

When he accepted that he was being tested, he relaxed and instantly found himself at ease and confident. He respectfully bantered with the director; he became analytical. He offered the vocation director tangible evidence of his excellent academic credentials, to which the man responded that it takes more than brains to be a priest. Tom agreed. He had leavened his intelligence with maturity, he explained, and had learned a lot in the school of hard knocks. The director's next tack was to focus on Tom's poor attendance at Mass, with which Tom had to agree but countered good-naturedly that as a parish priest, he'd have to attend every Mass, which elicited the director's only smile.

Finally, during an awkward silence when Tom felt his opportunity slipping away, he took an exceedingly practical approach; he cited statistics. He told the director he was well aware the diocese had not ordained one of its own as a priest in five years, and in the last decade, the diocese had produced only two ordained priests, and one of them left the priesthood and married.

"You need priests, Father," Tom finished, "and I want the job."

Within a month, Tom submitted his application materials to St. Meinrad Seminary. The diocesan vocation director provided a fine letter of recommendation which, Tom learned years later, placed a heavy emphasis on the applicant's perseverance and grit and very little emphasis on his spiritual endowments. Nevertheless, Tom was admitted to the seminary and on his way to becoming Father Thomas Abernathy, the man he secretly decided to become as he worked as a laborer in the days after his mother saved his life.

His mother was thrilled beyond words.

CHAPTER SEVENTEEN

I'm losing Naomi," Theo blurted out when Father Tom answered the telephone in his study. "She's dying."

Father Tom felt the now familiar and wholly expected catch in his breath when he heard Theo say her name, but this time, associated with words too surreal to believe, he required more time to catch his breath so he could speak calmly into the telephone. "What do you mean, Theo?"

"They did an ultrasound looking for gallstones. There weren't any gallstones, but they saw a mass on her pancreas. On her liver, too."

Tom lowered himself into his desk chair and said nothing. He was not a medical man, but he'd learned enough through his experiences with stricken parishioners to know cancer of the pancreas and liver, if that's indeed what she had, was a death sentence, and only God knows when it will be executed.

"Are you sure?"

"I saw the scans myself, Tom. They looked like a goddamned Rorschach test. Forgive my language."

"What you saw might be benign," said Tom irresolutely.

"It might be, but the doctors told us to prepare for the worst. Particularly with the spots on both organs. It looks like it's spread already."

"She can be treated."

"Yeah, but we all know how that turns out. They're going to biopsy her liver next week, and if it's cancer, start chemo. But it's so widespread, the doctor said the treatments might be palliative at best."

"I'll pray for you both, Theo." Tom felt tears pool in his

145

eyes, and he wiped his eyes on his shirtsleeve.

"Privately, I hope. Please don't put us on your prayer list at Mass, okay?"

Odd little man, Tom thought; his wife is dying and he's the ever-dutiful Lutheran worried about prayers for her healing said in the Roman church. He felt like saying, "Get a life, Theo," but he held his tongue. He knew when a man is stressed, he often retreats to the comfort of routine and dogma.

"As you wish, Theo," he said.

"Thanks, Tom." And after a pause, "I didn't know who else to call at this point."

Tom hung up the phone and sat at his desk, dumbfounded by Theo's news, his old anger slowly rising until his hands shook and rivulets of sweat crept down his forehead. He snatched his Catechism off the desk and threw it across the room, bouncing it off the window that overlooked the rose garden and Cat's grave. He immediately calmed himself, got up, and retrieved the book, placing it on the desk. He rested his damp forehead on the desk next to the Catechism and wept.

And contemplated death.

Whenever he contemplated the inevitability and finality of death, he always focused on one certain death, and, as if in rebuke to his faith and his training, it was not the death of Christ he fixated on; it was the death of his mother. When she was on the brink of death, he'd visited her one last time and performed the Rite of Extreme Unction. He anointed her forehead with the sign of the cross and prayed for the repose of her soul. And for an easy death, a prayer with aspects that haunted him ever after.

With his abiding love and respect for her, asking God for a merciful death was the best he could do since hers had not been an easy life. Her life certainly had improved after his father left, but there always was a struggle for money. Sometimes she worked two jobs to support them. She wore her clothes until they were threadbare and her shoes until the soles were thin. She drove an old car and maintained it herself, learning to change the oil and perform a minor tune-up. She never went out, except for church. Not even to a movie or a fast food joint. Yet, as he sat by her bedside in the deathwatch, he recalled he always had everything he needed—clean clothes, good shoes, money for an occasional movie, and tuition for Catholic school.

But her life had not been joyless drudgery, either. In later years, after he'd moved out and she had fewer burdens, she worked only one job as a cook at the local high school, ending her career as the head cook after thirty years' service. Her pay was adequate and she even salted away a few bucks but still lived austerely. The students and faculty alike held her in great esteem, appreciating her cheerfulness and kindness. She was feted upon her retirement with a reception, a dozen red roses, and a plaque with her likeness hung on the cafeteria wall for all to see. At her funeral, more than one former student told Father Tom how his mother would sneak a piece of cake or extra meatball onto a lunch tray when she knew the student was short on money or got little to eat at home.

In addition to her job at the school, she enjoyed her patch of land and her gardens, both her rose garden and her vegetable garden and her apple trees, all of which she tended faithfully until her health began to fail. For years, she supplemented her income by selling vegetables and apples from a roadside stand in front of her house. She didn't man it but placed the produce in an attractive array on an old table with handwritten prices per piece next to each variety, along with a coffee can for payment. It was an honor system, she explained to her son. When he was younger and more cynical, Tom thought it a foolish way to sell produce; he was certain the stand, with its lush vegetables and fruit, was a ripe target for thievery. His mother, on the other hand, had faith in human nature, and at

147

the end of each day counted the produce and accounted for each missing piece with coins in the can. At least that's what she always told him.

She also had her cats, which brought her pleasure by allowing themselves to be fawned over, at least occasionally, and serving as objects for her affection, particularly after he left home for the seminary.

And he knew her greatest source of joy in life was him, her son the priest. But perhaps it was he, the priest, who hurried her demise by praying so fervently by her side for a serene death, affecting the great harmonic to effect her death when she may have rallied and survived a good deal longer. The thought that he may have been implicated unnerved him and hampered for a time his ability to pray with and for the dying, one of his principal duties as a parish priest.

Now, as he tried to come to grips with Theo's news, Father Tom wondered if Naomi had any sources of joy in her life. Even though he'd gotten to know him a little better, Theo still seemed to him to be joyless, and during their conversation at the coffee shop had called into question whether their marriage was a source of pleasure or satisfaction for either of them. Still, the brief times Tom had seen Naomi outside church, she displayed a singular aura of happiness, smiling and laughing, and he wondered if there was a spiritual source of such good humor, or if she merely was maintaining appearances as the parson's wife. Still, it hardly mattered at this point; if Theo was correct, and Theo was not a man prone to hyperbole, Naomi soon would be dead.

After receiving the grim news regarding Naomi's illness, after weeping selfishly, and after revisiting his mother's death, Tom composed himself and called Brian Metzger to let him know that, for the time being, meetings of the St. Michael Poker & Drinking Club would be suspended. He told him only that Naomi Swindberg was quite sick, and Theo would be indisposed. Metzger replied that he'd heard Naomi had been ill, but he'd also heard her illness was not serious, and she'd be fine. Father Tom flushed at Metzger's comments, vexed that Naomi had been the subject of small town gossip, and he told Metzger, perhaps uncharitably, he reasoned later, that the minister should keep the information to himself and that he, Tom, would consider it a personal affront if word got back to him that Metzger had mentioned her condition to anyone.

Once he finished talking to Brian Metzger, he thought about calling Billy Crump, but he was conflicted. He needed to tell Billy the poker club meetings were canceled, yet he didn't want to give the smarmy little evangelical food for gossip. Nevertheless, he called Crump, who expressed surprise at the information, indicating to Father Tom that he, Billy, didn't get his news from the same circuit as other preachers in town. Before they ended the call, Billy said, "We should keep this under our hats, Tom. No need to subject Theo and his wife to the bedevilments of black-hearted gossips. You and me been in this business long enough to know there are folks out there who'd take great delight in talking about a good man suffering the pains of this life."

Father Tom was relieved to end the gatherings of the club. He was content to spend his evenings alone in contemplation and prayer, mostly for Naomi, and for Theo, too. However, his daily duties suffered from distraction. During Masses, his homilies lacked their old spark, and he went through the Rites and Sacraments in a rote manner. He visited the sick, but his visits were lackluster and short. He annoyed members of the Church Council by his inattention during meetings. And, for the first time, he considered his age and whether he should retire from the priesthood, rather than walk halfheartedly through his days of service, sinning grievously every day, inducing pain in others, so that he himself might suffer.

He also spent a lot of time questioning whether Naomi's

affliction was *his* punishment for *his* sins. When he heard confessions, he found the sins of his parishioners venal and trite
compared to the grievous sin he held in his own heart. He
dispensed lenient penances, believing he couldn't require more
from parishioners than he demanded from himself.

He'd not heard from Theo for almost a month when the
pastor called to tell him Naomi was bedridden. She was in
considerable pain, he said, and rarely lucid. He had called in
hospice, and hospice workers sat with her during the day when
he had work to do. He took care of her at night.

"She might only last a short while," he said. Tom then heard
Theo sob, and he too wanted to cry, so he put his hand over
the telephone mouthpiece.

"I didn't call till now because I didn't want to burden you
with my problems," said Theo.

Tom felt his stomach roil at Theo's last words and thought
he may have to excuse himself from the phone and vomit.
But he sat quietly until the nausea subsided. If, in the end, life
is just a blink of the eye, Tom asked himself, why must God
throw dust in it?

"You know, Tom, it's always been the Lutheran way to
accept and even rejoice in suffering. We believe suffering is
God's instrument of discipline and atonement. God disci-
plines those he loves. But it's always been someone else's suffering I've been asked to accept. Now it's me being punished
and I don't accept it."

Tom listened as Theo tried to stifle his sobs, sniffing his
loose snot, then coughing a deep, rattily cough. "I have a favor
to ask of you," said Theo after he composed himself.

"Sure, Theo."

"I want you to pray for her."

"I have been praying for her, Theo, and I'll continue to pray
for her."

"No, I mean *really* pray. Over her, to drive out the devil

that's rotting her body. Heal her with prayer."

Father Tom was taken aback by Theo's request. He didn't know what to say. "I don't think I can do that, Theo," was all he could muster.

"Why not?"

"First of all, I'm a Roman Catholic priest."

"I know what you are, Tom. That's why I want you to do this. You're a Catholic priest, a direct descendant of Peter, the Rock, aren't you? Didn't St. Peter receive his commission directly from Christ himself?"

"Well, Theo—"

"Didn't he?"

Father Tom felt terrible hearing the naive earnestness in Theo's voice. To what depth of despondency had the man sunk to allow himself to make this call? And what could he tell Theo to dissuade him? That there really is no direct lineage to Peter? That the road backward from himself, a mere parish priest, to St. Peter runs through centuries of popes and pretenders and is rocky and pocked with rents and schisms? That there is a long history of dissolution and corruption surrounding the Papacy itself that casts shadows over every pope and every priest?

He pondered the questions for a bit and realized Theo likely was aware of such criticism of the Roman Catholic Church and the Papacy. Theo's own church was founded on alleged iniquities of the Roman Church and the Papacy. He knew Theo, erudite and punctilious, probably had researched the matter and was sufficiently satisfied that the lineage from the local parish priest back to Peter to Jesus Christ Himself would allow him, Father Thomas Abernathy, pastor of St. Michael Catholic Church, to serve as a means to his desired ends. Or perhaps Theo's judgment was clouded by his despair. In any event, Tom decided he would not try to change Theo's mind about the tenuous relationship between himself and any saint, much less St. Peter, and try another tack.

"Surely there is a Lutheran pastor who could do this for you, Theo."

"No, Tom. I want you."

"There are priests specially trained for such practices."

"Your being a priest is not the only reason I want you to do this, Tom; you're also my friend."

"Yes, Theo, I am your friend."

"And I sense you're an instrument of God."

Father Tom didn't know how to respond to Theo's last remark. He'd always considered himself a servant of God, but not an instrument of God. The latter, he recognized, was a term of art, with specific meaning among the initiated. He started to mildly rebuke Theo. "Look, Theo, I'm not the man you think I am. I'm—"

"I need you to do this for me, Tom," Theo interrupted. "I've tried to pray for her myself but feel my faith wavering. I fear my affection for her is hindering my ability to pray as fervently and freely as I need to to help her. My love for her doesn't let me fully realize my faith. I need you to pray for her, Tom. Someone I believe in but who isn't emotionally attached to her."

Tom was shaken by Theo's reasoning which, if sound, raised the ominous specters of hypocrisy and certain failure if he complied with Theo's request.

"Are you sure this would be appropriate?" asked Tom, thinking he'd appeal to Theo's overwhelming devotion to Lutheran orthodoxy.

"No one needs to know. It'll be in the privacy of our home."

"Why don't you call someone at the Synod and see what they recommend?"

"Damn it, Tom, I want a priest! I want you!" Theo shouted, exhibiting another flash of frustration and anger of which Tom hadn't thought him capable.

"Okay, Theo, calm down. Just calm down."

"Forgive me, Tom. I'm distraught."

"I can understand that you are. Look, I need to think about this. I need to pray on it."

"Don't take too much time, Father. I don't know how much time she has," Theo replied before breaking down into a fit of bitter sobbing.

Tom held his tongue until Theo's sobbing devolved into a catarrh-like flood of sniffs and snorts and snot and then silence. "Theo?"

"Yes?"

"What is Naomi's birthday?"

"December fifth. Why?"

"Just curious," he responded, pleased she was a Sagittarius, a fellow Fire Sign quite compatible with Aries, which might be helpful if he agreed to Theo's request to intervene. But as he sat there, he saw no way he could agree to do what Theo asked; however, he didn't say no out of hand because he didn't want to add to the man's distress.

When he hung up the phone, Tom felt numb and lifeless. He sat at his desk, head in hands, and his only thoughts were of Naomi. What must she look like, he wondered, since this disease has ravaged her body? And the pain, the pain. Theo's pitiful sobs had had small effect on him, not that he was unsympathetic to his pain, but the realization of her pain was nearly unbearable, leaving scant space for any other feelings. In that scant space was his own pain and grief, a sense of profound loss of something he'd never had, the most difficult of all losses to mitigate.

He went into the kitchen and poured a glass of wine. He walked out into the back yard to clear his head. It was a typical Indian summer evening, warm, even at the end of the day, a vestige of summer melding into autumn. It was his favorite time of year. Temperate and dry, the roses still in bloom and fragrant. He sat down on the ground in the corner of the rose garden, adjacent Cat's grave, where he was indistinguishable from the shadows cast by the willow tree in the waning light of day to any passersby. The soil was damp from an earlier watering and he felt the dampness wick through his trousers and touch his skin, a cool and dank sensation. He looked around at the rose bushes which were fading into silhouettes in the twilight and tried to assess which would need an early pruning, which might continue to bloom into the cold weather, and which were old and woody and needed to be replaced.

"Do you like the roses?" he asked Cat in a near whisper. "Roses were my mother's favorite flower. She grew roses in our backyard. Red roses were her favorites.

"There's an old song, 'Red Roses for a Blue Lady.' When I was a kid, she had a record by Vaughn Monroe and she'd play it on the record player and sing along. She also used to sing it when she was working in the rose garden. A capella. She had a lovely voice, but she'd butcher the lyrics when she didn't have the record playing. Funny, the things that came out of her mouth. Anyway, the woman loved roses."

Tom sat silently watching the sun go down. He scanned the heavens, knowing at this time of year Sagittarius set at sunset. Did he really want to see Sagittarius set?

"Got a call from Theo Swindberg today," he said toward the dead cat. "Wants me to pray for his wife. Can you believe that? Me, praying *for* Naomi Swindberg. I've often prayed *about* Naomi Swindberg but not for her. Well, that's not quite true; I've been praying for her and Theo since he first told me she was sick, but now he really wants me to pray for her. To heal her. I don't know what to do, Cat. Don't know if I can do it," he added, exhibiting a malignant uncertainty of which the weak-spirited are prone.

"Why don't people want to die where they should and when they're supposed to anymore? You know how many parishioners I've had over the last ten years or so who've refused to accept the inevitability of their deaths? They traipse off to the Mayo Clinic or MD Anderson or some such place looking for a miracle cure and they die anyway, in a strange place, away from home. Seems to me they'd be better off if they'd just stay home and die in their own time, in their own beds, where their parish priest can perform the proper rites."

He sat in the twilight, sipping his wine.

"Their last exercise of free will, I assume," he finally said. "You understand that; cats have free will."

He grew pensive and contrite. "I suppose that's not a charitable way to feel on my part. Selfish. But if I pray for Naomi Swindberg, that would be selfish."

He took a last swallow of wine and held up his wine glass to reflect the last rays of the disappearing sun. "Shall I pray to have this cup removed from me, Cat?"

He set the glass in the dirt at the margin of the rose garden. Slowly, he felt his old anger rise as he contemplated Theo's request. Or was it a demand? A challenge to the primacy of the Mother Church? An invitation to failure? Or, was Theo asking him to atone for his own stuffy self-righteousness that invited God's retribution? As he sat there sweating in the warm evening air, he began to see the skinny Lutheran, along with his lovely wife, as a bane. Was Theo testing his faith? On whose authority? Who the hell does Theo Swindberg think he is that he can put me to the test, me a priest with almost twenty-five years' service to the Lord? Bastard. He grabbed his wine glass and threw it against the trunk of the willow tree, shattering it and sending shards of glass into the grass under the willow branches.

It was nearly dark. He got down on his hands and knees and crawled around in the grass, picking up the pieces. He put his palm down on a sharp piece and cut the skin. His palm bled and he held it up in the twilight and asked aloud, "Stigmata?" He laughed at his irreverence. He cursed Theo again, and then pulled himself up, walked to the alley, and dropped the broken glass into the trash can before returning to the rectory in the dark.

Chapter Eighteen

Back in the rectory, Father Tom's face was beaded with a funky sweat induced by the warmth of the evening and the heat of his ire. He went into the kitchen, pulled a paper towel from the roll, blotted the blood from the palm of his hand, and wiped the sweat from his face and head. Back in his study, he flopped down in a side chair, wiped his brow again with the paper towel, and stared obliquely at the bookshelves. He was troubled.

Although he believed in the salutary effect of prayer on the sick, he was a skeptic in regards to faith healing. Prayer, he knew, could give the ill strength of spirit to bear their illness and its inevitabilities, but proponents of faith healing avowed complete cures, and he wasn't sure if he believed their claims. Or had mastered their techniques. He was aware of the bevy of well-known faith healing priests—Richard McAlear, Hugh Thwaites, Andrew Apostoli—but he knew none of them personally and had no way to seek their counsel. And according to Theo, he had no time to make a trip to visit one of these priests before deciding what to do.

Father Tom got out of his chair, walked over and stood in front of the bookshelves. When he'd moved into the rectory, he'd conducted a brief inventory of the volumes left on the shelves by priests who'd lived in the house before him. He'd added a few of his own books to the collection. He looked over the titles until he located his copy of *Anointing and Pastoral Care,* a study text he'd owned since his days in the seminary but had consulted only a few times as a parish priest, believing as a practical priest, proper pastoral care of the sick was a practical art, often a matter of common sense and common compassion. He didn't feel ministration to the sick a proper subject of pedagogy. Nevertheless, he took the text from the shelf and held it in his hand as he continued to peruse the book titles.

He found, on the bottom shelf next to collection of books by Bishop Fulton Sheen, an array of books covering subjects generally associated with the black arts, mysticism, and charismatic practices. Looking over the dusty spines he saw volumes dedicated to paganism, witchcraft, possessions, exorcisms, and mystic practices of every ilk. He ran his fingers through the accumulated dirt on several titles attributed to Edgar Cayce and assumed from the period graphics on the dustcovers that the priest who'd donated them to the rectory library probably procured them sometime shortly after the double-barrel blast of the Vietnam War and the Nixon presidency crippled his faith in God's good guiding hand in the affairs of man. Perhaps the priest who read Cayce began looking outside the Mother Church for reassurances and took some comfort from the nebulous concepts of clairvoyance, reincarnation, and karma.

Father Tom moved past the Cayce bibliotheca and pulled from the shelf a book entitled *Healing* by Francis MacNutt. He stared at the author's photograph on the cover and tried to recall if he'd ever heard of the man before but didn't think he had. Had he heard of a man named MacNutt, he likely would have remembered him, he reasoned and, as he was wont to do when he was under stress, his sense of humor took a dark turn and he wondered if his name, MacNutt, considering the subject matter, was in some way eponymous or simply a happy coincidence.

He took both the MacNutt book and *Anointing and Pastoral Care* to his desk, turned on the desk lamp, and sat down to read the notes on MacNutt's book jacket. MacNutt was billed (or billed himself, Tom figured with cynicism) as an expert in the healing ministry. He was ordained to the priesthood in

1956 but married in 1980. The notes were sketchy, and Father Tom reckoned somewhere between his ordination and his marriage some event took place that caused MacNutt to leave the priesthood, casting some doubt on his bona fides. Nevertheless, he turned to the table of contents, and with Theo's comment that his faith was wavering fresh in his mind, Tom's eyes were drawn to a section heading devoted to the issue of faith, including the faith to be healed and the mystery of faith.

He skimmed through the pages dedicated to issues of faith and found them unsatisfying. MacNutt, in his opinion, focused too much on the faith of the subject and whether the subject had sufficient faith to be healed. Father Tom believed Naomi must have sufficient faith to be healed, if her faith was required, but she likely was insentient at this point and wouldn't be an active party to any faith healing. On the other hand, Theo, as her surrogate, had great faith that she could be healed but lacked sufficient faith in himself to mediate the healing. For that task, Theo wanted him, Father Thomas Abernathy, a poker-playing priest near the end of his career. Father Tom wondered if the stress of Naomi's terminal illness, along with his inherent anxiety and morose worldview, had addled Pastor Swindberg's mind.

Nonetheless, Father Tom had not refused Theo's request out of hand, which, he conceded, said something about his own mental status. He questioned his own motives for even considering the request. Did he leave the door open because he wanted to spend Naomi's last days at her bedside, praying disingenuous prayers, sharing her last gasps of life with her husband? He shook his head to rid himself of the thoughts, which were, he knew, both melodramatic and morbid. Not to mention covetous and sinful.

He had MacNutt's book in hand and his finger between the pages, so be began to read the section dedicated to the issue of the faith of the healer, rather than the healed, but found the text unsatisfying. It begged the question: what faith is sufficient? If he were to accede to Theo's request, and if faith healing were to be effective, it only would be so if his faith were unassailable and powerful enough to prompt God to affect the great harmonic sufficiently to reverse the course of her disease. That was a pretty tall order, and he again couldn't believe he was considering it.

But he was.

Closing MacNutt's book on his lap, Father Tom decided to look at the question of the sufficiency of his faith in the same practical way he'd looked at other issues over the years of his priesthood. He recognized the issue had two aspects: the amount of faith he held in his heart and the strength of that faith. Even if he had wholehearted faith that he could heal Naomi through his intervention as an instrument of God, as Theo referred to him, he still was troubled. He needed his faith in the healing power of prayer, through the Holy Trinity, and ultimately through himself, to be above reproach, and he conceded it was not.

Theo's comment, "My love for her doesn't let me fully realize my faith," was uppermost in his mind, and it flummoxed him. Just thinking of Naomi, just hearing her name, revved his pulse, causing a tightness in his chest that robbed him of his breath, forcing him to pant to take in air, and it had been that way since the first time he saw her in front of St. Paul's. But Theo's implication was another matter. It compounded his distress, particularly in view of the fact he was actually considering Theo's request. Alone in his study, he concentrated on his breathing, trying to push Theo's comment and his own feelings for Naomi out of his mind. His respirations slowed along with his heart rate. In a state of quietude, he admitted to himself that if he was going to help Naomi, he had to squelch all feelings for her. If not, he could not, as Theo could not, fully realize his faith.

Tom placed MacNutt's book on the corner of his desk. He walked across the study, picked up the end table that sat next to the wingback chair, carried it to the middle of the study, and set it down about three feet away from the bookshelves. He closed the window curtains, went back to his desk, and disconnected the telephone. He trundled upstairs to his bedroom, unplugged his bedside telephone, turned to his dresser where he took his pocket knife from the drawer and slipped it in his trouser pocket. He then picked up a neatly folded cloth from the drawer and carefully unfolded it on the palm of his hand, exposing a medal about the size of a quarter. He rubbed his thumb across the medal, which bore a relief of St. Rita of Cascia, patron saint of the impossible. It was an icon he'd carried in his pocket every day during his years at the seminary and one which he'd retired to one of his mother's hankies upon his ordination in honor of completing a task he'd viewed, at one time, as impossible for a man of his background and temperament.

Back downstairs in the library, he placed a votive candle, the St. Rita medal, a rosary, the photograph of his mother, his Bible, and the Virgin Mary statue on the end table. He went out the back door and walked through the darkness past Cat's grave, where he made the sign of the cross, to the willow tree where, amid the mass of dangling branches, he could barely make out the arrangements of the stars overhead. He took out his pocket knife and felt around among the branches until he found one to his liking. He cut off a section about four feet long and about as big around as his little finger and used his knife to strip it bare, letting the leaves and bark fall in the grass under the tree.

Back inside the rectory, he placed the willow switch on the floor next to the table, locked the backdoor, lit the votive candle, and turned off all the lights, leaving the study sparsely lit by a flickering flame. The room was warm and stuffy. He took off his shoes and socks and stripped to the waist, tossing his dress shirt and T-shirt into the corner. He knelt before the table and faced the bookshelves. In an amorphous pool of yellow candlelight, he prayed.

He admitted, in his opening prayer, that he wasn't properly prepared, in a classical sense, to effect the healing of Naomi Swindberg through prayerful intervention. What he confessed was true. He'd had no education or training in the process; his area of formal study had been Pastoral Theology, and little of his coursework was relevant to the present problem. Prayers for health and healing were a routine service offered by all priests, but intense concentration on the healing of a damaged human was the purpose of a healing novena, he reasoned, and sending a sick parishioner to a novena was the pastoral equivalent of a family practice doctor referring a patient to a specialist.

Nevertheless, Theo had given him a commission, he prayed, but he'd not yet agreed to take on the task and he was praying for guidance. Or perhaps a sign. He began earnest contemplation by reciting aloud an Our Father and a Hail Mary and then another Our Father. It occurred to him, as he recited the second Our Father, that the first thing he needed to do was clarify in his mind the genesis of Naomi's affliction so he could focus on the proper approach if he acceded to Theo's request. Determining the approach might help him decide whether he should even get involved. He admitted it was a tail-wagging-the-dog approach, but he was empty of ideas. So he cleared his mind of all thoughts and listened to the voice of his heart. After at least an hour of deep contemplation, the voice kept calling him back to the saving grace of Jesus Christ, but he wasn't sure if that was merely an artifact of Christian dogma or a genuine guiding voice.

Still, he plodded on. Surely, despite her bodily affliction Naomi was held gently in Christ's good graces. In light of such grace, he concluded, Naomi's illness could not be the work of the Devil, so an exorcism was not warranted. Neither was her cancer divine retribution for some personal sin, nor God's method of disciplining her, conclusions which negated the dogmatists' and fundamentalists' arguments as to the cause of her cancer which plagued him as he prayed. What it was, he finally concluded, was simply an unhappy accident of nature, a biological or genetic time bomb, randomly planted in her otherwise perfect body at birth, that finally exploded, sending its murderous shrapnel into all her vital organs.

This, his heart told him, was most certainly true.

But what was to be done for her? His heart told him he had the answer, he just had to find it. He considered the question for another hour or so, until his head pounded and his body stunk in the heat of the study. If, as he fervently believed, God made man, God can rectify any defects in a man, genetic or biological or accidental, if one could move Him to do so, without putting Him to the test. Tom saw his clear path: he would, if he determined he could, beseech God to heal her with complete faith that He will heal her, not to prove anything to him or to Theo about the nature of God, but only because she, as one of God's finest creatures, deserved healing.

Once he settled on the proper path, he again questioned whether or not he should be the one to go down the path. He opened his Bible, and by the flickering candlelight, turned the pages until he found Matthew 17:31, which he read aloud: "For truly I tell you, if you have faith the size of a mustard seed, you can say to this mountain, 'Move from here to there,' and it will move. Nothing will be impossible for you." He questioned whether his faith was sufficient, like that of the mustard seed, sufficiently strong to move the mountain Theo had asked him to move.

He understood the conventional teaching of the parable, yet he knew there had to be more to it. At times, Christ could be subtle. He wanted to divine the subtler meaning of scripture as instructed by Augustine. He closed his eyes and visualized the mustard seed itself: small, hard, spherical, with the beeswax hue of a dead body. He intently concentrated on the image of the seed, praying that the inherent quality of faith would leap out at him. He lost track of time. He was sweating and thirsty but vowed he'd not take a drink until Christ opened his eyes. His knees ached from kneeling on the floor, and his back and shoulders were sore from hunching over the table in prayer. The votive candle was nearly sputtered out. He doubted himself and considered it folly, at his age, to punish himself in this manner. He considered getting up from the floor and calling Theo to tell him to find another man. But as he felt the hard surface of the table under his elbows, it came to him: the mustard seed is small, but hard and solid. Even though it is small, faith like the mustard seed is hard and solid, with no interstices in which doubt or the Devil could hide.

Once he was satisfied with his divination of the subtle meaning of the mustard seed parable, he next needed to determine if he possessed such faith, hard and solid though small, that would warrant agreeing to Theo's request. If he prayed fervently enough, he assumed Christ would disclose the strength of his faith the same way he disclosed the inherent mystery of the mustard seed.

"Forgive me, Christ Jesus, for I have sinned," he recited out loud. "I am a bad man, a known sinner, a sinner worse than St. Paul and not worthy of your intervention. But it's not for me that I call on you. It's for her, and she is good."

He held the rosary in his hands and concentrated on the recitation bead by bead, trying to drive all other thoughts out of his mind. He began to fervently pray to the Holy Mother for guidance and asked that she instill in him just half the faith his own mother possessed when she had prayed that he would call after he'd abandoned her, He had called, and she came and saved him. With prayers to Mary, Mother of God, his mind had drifted to his mother and then to women in general and then to the image of Naomi standing in front of the Lutheran church, her soft skirt billowing in the breeze. He didn't know how to rid his mind of the simulacrum that now stood lewdly at the forefront of his thoughts so he banged his head viciously against the tabletop and reveled in the pain. "Get behind me, Satan!" he shouted.

"Oh God," he prayed aloud again, his head throbbing, "who didst break the chains of blessed Peter the Apostle and didst make him come forth from prison unscathed, loose the bonds of Thy servant, held in captivity by the vice of lust and by the merits of the same Apostle, do thou grant me to be delivered from its tyranny."

He knelt in the waning light of the small candle and begged for abnegation of his self-interests, of his sinful feelings. His head ached from striking it against the table, but he still felt Naomi encroaching on his consciousness. He grabbed the willow branch and sat on the floor and beat the soles of his feet with the thickest end of the branch until he thought he was going to piss his pants from the pain, but he held his water and rolled onto his knees, leaned his elbows on the table, and recited another decade of the rosary. Between the nettling pain in his feet and the words of the rosary, he lost all thought of Naomi and began to feel self-satisfied, which he knew was, in itself, another sin, and at his realization that she'd abandoned his thoughts, she returned.

I sought pleasure, sublimity, and truth not in God but in his creatures.

He picked up the willow switch and flogged his back. With the switch in his right hand he beat his bare back as hard as he could until he felt fluid trickling down to his waist. He couldn't tell if it was his heavy sweat or blood or both, and he reached around and ran his finger through a rivulet, touched it to his lips and tasted the metallic taint of blood. He took the switch in his other hand and proceeded to mercilessly whip the skin on the other side of his back to drive out his impure thoughts.

He also wanted to remove all questions regarding the solidity of his faith through the application of the willow branch. His faith needed to be that of the mustard seed, but he stopped flogging himself when the pain nearly robbed him of reason; he couldn't continue, he knew, if his self-abuse distracted him from his contemplation and inquiry. It was a damning dilemma.

So intense was his pain and so deep his concentration and so fervent his prayers that he began to hallucinate. Alone in the dark library, he heard raspy voices muttering rough oaths; he felt the jostling of grimy bodies against his own; he felt acrid cigarette smoke curling into his nose; he had the taste of whiskey on his tongue. From across the room, he saw a group of men lazing against the bar which stood in place of the bookshelves, drinks in hand, smirks on their faces.

"I am Little Shithead, and I can whip any son-of-a-bitch in the place," he shouted toward the men, but they only laughed and mocked him with obscene movements of their hands.

You promised no fighting, Tommy, echoed through the room.

"Mama?"

No fighting.

"But I have to."

No fighting.

"It's different this time."

Fighting is fighting.

"I fight for God, Mama."

You're not fighting for God, Tommy. God did not ask you to take up this fight.

"You're right, Mama; you're always right."

Then who is it that asks you to break your promise to me?

"Just a man, like me."

Just a man?

166

"For his wife."

Another man's wife?

"Not just for another man's wife, Mama; for another of God's creatures."

But you promised no fighting.

"I swear on your grave this is the last time."

Is this the last time?

"Yes, Mama, I promise."

That's Mother's precious little lamb.

"Oh Little Therese of the Child Jesus, please pick for me a rose from the heavenly gardens and send it to me as a message of love," he prayed aloud.

He rubbed his eyes and shooed the voices and visions from his head and looked about the room to get his bearings. He still was on his knees before the prayer shrine. He tried to lift his arms but couldn't. He ached physically. His knees and elbows were numb from pain. The welts on his back burned and itched. He ached emotionally, as well. He sat on the floor and felt impotent, felt that his efforts were weak, and that he was not up to the task Theo had asked him to perform. He rebuked himself for his failure to solidify his faith, like Christ's Disciples in the Book of Matthew. He had the Bible verses in his memory but didn't trust his memory in such a state.

He picked up his Bible from the table and turned again to chapter 17 of Matthew and read: "Afterward the disciples came to Jesus privately and asked, 'Why couldn't we drive it out?' 'Because you have so little faith,' He answered. 'For truly I tell you, if you have faith the size of a mustard seed, you can say to this mountain, 'Move from here to there,' and it will move. Nothing will be impossible for you.'"

He again recognized that such a faith may be small, as small as a mustard seed perhaps, but that small faith must be absolutely solid and not circumscribing any doubt that could make it porous and fragile.

"Truly I tell you," he continued reading in the waning candlelight, "if you have faith and do not doubt, not only will you do what was done to the fig tree, but even if you say to this mountain 'Be lifted up and thrown into the sea,' it will happen."

He dropped the Bible on the tabletop and stared at his mother's photograph.

Who do you think you are? he heard her say.

"Tommy. Tommy Abernathy. Mother's little lamb."

But who do you think you are?

"Father Thomas Abernathy, pastor of St. Michael Catholic Church."

But who do you think you are? she asked again, continuing his internal dialectic.

"Just a man."

Why are you even considering this?

"Because Theo asked me."

But why are you considering this?

"He says I'm an instrument of God."

Aren't we all instruments of God?

"Yes, we are all instruments of God, Mama, and therefore I'm an instrument of God."

Why save her from death? Isn't the release of her soul to God preferable?

"Theo needs her to help him through life."

Do you love her?

"Christ said love one another."

Do you love her?

"There are many types of love."

Do you love her?

"Yes."

Is that why you're willing to do this?

"I want to save her."

For Theo?

"Yes."

Or for you?

"For God. She is one of God's most perfect creatures. God will save her through me."

But who do you think you are?

"Just a man who loves one of God's most perfect creatures."

You will save her even if you can't have her?

"Because I can't have her."

You will save her even if you can't have her?

"I will save her because I can't have her; and when I save her, I'll never look at her again. I will never again think of her in any way."

Then why save her?

"When I save her, I'll know the world is more beautiful because she's in it, even though I'll never look upon her beauty again."

Who do you think you are?

"I am merely a man, yet an instrument of God."

How strong is your faith?

"Strong enough to save her."

But how strong is that faith?

"My faith is like that of a mustard seed."

It was with this thought he nodded off to sleep, exhausted from the rigors of contemplation and fervent prayer and flogging. He woke with his head resting on the tabletop. A shard of sunlight slipping through a gap in the curtain panels settled near his cheek. He raised up slowly; he was cramped and stiff. His knees and elbows ached, and he had a pounding headache. His back burned and itched. His prayer books were scattered across the tabletop. He rested his head in his hands and conjured up the previous night, how he had prayed, and the hallucinations which indicated what God had decided for him. He eased up from the floor and limped on sore feet to the telephone on his desk. He connected the phone jack and dialed St. Paul's parsonage.

"I'll do what you asked me to do," he said when Theo answered, "but only if I can do it alone, with no interference. And you can't question my methods. Also, we must give each other our solemn promise we won't tell a soul."

"As you require, Father," Theo responded. And after a short pause, he added, "You are the instrument of God."

Tom winced at his last remark, a remark which caused his back to sweat and smart as if freshly flogged by the willow switch. Yet he accepted the remark without comment. He needed to accept it with unquestioned faith. If he had any doubt whatsoever, all would be lost.

"We'll begin tomorrow afternoon."

He next placed a call to the bishop's office but got no answer. He left a message on the secretary's answering machine, instructing the secretary to tell the bishop he needed to take a short leave of absence and that the bishop needed to find a temporary replacement for St. Michael. He could be gone a couple days or as much as a week, beginning today. He provided no further explanation, hung up, and disconnected the phone line.

Perhaps he did have faith like a mustard seed, he reasoned, but he had little faith that the bishop would respond fairly to his message. Since being named bishop of the diocese, the man had displayed a capricious and arbitrary turn of mind, even in small matters. In large matters, he could be petty and demanding, favoring those who displayed obsequious fealty and ignoring those with an independent approach to priestly duties. Despite his many years of dedication to his parishes, Father Tom had been passed over for Monsignor several times for reasons he could attribute to nothing other than having earned the bishop's disfavor. Now, in view of his commission from Theo, he wasn't concerned about the bishop's favor or his obsession with hierarchy and protocol. Nor was he concerned about the ramifications of leaving St. Michael without an explanation. He understood, under the circumstances, a temporary replacement at St. Michael could turn out to be permanent if the bishop decided to retaliate, which he was prone to do, but Father Tom believed the stakes were too high to worry about what his disappearance from St. Michael for a few days might mean to his middling career.

Father Tom went upstairs to take a shower. Naked, he stepped into the bathtub and turned his head to look at his reflection in the big mirror over the sink. He stared for a minute at the welts and cuts and blood on his back.

Ecce homo.

After he showered, he donned his pajamas, put a few pairs of clean briefs, two T-shirts, and his toiletries in his grip. He would pack more accoutrements before he left for Theo's. And although it was only mid-morning, he pulled down the window shades and darkened his room and went to bed. He knew he needed to rest; he didn't know after today when he would sleep again.

CHAPTER NINETEEN

Father Tom called a cab to take him to the Lutheran parsonage. When they pulled up to the curb, he saw Theo peeking through the front window blinds. He got out of the cab as quickly as his sore legs allowed and paid the driver. He knew Theo would be skittish and uncomfortable having a priest in front of his house in broad daylight, dressed in a soutane, band cincture, and Roman collar, and he didn't want to make the poor man any more uncomfortable, so he jogged up the sidewalk to the parsonage as quickly as he could.

Once inside the house, Theo led Father Tom to the master bedroom where Naomi lay in a hospital bed provided by the hospice service. He found the room warm and stale, and he began to sweat under his soutane, causing the welts on his back to smart as if fresh. A good sign, he thought, a good reminder. The only aspect of cheeriness in the room was the late morning sun shining through an east window. He told Theo to leave the room and lock the door behind him. He warned him to not interfere, no matter what, and to stay out unless called for.

Once Theo left the room, Father Tom walked over and lowered the window shade, leaving the room dimly lit by seeping yellow light. He looked around and saw the room was well suited to his purposes. It was intimate and clean, and there was a comfortable side chair adjacent the hospital bed and an adjoining bathroom for his personal needs. He stood quietly next to the bed and listened. He could hear Naomi's shallow breathing, very likely slowed by morphine drops, liberally dosed by the hospice nurse, as he'd seen in other cases, ostensibly to relieve discomfort but also to augment the natural, sometimes reluctant, pace of death. Naomi's skin had the beeswax color of the living dead. Her hands were outside the sheet, and he saw they were thin and veiny but beautifully manicured. The nail beds had begun to turn blue.

Death used a varied palette, and he had seen its work before: the mottled gray of the old dead, the saffron-skinned cirrhotic, the cherry red faces of the sweet family of five who'd died in their sleep from a faulty furnace flue. One of the worst he'd seen was early in his priesthood, back in the 1980s, when a distraught wife asked him to say a funeral Mass for her husband, an accountant named Ferguson who'd hanged himself. By the time they'd cut him down from the garage rafters, he was as purple as a plum, and no amount of mortician's makeup could make him sufficiently presentable for an open casket. He'd said Mass for Ferguson and prayed for the repose of his soul, which was not routinely done for a suicide in those days, and for the first time, he'd incurred the disapprobation of the diocesan hierarchy. That act, along with subsequent others, earned him the reputation as a maverick, and he maintained a reputation among succeeding bishops as a priest to keep one's eyes on.

Now his eyes were on Naomi. He could see she'd been prepared for him. The hospice worker, who'd left just before he'd arrived with instructions not to return until called, had given her a sponge bath and washed her hair, which was still damp and brushed straight back away from her face. She had faint, pleasant odors of soap and shampoo about her. Her eyes were closed, and she appeared insentient, much as he'd anticipated. She was covered to her neck with a sheet, and her citrine cheeks were crisscrossed by prominent blue veins which gave her face a pale yellow-blue cast. Under the sheet her arms were crossed on her chest, like a corpse. Father Tom observed that her arms were quite thin, and he also could see the outline of her knees under the sheet. She was much thinner than the last time he'd seen her standing in front of St. Paul's. Yet, despite the wasting and discoloration, he still thought her lovely, and at the thought of her loveliness, he felt the burn and prickle of the welts and wheals on his back, and he easily shoved the thought from his head and prepared for his work.

He opened his grip and looked at the items he'd piled on top of his underwear that morning. He had packed his Bible, the copy of *Anointing and Pastoral Care*, his rosary, the St. Rita medal, the Virgin Mary statue, a glass vial of olive oil, and a small, plastic bottle embossed with the words "holy water" in gold paint. He carefully placed his books and icons on the bedside table. Next, he lifted out a silver aspersorium and an aspergillum. Finally, he took out a clean T-shirt which was wrapped around a full bottle of Jameson Irish Whiskey, two bottles of drinking water, three packages of beef jerky, and four Almond Joy candy bars and set them in a neat arrangement on the dresser top. Once he had all accoutrements in place, he sat in the side chair and contemplated Naomi and her tenuous hold on life.

After about ten minutes of staring, he took the vial of oil in his hand to warm it, opened it, poured a dollop on his thumb, and anointed her forehead with the sign of the cross. He then recited the older, shorter prayer for the anointing of the sick he held in his memory: "May the Lord who freed you from sin heal you and extend his saving grace to you. Amen."

Dissatisfied with the brevity of his prayer, he picked up the copy of *Anointing and Pastoral Care of the Sick,* opened it to a marked page, placed his oily thumb on her forehead, and read aloud, "Lord God, all-comforting Father, you brought healing to the sick through your Son Jesus Christ. Hear us as we pray to you in faith and send the Holy Spirit, the Comforter, from heaven upon this oil, which nature has provided to serve the needs of men."

Naomi didn't move under his touch nor respond to his

voice. Her face was impassive, and her breathing remained shallow and labored. He stood at the bedside holding the bottle of oil, considering her shaky hold on life, and contemplated performing the Sacrament of Extreme Unction. But he wavered. Extreme Unction was a sacrament for Catholics, not Lutherans. Moreover, performing the rite was not what Theo had asked him to do. Although he understood the commission Theo charged him with, he also considered his obligation to Naomi and her immortal soul. He finally concluded that performing the sacrament might be a concession to the power of death, a pre-emptive admission his faith was porous and weak, so he put the vial of oil back in his grip and resolved it would not be needed.

"Oh, my Jesus," he prayed as he stood over her, "thou has said: 'Truly I say to you, ask and it will be given, seek and you will find, knock and it will be opened to you.' Behold, I knock! I seek and ask for the grace of healing for your child, Naomi. Our Father, Hail Mary, Glory Be. Sacred Heart of Jesus, I place all my trust in Thee."

Next, he opened the bottle of holy water and poured it into the aspersorium. He dipped the head of the aspergillum into the holy water and slowly flicked the water onto Naomi from her feet to her head. Fine droplets landed on her chin, her eyelashes and her lips, but she showed no reaction to the asperges, so Father Tom made the sign of the cross on her behalf. It was at that moment when he felt the awful weight of responsibility settle on his sore back.

He pulled the chair closer to her bed and sat down. Picking up his Bible, he opened it to where he'd placed a bookmark and lay it on the bed next to her hip and began to read aloud:

"Verily, verily I say unto you, He that believeth in me, the works that I do shall he do also; and greater works than these shall he do; because I go unto my Father. And whatsoever ye shall ask in my name, that will I do, that the Father may be glorified in the Son. If ye shall ask anything in my name, I will do it."

He closed the Bible and placed it back on the bedside table. He stood up and raised his eyes and arms toward the ceiling and in a loud voice prayed, "Lord Jesus, in your name I ask that this woman, your sister Naomi, be healed of all afflictions and returned whole to her good husband Theo and to her church. I ask this of you, Father, in your name. I have unshakable faith you will do as I ask."

He made the sign of the cross over Naomi's face and breast. Although he'd prayed loudly, Naomi, so deep in her hebetude, was unmoved by his voice. He sat down in his chair, knowing it was necessary to conserve his strength, and took a notecard out of his pocket and his St. Rita medal in hand and moved into his prayer vigil in earnest by reading a prayer to the saint he'd written on the card:

"O excellent St. Rita, worker of miracles, from thy sanctuary in Cascia, where in all thy beauty thou sleepest in peace, where thy relics exhale breaths of paradise, turn thy merciful eyes on me. Weary and discouraged as I am, I feel the very prayers dying on my lips. Must I thus despair in this crisis of my life? O come, St. Rita, come to my aid and help me as you did before, in my youth. Art thou not called the Saint of the Impossible, Advocate to those in despair? Then honor thy name, procuring for me from God the favor that I ask. That my faith be like that of the mustard seed, strong enough to move a mountain, and that my prayers restore your sister Naomi to good health. Everyone praises thy glories, everyone tells of the most amazing miracles performed through thee, must I alone be disappointed because thou hast not heard me? Ah no! Pray then, pray for me to thy sweet Lord Jesus that He be moved to pity by my request for her and her alone, and that, through thee, O good St. Rita, I may obtain what my heart so fervently desires."

He gently placed the St. Rita medal in Naomi's right hand and folded her fingers about it, marveling at how delicate and pale her young fingers looked in his rough hand. As he held her hand in his he felt the sores on his back burn and smart and he immediately said loudly, "Get behind me, Satan! You're a stumbling block to me!" He lay her hand holding the St. Rita medal gently on the bed, close to her side.

Father Tom picked up his rosary from the table, and with it in his right hand, made the sign of the cross over Naomi. He began reciting the Apostles' Creed while watching her face closely. It was a creed also recited by Lutherans, and he figured she knew it intimately, and he was hoping the familiar words would draw a response from her, but she slept on. Once he finished reciting the Apostles' Creed, he started on the Our Father, speaking slowly and clearly, not hurrying through the prayer as he often did when reciting from memory at Mass or alone in his study. Again, he hoped the Lord's Prayer would provoke a glint of recognition, but she didn't open her eyes. He next introduced the heart of his Catholic doctrine by reciting the Hail Mary. Naomi shifted her weight in bed, and Father Tom stuttered over "Blessed art thou among women," thinking, perhaps, this most Catholic of prayers provoked some discomfort. However, she moved no more, and he didn't stop reciting until he'd repeated the prayer two more times.

Discouraged because he already found his tongue dry and his voice weak, Father Tom took a swig of water from one of the bottles and chanted, "Glory be to the Father, and to the Son, and to the Holy Spirit. As it was in the beginning, is now, and ever shall be, world without end. Amen." He found his voice and said, "This is the First Joyful Mystery, The Annunciation," and repeated the Hail Mary ten more times, which took considerable concentration, particularly each time he recited, "Pray for us sinners, now, and at the hour of our death." Despite his intense concentration, at least three times he stumbled over the word "death." After completing the ten Hail Marys, he repeated "Glory be to the Father" and announced the Second Joyful Mystery—The Visitation.

He looked at his watch and realized he had been at his task barely two hours. He removed his watch and dropped it in his grip. He got up from the chair and walked to the dresser where there was a clock, and he turned it around so it faced away from him. He didn't want to be distracted from his obligation by the slow passage of time. He wanted to be suspended in time, not subject to it.

After reciting the Second Joyful Mystery, Father Tom repeated the Our Father and moved slowly through another decade of Hail Marys, this time concentrating more fervently to avoid stumbling. He was pleased with himself for reciting flawlessly, then rebuked himself for his vanity. He'd begun to sweat from the intensity of his prayer and the warmth in the room, but he accepted that it was Naomi's comfort which was important, not his own. He knew when death crept near, it dragged along the cold like a bride's veil of ice. He removed his collar tab and put it on the table, undid the cincture and methodically unbuttoned the thirty-three buttons down the front of the soutane. He removed it and placed it, already heavy with sweat, over the back of the chair to dry. In the event Naomi awoke, he wanted to be able to clothe himself quickly and properly. He sat in his black trousers and damp T-shirt and continued to pray, "Glory be to the Father, and to the Son, and to the Holy Spirit. As it was in the beginning, is now, and ever shall be, world without end. Amen."

As he prayed, he was transfixed by the familiarity of the face on the pillow. Gazing at her on her deathbed, he understood, subliminally at least, what it was about the woman that had captured his imagination and roiled his feelings.

"I am faithful, Lord," he said. "I have faith. I know all of your prayers and the proper invocations. Please hear me. Mother Mary intercede for her."

As he prayed, he watched the daylight beyond the window shade dim into twilight. He'd lost track of time, as he had wanted. He repeated each decade of the Rosary. In between the decades, he improvised lamentations regarding her loss to Theo, to her church, to the world itself. But never to himself. As he methodically continued with his formal prayers interspersed with his improvised prayers and supplications, he saw the shadows cast by the sunrise play on the window shade. Yet he didn't waver, didn't stop; he felt strong and robust, more vigorous and more intuitive of his calling than ever before in his ministry. His spirits buoyed, he continued to beseech Jesus Christ, the Lord and Savior of the universe, to heal the child resting in front of him. He had pangs of hunger and his hands were shaking, so he stopped praying briefly and ate a candy bar, chewed a stick of jerky, and washed it all down with three fingers of Jameson. He felt the glow of the whiskey spread from his belly to his limbs, and fortified by another light, he plodded on with his prayers.

As he leaned forward in the chair praying, a random thought entered his mind and disrupted his prayer. He wasn't sure if it was a vestige of a precept he'd learned years ago or a novel insight which had insinuated itself into his consciousness. In any case, he realized for the first time that Naomi's illness might be a manifestation of a troubled marriage. Theo had hinted at problems the day they met in the coffee shop. He wasn't sure, but he decided that rather than praying for Naomi alone, he might better serve her by praying for Theo as well. And their marriage. He began to diligently pray for emotional healing of both man and wife; he prayed that any iniquities which were troubling them and their marriage would be forgiven; he prayed for each spouse to forgive the other for any real or imagined failing; and then prayed relentlessly for their relationship to be healed, along with Naomi's body, if that relationship indeed needed healing. Once he added Theo and their marriage to his prayer vigil, he felt as if an unacknowledged nettle that had been irritating the wounds on his skin was lifted off his back, and he continued praying with renewed vigor and purpose.

According to the clock in Theo's parlor, twenty-four hours passed and then thirty-six. Theo was nearly overwhelmed by the anxiety felt by a man when there were matters of great consequence afoot affecting his life and all he can do is sit idly by and let matters run their course. He was so agitated by his inactivity he couldn't eat or sleep, although he'd dozed briefly on the sofa in the parlor when nervous exhaustion overtook him. More than once, as he waited, he started to chew the fingernails on his left hand, but he stopped, offering his minor demonstration of willpower as penance for his failures as a husband and as minister of the Lord. Under the stress of sleeplessness and plummeting blood sugar, his mood swung back and forth between a feeling of self-satisfaction that he'd risked everything—his education, his reputation, his position, his sense of moral superiority—to save his wife, to abject self-loathing for relying on another man to stand in his stead.

Once, when his anxiety nearly caused him to vomit, he crept on his hands and knees to the bedroom door and strained to hear Father Tom's prayers and supplications. He couldn't make out the words, but he heard the priest's voice as it rose and fell in a hypnotic rhythm, and reassured, his nausea subsided, and he stood up and walked quietly back to his chair in the parlor to read his Bible. However, as soon as he sat down, he was immediately embarrassed by his comparative fecklessness, and he got down on his knees in the middle of the room and recited aloud a Lutheran prayer for healing:

"Dear heavenly Father, you intend her body to be a temple of Thy Holy Spirit. May it be Your gracious will that she enjoy Your healing power, that she may seek You, serve You, enjoy You and depend on You, through the physical life You have given her and shared with her, in Jesus Christ, my Lord. Amen."

The words were no sooner said when he realized the reedy timbre of his little man's voice offering an insincere, canned prayer was worse than not praying at all. He was on the floor contemplating his weakness as a man when he was startled by a loud thud. A minute later, he heard Naomi calling him from their room: "Theo! Theo, come here, I need you!"

Theo scrambled to his feet, ran to the bedroom door, took the door key from his pocket, and let himself into the room. He nearly gagged from the staggering stench of excrement and raw body odor. Naomi was out of bed standing over Father Tom, who lay motionless on the floor. She held one of his arms in her hands. "He fell out of the chair," she said. "Help me get him up."

Theo got down on the floor next to Father Tom and felt his neck for a pulse and found it to be weak and slow. He called his name, but Tom didn't respond. For a brief moment he thought the priest was dying and in his anguish and confusion, thought little of Naomi, of her being out of bed standing next to the priest, the back of her nightgown streaked with runny shit.

"I need to call an ambulance," Theo said.

"Wait," Naomi said. "I think he just passed out."

She walked into the bathroom, soaked a washcloth in cold water, and kneeled on the floor next to Father Tom, wiping his forehead and temples with the cloth. Awash in a rich damask fragrance emitted by Mister Lincoln roses, the priest opened his eyes, and seeing Naomi leaning over him, smiled, thinking her his mother and that he was dead.

"I'm calling an ambulance," said Theo. "Naomi, get back in bed."

"I think this man is a priest," Naomi said blankly. "Why is there a priest here?"

"I'll explain it all to you after I call an ambulance."

"Was he praying?"

Theo didn't respond.

"Was this priest praying for me, Theo?"

Theo couldn't respond. Naomi's comportment both elated and dumbfounded him. And he had presence of mind enough to understand an admission of Tom's purpose would be an admission that he'd abdicated his duties both as a husband and a pastor and would distance himself even further from Naomi. But it really didn't matter now. He could only stare awkwardly at Naomi, who was silently staring at Tom lying on the floor. She finally said, "I understand."

"No, Theo, don't call an ambulance," Father Tom said weakly from the floor. He propped himself up on one elbow. "I don't need an ambulance. Just get me into the chair."

Theo struggled to lift Father Tom, so Naomi grabbed an arm and together they lifted him into the side chair. Father Tom looked up at Naomi standing over him, hands on her hips, her gown soiled and stinking. At that moment, Tom thought she still was perfect. But he felt nothing for her but hope.

"Oh, my, how embarrassing," she said when the stench informed her of the soiled condition of her night clothes. "I need to get cleaned up. I'm so embarrassed you saw me like this."

Naomi hurried into the bathroom and closed the door. Father Tom heard the water from the shower. He realized his own body stunk from sweat and whiskey. He looked around the room at the mess he'd made. The half empty bottle of Jameson's sat in a puddle on the dresser top; there were shards of beef jerky strewn around the room, along with discarded water bottles and candy wrappers. His soutane hung on the chair back. His T-shirt was yellow with sweat, and while Naomi was in the shower, he put on the clean T-shirt, donned the soutane and inserted his collar tab. He looked in the mirror and saw that he needed to comb his hair, which he tried to do with little effect, and he also needed a shave.

"I need to go home," he said to Theo as he packed his books and icons in his grip. "It's finished."

When Theo arrived back at the parsonage after driving Father Tom to the rectory, Naomi was back in her bed, showered and fresh and wearing clean night clothes. He heard the rhythmic whirl of the washing machine in the laundry room. He looked around the bedroom and saw that she had straightened it: the trash was gone, the furniture tops wiped clean, and the bottle of Jameson's was capped and sitting on the dresser. Without opening her eyes, she told him she was tired and needed to rest, so he left and went to the parlor to pray and contemplate what he'd been a party to.

Theo gave Naomi's improved condition short shrift. He assumed her flurry of activity—the cleaning up the bedroom, showering, dressing, doing the laundry, not to mention her ministrations to Father Tom as he lay on the floor—was nothing more than an example of the paradoxical effect of stress on a weakened body. Her display of vigor likely resulted from being startled out of her lethargy by the great clomp of the priest falling down on her floor. He assumed, now that she was back in bed, she'd slip back into her torpor until the angels called for her.

Oddly, he was more worried about Father Tom's well-being. Once he'd gotten him back to St. Michael, it took all his strength to help him up the rectory stairs to his bed, and as soon as he fell on the bed, he began to snore loudly and irregularly. Theo had removed the priest's shoes and collar tab and loosened the buttons on his soutane. He wanted to sit with him for a while, but Naomi was home alone, and he'd already bailed on his husbandly responsibilities too readily by driving Father Tom to the rectory, so he went home to be with his wife.

As Naomi slept, Theo spent his time scouring his memory for scripture passages relevant to the emotional upheaval in his life. His wife was still going to die, he knew, and through his selfishness, he likely damaged the health of the only friend he'd ever had. Although his memory was impaired by his pothered emotions, he still knew there was nothing in the Bible applicable to the mess he'd caused. Nevertheless, he combed through the Bible and *Luther's Small Catechism* and pondered the events that led up to his finding Father Tom collapsed on the bedroom floor with Naomi standing over him, soiled and stinking.

He looked up from the texts as if he'd had a revelatory thought. The thought occurred along with the image of the sweaty priest sprawled on the bedroom floor with his wife tugging mightily on one arm to move him. It was at that moment he considered for the first time the possibility that Naomi might be healed, and with that epiphany, he felt a presence in the parlor, looked up from his Bible, and saw her standing near the doorway. She was hungry, she said, and was going to fix a bite to eat. She wanted to know if he would like to join her. When he told her she should go back to bed, and he would make her something to eat, she just giggled and said that was nonsense; she was perfectly capable of making a sandwich. She laughed again and walked out of the parlor.

Theo got up from his chair and followed her into the kitchen. He was weak from hunger but had no appetite, so he flopped down in a kitchen chair and watched her going through the wonderfully mundane motions of taking two slices of bread from the loaf, rummaging through the refrigerator for cold-cuts, mustard, and pickles, and placing her plate on the kitchen table across from him. She sat down and ate. Although he'd seen her eat a sandwich countless times, he was now fascinated by her ritual: first, she cut the sandwich in half, cross-corner; she took one half and nibbled evenly from each corner. He realized it was the manner in which she always ate a sandwich, an everyday act he'd never really appreciated before. He wondered if she knew she was slowly destroying the hypotenuse of the triangle eating it that way, and then he silently cursed his own erudition, and cursed his other niggling traits that took the joy out of so many simple acts of their married life.

Naomi ate and didn't speak, her eyes scanning the room, taking in every appliance, utensil, plate, cup, condiment, canister, and knickknack as if she were inventorying the kitchen to see if everything had remained in the place it occupied before she took to her deathbed. Theo sat across from her in awkward silence and tried to think of a response to the inevitable questions as to why she'd awakened in her bed to find a Catholic priest in his trousers and T-shirt, sweaty and foul, on their bedroom floor. And why was it she now felt well enough to clean the room and do laundry and shower and dress and fix her own sandwich and eat? However, as they sat at the kitchen table, there was a sweet quietness between them. Naomi raised no questions about the events of the past couple of days, and Theo decided not to broach the subject with her as she ate. He focused on her and her alone as she relished her food and didn't worry about how he would best explain the details of the affair if she asked.

Yet, he couldn't stop being himself for very long. He was uncomfortable with dissimulation and felt like he needed to say something to his wife, this woman who now sat across the table from him as she had most mealtimes through the many days of their marriage, eating a sandwich, seemingly oblivious to the profound event that moved her from her deathbed to a kitchen chair, leaving her whole and hungry but incurious. His prodigious memory failed him as he searched for a snippet of scripture to put events into perspective, to segue into the less-than-believable story of her unexpected flush of good health, which he was not quite ready to believe was a healing. When he couldn't think of something scriptural to say to her, all he could blurt out was, "I love you, Naomi," to which she replied through a mouthful of food, "I know, Theo. I know."

CHAPTER TWENTY

Across town, Father Tom slept. He later awoke to pounding on the rectory door. He looked at his alarm clock and realized he'd been in bed for almost twenty-four hours. He crawled out of bed and put on his bathrobe and went downstairs. He looked out the front window before he answered the door. Monsignor Manring, the Coadjutor Bishop for the Diocese, was standing on his stoop. Tom knew Manring to be a shameless toady, a man perversely titillated by delivering distasteful messages from the bishop. Father Tom opened the door, and Manring greeted him with a quick nod of his head. The coadjutor did not deign to step inside the rectory, and in his characteristic brusque manner he announced from the stoop that he was at St. Michael to summon Father Tom to a meeting with the bishop at the cathedral and provided no details, save for the day and time.

The meeting between Father Tom and the bishop was to be held in about a week. As he had promised himself, and his mother, in the intervening days, he rid his mind of thoughts of Naomi. He didn't inquire as to Naomi's health; he didn't drive by St. Paul's; he didn't whisper another silent prayer for her. He didn't need to; his soul informed him of the certainty of her recovery, and he was content.

For the next week, he focused on his duties as pastor of St. Michael. There indeed had been a temporary priest when he was gone, a native of Kenya who, he learned from his parishioners, had a pronounced accent which he aggravated by speaking very rapidly, rendering him doubly difficult to understand. Father Tom had only been gone a few days, but his old parishioners fawned over him at morning Mass, and he was happy to be back. They inquired tactfully about his absence, but he deflected their questions by merely saying "priest business."

He found renewed enjoyment in the mundane tasks of a parish priest, more enjoyment than he'd found in years, and attributed his pleasure to the realization, because of his impending meeting with the bishop, his days of doing the work he'd loved for decades were coming to an abrupt and ignominious end.

In the evenings during that interval before his meeting with the bishop, when he didn't have parish business to attend to, he worked in his rose garden, raking together small piles of dropped petals, and pruning the bushes for winter. He mulched the plants, pulled weeds, and generally tidied the flower bed. He sprayed his concoction on the occasional vagabond aphid or thrips. He found working around the plants satisfying, and the pleasure of the tasks was compounded by the constant thought of his mother and the lessons of husbandry she'd shared with him years ago. The pleasure also was augmented by the sweet rose scent that still was pervasive even though the growing season was coming to an end. The morning of his meeting with the bishop, as he walked to the garage, he stopped at the rose garden and grasped the stem of a late-blooming yellow hybrid tea rose, bent down to sniff its fragrance, and as he did, petals fell to the ground. He picked them up and put them in his trouser pocket.

As he drove downtown, Father Tom assumed the meeting would be formal, yet brief, with the outcome preordained. His first assumption was confirmed when he approached the front door of the cathedral wearing simple black trousers, his black suit coat, a black cotton dress shirt, and his Roman collar, while Father Gregory, one of the bishop's many assistants, was dressed in a formal black cassock and black skull cap as he unlocked the massive front door and allowed him in. The two priests exchanged nods but no spoken greetings. Father Gregory locked the door behind them and the two remained silent as they walked together up the main aisle, through the nave to the chancel, where the bishop was seated on his cathedra.

The bishop was wearing his violet mozetta and skullcap. His large pectoral cross was well polished and blindingly reflective in the chancel lights. On the bishop's left stood Manring, the coadjutor, wearing an ornately embroidered chasuble over a starched snow-white alb. The bishop's secretary, whose name Father Tom couldn't recall, dressed in a formal black cassock and skull cap, was seated at a small table positioned below the chancel, adjacent the nave, three steps down from where the bishop sat, prepared to record the proceedings. Looking back and forth from the bishop to the coadjutor, Father Tom thought it fortunate he had bothered to iron his trousers and shirt and insert the tab. His uncharacteristically presentable dress and Roman collar were, however, the only outward signs of respect for the bishop he could muster. But he was the bishop, after all.

At the chancel steps, Father Tom genuflected before the bishop, who, in turn, nodded his head and beckoned him to move up one step toward him. Monsignor Manring stood with a smug and self-satisfied smirk, and Father Tom felt a powerful urge to bound up the steps and punch him in the face. The old secretary, on the other hand, sat at his table with a look of sad resignation on his.

The proceedings began abruptly, with no introductory comments. In response to a backhanded wave by the bishop, his secretary began reading a list of grievances against Father Thomas Abernathy, some going back many years, none especially serious by itself. The list included the Mass he'd held for the suicide almost thirty years prior, a proscription in place when Father Tom performed the rite, but which had fallen into disfavor in the intervening years. Nevertheless, the admonition remained in the record. Other transgressions included his slovenly appearance, his lack of collegiality, and frequent backhanded slaps at the bishop in his weekly homilies. None of the grievances on the list read so far were particularly offensive, yet all of them were makeweight in a bundle.

The last and most serious accusation was his purported abandonment of St. Michael for several days without explanation. Tom silently accepted the accusation, but felt, as he was being accused, that leaving the voice message for the bishop's secretary should, in a small measure, mitigate this transgression. However, the secretary made no mention of the message, and Tom remained silent and didn't offer any reference to it as evidence in mitigation of the offending behavior. As he listened, Father Tom stood with his hand in his pocket and fingered the yellow rose petals he'd picked up in his garden and held his tongue.

After the grievances were read, the bishop asked Father Tom if he had anything to say in his own behalf.

"No, Your Excellency," he responded, using a term of address he'd not used since he was a young priest. He was puzzled as to why these words popped into his mind at this time and even more than puzzled, he was chagrined he'd used them under the circumstances.

"Come, now, Father Abernathy, you've never been one to mince words. If you have something to say, now is the time to say it."

Father Tom again demurred, this time addressing his accuser only as "Bishop."

"Do you deny you left St. Michael without explanation as to why?"

"No, Bishop, I don't deny it."

"Would you like to explain yourself?"

Father Tom chafed at the bishop's tone. His anger informed

him to remain quiet, however, and not to respond, lest he say something he might regret. Nevertheless, with his years of service to the church and adherence to its formalities, he was inculcated with the rules under which the hierarchy functioned and understood the relationship between a bishop and a parish priest. As much as it displeased him, he reflexively felt he owed the bishop, his superior, some explanation as to his absence from St. Michael.

"I had to attend to the sick," he said.

"To the sick? How many sick? Was there a plague that passed through Belle City I wasn't aware of?" the bishop asked, drawing a wry smile from the coadjutor.

"I misspoke. I had to minister to one person who was very sick."

"I see. You abandoned your parish to minister to one very sick person?"

"Yes."

"What was the result of your ministrations to this very sick person?"

"She's well now."

"She?" he asked, raising his eyebrows in the direction of the coadjutor, who issued a barely audible snicker at the bishop's implication. Again, Father Tom had the urge to bash Manring in his nasty mouth.

"Yes, a woman," he answered.

"So let me be clear about this: you abandoned your church without explanation to minister to a woman, a very sick woman, as you described her, who now is well?"

"Yes."

"You healed her by your ministrations?"

"I was only an instrument of God."

"You deem yourself an instrument of God?"

"Not I."

"Who then?"

"Her husband."

"Who is this woman?"

"I can't say."

"As the bishop of this diocese and your superior, I insist you to tell me who this woman is," the bishop said loudly, leaning forward on the cathedra.

Father Tom didn't respond. The bishop beckoned Father Tom to move one step closer to him such that the bishop's face was so near him Tom could see the tension and frustration in the man's eyes and count the beads of perspiration on his upper lip. Father Tom studied the bishop's face for a quarter minute and as he did he saw the bishop's tension and frustration begin to dissolve away. At that point, he knew the bishop would not press him for more information. Father Tom understood that the bishop's demeanor changed with the realization he had Father Thomas Abernathy right where he wanted him, and being a talented inquisitor, the bishop knew better than to ask one more question, one which might afford his subject the opportunity to wriggle free with an exculpatory answer. They maintained their positions in awkward silence for nearly a minute longer. The bishop closed his eyes and rested his chin on his chest in what Father Tom knew to be mock contemplation.

"My preliminary decision is to remove you as pastor of St. Michael," the bishop finally said, without looking up. "You can respond in writing to the list of grievances, if you so choose. In any event, I'll give this matter due consideration and render a final decision. In the meantime, attend to your duties. You are dismissed."

The bishop made a sign of the cross in Father Tom's general direction, and Tom genuflected, turned around, walked down the long aisle escorted by Father Gregory. He exited the cathedral without a word to anyone.

On the drive back to St. Michael, Father Tom considered

whether he should have addressed the bishop, in a general way, in his own defense. The bishop had complete power over him and could subject him to a spectrum of punishments from a mild rebuke to laicization. But only if he remained a parish priest. He'd always been a pragmatic parish priest, he reminded himself, and as such concluded he'd followed the proper course of action. Nothing he could have said would have dissuaded the bishop from implementing punishment. For the first time in his life, he just didn't feel like fighting.

Father Tom didn't like it, but he admitted to himself his soul was tired; an acedia had set in as soon as he walked into the cathedral nave and saw the bishop on his cathedra. The entire experience—the preparation, the ritual, the bishop's reaction—had taken a toll on his spirit, as well as his body. It wasn't that the effort had not borne fruit; it was, in truth, a vindication of faith and depth of spirit beyond all earthly powers. However, where before he would have been combative in his interview with the bishop, with a tired soul, he'd accepted his fate without a whimper. He concluded his acquiescent behavior in the face of the bishop's charges was an appropriate reaction. He knew his purpose for becoming a priest was fulfilled, and he had nothing else left to do. He decided not to respond in writing to the list of charges. Instead, when he returned to see the bishop, he'd hand in his resignation and retire.

During his second meeting with the bishop, before the bishop could make any pronouncement, Father Tom handed him his notice of retirement, which the bishop read with thinly veiled pleasure. In response, the bishop gave him two weeks to get his affairs in order, with instructions to be out of the St. Michael rectory after 10:30 a.m. Mass two Sundays hence.

Father Tom knew he needed to make good use of his time. When he arrived in the rectory garage, the first thing he did was find his garden trowel and gloves. He went into the kitchen and picked out an appropriate piece of Tupperware. He got a roll of duct tape out of the junk drawer. He walked out to the rose garden and sat down on the dirt under the willow tree, donned his gloves, and dug up Cat's body. He was careful with the trowel so as not to do more damage to the animal than nature had already done. He opened the handkerchief and found rigor mortis had set in. The fur was matted and patchy; there were various insects infesting the flesh. The body was beginning to putrefy and was malodorous. He secured the shroud and placed Cat's body in the Tupperware container, closed it tightly, and wrapped several lengths of duct tape around the seal to make sure it was airtight.

CHAPTER TWENTY-ONE

Although intended to be confidential, news of Father Tom's meeting with the bishop seeped down through the levels of church hierarchy until it dripped into the receptive ears of an elderly, retired priest, one of Brian Metzger's golf buddies. Metzger had played golf with the old priest and two other men at least once a week during fair weather ever since the course marshal grouped them together on a crowded day to speed play. The priest's mild senility, along with his proximity to the seat of Catholic Church power, made him a favorite of the foursome when they were on the course. He was an entertaining raconteur, except when he babbled during another player's putt, and he had an endless supply of anecdotes and gossip. And Metzger loved gossip, particularly gossip about local clergy, and he was sure the retired priest, who seemed to filter nothing he said, would share with him any aspersions on his own character and considered the old man a canary in the mineshaft of his own behavior.

In any event, during their Wednesday morning round, the old priest began talking about Father Tom's situation as the players stood on the second tee. As always, he began his story with this prefatory, "You didn't hear this from me," and as always, each member of the foursome swore himself to secrecy. As he withdrew his ancient persimmon wood driver from his golf bag, the old priest asked if any in the group knew Father Tom Abernathy. The other two of the foursome, not being clergy nor even lay Catholics, remarked in a disinterested way that they only knew him to be the pastor of St. Michael, but neither had formally met the man. Metzger, holding back until he heard the substance of the old priest's gossip, admitted only that he'd met the man a few times, but didn't know him well.

The old priest carried his ball and driver to the tee box, resulting in a maddening pause in his story as Metzger waited for him to hit. As he usually did, the old priest sliced an errant drive to the right, barely the distance of the ladies' tee. Metzger, always the proficient golfer, teed off next, hitting a nice drive about 260 yards down the middle of the fairway. After the two other golfers hit their tee shots, they climbed into their golf carts and headed toward their balls.

The old priest always rode in the golf cart with Metzger. The other two golfers felt self-conscious riding with a priest and thought Brian, himself a clergyman, best suited to chauffeur the old cleric around the course. Once they both were in the cart and Metzger started down the cart path, he looked expectantly at the old priest, whose only comment was, "I think that's my goddamned ball over there" as he pointed to a ball near the cart path. In his decline, the priest had become foulmouthed, even blasphemous, a condition the other golfers considered humorous and endearing in an old man of the cloth. Metzger just wanted the old priest to get on with his story about Tom Abernathy. After the old man hit an acceptable three wood, and Metzger caught up with his own ball and played it within twenty yards of the green, back in the cart, he looked over at the priest and asked, "What were you saying about Father Abernathy?"

"I mentioned Tom Abernathy?" he asked with a befuddled look on his face, and then sat quietly, the befuddled look changing to one of pensiveness, until his eyes flashed, and he said, "Yes, good man, that Father Tom. We're gonna miss him."

The man's words caught Metzger off guard. Although the old priest's decline had markedly accelerated of late, his stories, sometimes banal, sometimes salacious, were always founded in fact, often facts few others were privy to.

"Is Father Abernathy leaving?" asked Metzger, gently prodding the old man.

"Yep. The bishop shitcanned him."

"You're kidding."

"I don't kid around about things like that, Brian."

"Why'd the bishop do that?"

"Father Tom is a heretic, or so the bishop thinks. Bishop never cared much for him. They've butted heads in the past. Anyway, rumor is Tom abandoned his church to go around doing faith healings and other miracles. Guess old Tom thinks he's Jesus Christ himself."

Metzger was so flummoxed by the old priest's disclosure, he nubbed his pitching wedge and then on his second try, hit the ball over the green. He couldn't concentrate on his golf game, and over the next sixteen holes shot the worst round of golf of his life.

Once he was back at his church office, Metzger closed the door and sat at his desk staring out the window and tried to make sense of the story the old priest told him. He knew Tom to be a steadfast and traditional priest, not one to dabble in charismatic practices or chicanery. It just didn't make sense that he would have abandoned his parish to engage in ontological rites. Nevertheless, if what the old priest said was true, as most of his scuttlebutt usually proved to be, he was faced with daunting questions as to whether he should somehow involve himself in Catholic Church politics and, if he got involved, what could he do on Father Tom's behalf anyway? He knew a lot of people; a lot of influential people in town, but none near the seat of power in the Catholic Church.

Metzger looked down at his feet and realized he'd been so distracted by the old priest's news he'd not taken off his golf spikes when he left the country club. It was then he appreciated the depth of feeling he had for Father Tom, and a sense of awe overwhelmed him. If what the old priest professed was true and Tom had dabbled in faith healing, it was an act of profound transcendence which called into question his own dedication to the cloth. As he looked down again at his big feet and the wide hands resting on his legs, he admitted what he'd before been able to fight shy of: after so many years as a minister, he now cared more about improving his golf game than improving his pastoral care to his congregants. And when he was grinding himself to dust, as he now was, sitting in his office, awkward in golf attire, contemplating the possible end to his friend's long career as a parish priest, he broadly chastised himself for failing to find most matters in life more important than his handicap.

The longer he sat at his desk considering the situation, the more conflicted he became. Father Tom's removal from St. Michael was a matter of great delicacy, but he couldn't make up his mind whether he should act, and if so, how to act. He felt as if his large body was now a liability, hindering not only movement of his limbs but delicate workings of his mind. He was tormented by indecision, a personality flaw he previously considered aggravating in others but recently claimed as his own.

He'd thought it a godsend when the assistant minister was assigned to his church, at least at first. Under the auspices of on-the-job training, he allowed her to handle all the awkward and painful and time-consuming situations that called for warmth and compassion, such as counseling the bereaved, visiting the terminally ill, or meeting with couples whose marriages were shattered beyond repair. She, unlike he, was warm and compassionate. She had the patience such situations called for, where he could be graceless in his haste and artless in his sincerity. But he soon learned her personality made her vulnerable, and her training put them in close proximity, and that combination was problematic for them both. He erred

197

in a way he'd never erred before, and as a result, questioned every decision he made, large or small, and lost all sense of self-assuredness and right.

In regard to Father Tom's problem, Metzger well understood the dispassionate aspects of church politics, whatever the denomination, where decisions were coldly made to move or dismiss pastors for myriad reasons unrelated to the pastor's ability to lead his flock. In his own church, however, there was not a single autocrat like the local Catholic bishop. The Methodist Church employed a Council of Bishops, and a decision such as the one to shitcan Father Tom would be based on a consensus of bishops. Moreover, his church employed a Judicial Council made up of clergy and lay persons that reviewed cases referred by the Council of Bishops. In the case of a pastor's removal, there were several levels of oversight and appeal, and no pastor was subject to the capricious actions of one person.

But that was how his church operated and not Tom's. He'd heard comments from his old golfing pal that the bishop was a difficult man, highly educated but vain and temperamental, much taken with the power and ceremony of his office. However, even such a man wouldn't make an impulsive decision to remove a popular parish priest, Metzger reasoned. One thing that Metzger was able to decide is that there had to be reasons beyond his ken on which the bishop based his decision to remove Father Tom from St. Michael.

Hence, Metzger was troubled by a specific aspect of the old priest's gossip. Sitting in his office he recalled it word for word: "He abandoned his church to go around doing healings and other miracles." As he pondered the import of the comment, he wracked his brain trying to figure out if Father Tom might have engaged in some sort of conventional intervention or rite which a distraught individual may have confused with a miracle or healing. Every congregation and parish had its sick, and visiting and praying with the sick were ordinary pastoral duties. Perhaps a grateful but overwrought parishioner made bold assertions about Tom's powers.

On the other hand, if there was a scintilla of truth in the old priest's accusation, Father Tom's activities would have been extraordinary. He knew from his many years at First United Methodist Church that Belle City was like any small city. It countenanced its fair share of chin-wagging. And miracles were rare. Had Father Tom actually been involved in faith healing, it had to have been a clandestine affair and the object of his ministrations had to be a person of unquestioned rectitude whom the priest could trust to not disclose his involvement.

At a loss for ideas and feeling impotent in the face of his friend's pending dismissal from his parish, Metzger decided to call Theo Swindberg and Billy Crump to see if they had any thoughts on how to intervene on Tom's behalf. He was just about to dial Theo's number when he put down the phone. He remembered Theo's wife Naomi was very ill, perhaps on her deathbed, and he didn't want to disturb them with Tom's problem. However, the recollection of her grave situation gave him pause. Yes, Theo's wife has been very ill. And who would demonstrate greater rectitude under the circumstances than a prissy little Lutheran and his wife? At that moment, he allowed himself to consider the accusations made against Father Tom as true. And if so, they very likely could involve Naomi Swindberg. As fantastic as the thought was for a number of reasons, it made sense to him. He picked up the telephone and called Billy Crump.

Chapter Twenty-Two

In response to the doorbell, Theo opened the parsonage door to find Brian Metzger and Billy Crump standing on his front porch. "We need to talk to you," said Metzger.

Theo looked up and down the street and then invited the men into his parlor. Once they were settled and declined his offer of a cup of coffee, Theo asked them the purpose of their visit, abruptly and nervously, like an anxious man who delved into the formality of asking questions while worried about the import of the answers he might receive.

"Father Tom," answered Metzger

"What about Father Tom?"

"He's been called up before the bishop," said Crump. "It's serious."

"Who told you that?"

"Tom Abernathy's not the only Catholic I know in this town," Metzger replied.

"I'm sure it's just a rumor. Maybe a little dustup blown out of proportion."

"The bishop said he abandoned his parish for days and dabbled in some heresy or the other," Crump said.

"Rubbish."

"The word I heard was, quote, 'The bishop shitcanned him.'"

"Scatological rubbish."

"My sources are pretty reliable."

"Well, if Father Tom is in some sort of pinch, I'm sure it will all work out. I'm sure the bishop is a reasonable man."

"Not this bishop. He's an arrogant, preening bastard, and according to my sources, Tom and the bishop have butted heads in the past. Now the bishop thinks he has Tom by the balls."

Theo raised his eyebrows at the Metzger's last remark. "Please, Brian, Naomi is in the other room."

"Sorry, I'm upset."

"We need to pray for Tom," Theo said.

"We need to do more than pray, Theo," Crump butted in. "He could lose his parish, maybe even his commission. And we think you know something about Tom's whereabouts when he was away from his church that could help his case."

"Why would you think that?" asked Theo, his pale cheeks flushed and warm.

"Lucky guess," said Crump.

Theo began to fidget and twitch, sweat beads formed on his forehead. He coughed nervously and started to chew the nail on his right ring finger. He finally said, "There is nothing I can tell you."

"Looky here, Theo," said Crump, "me and Brian don't know what you know, but if you know something that'll get Tom off the hook with the bishop, you better spill the beans."

"I...I can't."

"Jumpin' Jehoshaphat, Theo, the man's life's work is on the line!"

The two visitors sat staring at Theo who, for his part, sat pensively in his armchair, left leg crossed over the right, his left foot waggling nervously, his right hand hovering about his mouth.

"I took a solemn oath," he finally blurted out. "I can't tell you anything."

"I took no oath," Naomi said as she entered the parlor, chin up, an impish glint in her eye.

"Hush, Naomi," said Theo. In the instant he'd heard her words, the terrible ramifications of the truth cascaded through his mind. He had a life's work, too, and it all could come to naught. The Synod surely would remove him from his office for his dalliance with a priest from the Roman church. What would he do? What would they do? "Just hush."

"Don't you hush me, Theo Swindberg. These gentlemen have a right to know their friend is a saint."

Theo placed both feet on the floor and rested his elbows on his knees, head in hands, looking blankly at the floor as Naomi matter of factly told the story of how she was dying, that she was filled with cancer, that she had scans that showed all her internal organs being eaten away by the cancer, and how Father Tom came and prayed over her, how he suffered for her, how his faith healed her. And how she knows him to be a saint.

"Father Tom was right here, where God wanted him to be," she added. "And you can tell that bishop he can go straight to hell."

"Naomi!"

"Oh, Theo, you silly little man," she said, and laughed a sardonic little laugh. "Did you offer our guests some coffee?"

Metzger and Crump sat dumbfounded as they watched Naomi walk out of the room. She was thin, they noticed, but graceful and composed, and her skin was flush with a healthy pink color. After she left the room, Theo slumped back in his chair, closed his eyes, sighed a long, relieved sigh, calm and relaxed.

"It's true," he finally said. "Everything she said is true."

"Was there some mistake?" asked Crump. "I mean, could the doctors have been wrong from the get-go?"

"No," said Theo, without opening his eyes. "I saw the original scans myself. They pointed out all the dark blotches. Told me she had only a short time to live."

"And now?"

"Her scans yesterday were as clear as Christ's conscience."

"It's a miracle for sure," said Crump. "Praise be to God!"

The three men sat silently contemplating the profundity of what they were privy to. "What do we do with this information?" Metzger finally asked.

"Nothing," Theo answered. "Nothing. I promised Tom."

"Looky here now, Theo. I'm not one to have a man break a solemn oath, but folks need to know about this. That bishop needs to know about this. Like your wife said, she never took no oath. Me and Brian never took an oath—"

"Billy, please," Theo said. "Please."

"Well, I don't know about you," Crump said to Metzger, "but I'm gonna go home and pray on this. Pray hard. And hope the Good Lord guides my footsteps. Somebody has to do something about this situation. Yes, sir. Gonna ask Jesus what to do about this."

"And I'm sure he'll tell *you*, Billy. You're an instrument of God," Theo said in a voice struggling under the weight of sarcasm. "A bona fide instrument of God."

CHAPTER TWENTY-THREE

After he'd finished packing the few personal belongings he had at the rectory, to take his mind off his trouble with the bishop and the end of his career as a priest, Father Tom decided to attend the tent revival Billy Crump was holding on the grounds of the Grand Hope Nondenominational Family Church. What the hell? He was practically a layman, free to consume his spiritual sustenance anywhere he wished. Besides, he'd only heard about such spectacles and wanted to see one for himself. He found a passably clean sport shirt and khakis, and remembering the bishop's comments about his appearance, skimmed them with an iron to flatten out most of the wrinkles. He walked out of the rectory door and sniffed the rose garden, thinking it as fragrant and sweet as he'd ever smelled it for so late in the year. Out of habit, he made the sign of the cross over Cat's empty grave, walked to the garage, and climbed into his automobile.

Father Tom arrived late to Billy's church and couldn't find a place to park his car. The parking lot was full, and the ushers had directed drivers to park on the grass in the church yard, but the church yard was also packed with cars, requiring the ushers to send him in search of street parking several blocks away. There were cars parked up and down the street as far as he could see, so Tom drove nearly a quarter mile away before he found a spot. He walked quickly in the direction of the church amid clumps of others who also were hurrying to the tent revival. Most were strangers to him, except for a handsome family consisting of a young father, a mother and two cute little kids, a family who regularly attended 10:30 a.m. Mass at St. Michael, but who were at that moment so intent on their walk and keeping the kids out of the traffic, they didn't recognize him.

Tom eyed up the tent as he neared it. It was an impressive structure; but rather than a canvas tent, as he expected, it was a blue-and-white-striped canopy held up by an array of spaced-apart aluminum poles and secured in place by ratchet straps extending between the tops of the poles and tent stakes in the ground. Tom estimated the canopy to be about sixty feet long and about forty feet wide. There was portable picket fencing extending around an end and both sides, leaving one end open so the attendees could be herded under the canopy. Tom stood in line and made his way in and noticed strategically placed five-gallon plastic buckets adjacent the entryway, already seeded with loose cash.

There were rows of rented folding chairs neatly aligned under the canopy, the rows divided in half by a center aisle. Tom figured there were a couple hundred folks in the seats, leaving only a few open singles about the array. The vinyl canopy was holding in the body heat, and despite the open sides, the scant breeze did little to cool the air, and he sweated through his shirt as he wandered around looking for a vacant chair. He nearly walked out before he found one in the middle of the last row, near the entrance.

At the front end of the aisle was a riser occupied by an odd assortment of musicians playing an odd assortment of instruments, including a banjo, a bass guitar, a zither, an electric keyboard, and a snare drum. Immingled with the musicians were several singers, both young and fresh-faced boys and girls and some old codgers and crones. The musical act started the revival by warming up the crowd with old-time gospel music. Tom recognized the first few songs, although he'd not heard them since he was a kid. He found the banjo picker, who reminded him a bit of Earl Scruggs, most entertaining, particularly during his solo in "Are You Washed in the Blood?"

A young girl, perhaps ten or twelve years old, had an amazing voice, untrained but pitch-perfect as she belted out "Jesus Loves Me" with abandon.

When the last tune was winding down, Tom could hear murmuring from the front rows. He craned his neck to see Billy Crump off to one side of the stage, pacing nervously until the musicians laid down their instruments, locked arms with the singers, and bowed to the crowd. In an instant, Billy bounded onto the stage and stood with his arms spread wide, a great smile on his face, soaking up the raucous adulation of the people.

"Praise the Lord!" he shouted over the cheers and applause. "Looky here, looky here, looky here! Praise Jesus! What a crowd! Am I blessed or what?"

"Yes!" the audience shouted. "Blessed!"

"Praise and hallelujah!" he shouted back.

Tom focused on Billy as he moved across the stage, floppy old Bible in his left hand, waving with his right, pointing to spectators, offering random words of recognition such as, "Good to see you, brother." "Howdy do, sister." "Good to see you, friend." He had a way about him in front of a crowd, Tom had to admit. And he looked good. The short hair on his great round head was neatly trimmed; he was wearing charcoal gray slacks and a wine-colored sports jacket over a snow-white mock turtleneck. Tom looked him over head to toe, trying to figure out what was different about his poker club buddy, other than his clothes, until he settled on his feet. Billy was wearing steel gray western boots with massive heels that made him stand at least two inches taller than his normal height. Elevated as he was, with his short legs and outsized head, he had the comical look of a malformed homunculus, and Tom could not help but chuckle out loud.

When the crowd settled down, and after he introduced and thanked the musicians and singers, Billy launched into a long and earnest prayer of welcome and guidance, and if he ad-libbed, as Tom suspected he had, he had to credit the man with an enviable ability to fly by the seat of his pants, an ability Tom, who lately always stuck to the written script of his homily, no longer possessed.

As the revival progressed, Tom decided he admired the format: the musicians played a good old-fashioned hymn, and Billy would urge the crowd to sing along. Each hymn had a signature theme, and when the singing ended, Billy would ignite a short, fiery sermon on the theme. He repeated the sequence several times with several different themes, keeping the listeners engaged and allowing Billy to tackle multiple sins and iniquities in a fresh way in a limited amount of time.

The first gospel hymn was "Leaning on the Everlasting Arms," and although he didn't know all the words, Tom enjoyed the melody and sang in a low, reserved voice, "Leaning, leaning, leaning on the everlasting arms" when the refrain rolled around. What intrigued him most, however, was when Billy took to preaching, he segued "leaning on the everlasting arms" into the acceptance of Jesus Christ as their Lord and Savior and, by implication, informing his audience that Grand Hope Nondenominational Family Church had its arms out to them as an instrument of salvation, but one which couldn't survive to save their eternal souls without the generosity of sinners such as themselves.

Billy's backup band next played "Amazing Grace," and after the final verse, he launched into an impassioned speech explaining how Jesus worked through grace, and his amazing grace saved a wretch like him. Tom's ears perked up at the comment, thinking Billy might just reveal something salacious about himself, perhaps about his past, perhaps the basis for proclaiming he himself was a wretch. But Billy stopped short of any personal revelations, much to Tom's disappointment. Nevertheless, Tom himself, having been a miserable wretch saved by grace through his mother's intervention, found Billy's words both applicable and inspiring. Moreover, he thought Billy's format was well-played. Crump used his words to prod and cajole and shame, but always in the end, to praise and uplift and announce the gift of grace.

Tom also picked up on, and mildly admired, Crump's tactic of using old gospel music to shoehorn in his teachings on hot topics of the day. They were awkward transitions, but they didn't deter Billy who, with garbled phrasing and tortured syntax, made each uncomfortable subject fit into a lyric frame. Since most of the hymns were old Protestant standards, many originating in the Southern or Appalachian regions of the country, Tom had a lack of familiarity with the words, which only enhanced his acceptance of the allusions. Crump first preached that unrepentant homosexuality was a learned behavior that consigned the practitioner to a seat in hell. And he bolstered his pronouncements with at least a half dozen references to scripture, from verses in Leviticus to Romans, which Billy had marked in his old Bible with yellow Post-It notes, and which Tom recognized as authentic and literal. Billy ended the discussion on the subject by shouting out Paul's condemnation of the homosexual act from Corinthians and saying the saint's use of the original Greek word *arsenokoitai* could not be clearer or more graphic.

Crump displayed, Tom thought, good insight into the hearts of the men and women in his audience. He played to the audience and plowed into a fertile field of proselytization. His next topic was lust, in general, and then lust specifically, citing First John, the lust of the flesh, the lust of the eyes, and the pride of life. At the mention of lust of the flesh, Tom felt a little uncomfortable. But as he thought about Naomi, he felt nothing but joy in her healing and he let the discomfort pass. However, thinking about her caused him to miss most of Crump's words of warning and condemnation regarding lust of the flesh.

Billy next moved on to the evils of pornography, which he condemned as causing the Lord's people to lust after flesh, but further added that pornography was undeniably lust of the eyes. Pornography is addictive, he warned, and destructive. Lusting after another in our minds is the essence of pornography, he explained, and is offensive to God. Tom again felt a pang of self-consciousness hearing Billy's words. Billy then skillfully worked his way to a logical and practical conclusion: the proliferation of pornography and licentious behavior leads to the degeneration of the soul, resulting in the disintegration of the family in some cases and rape in others.

Tom noticed Crump had begun to wander off topic when he started in on a mishmash of hot-button issues, and he wondered if fatigue was setting in and old Billy was wearing down, causing a lapse in discretion. The little evangelical exhorted the young women in the audience to remain chaste and then reminded them abortion, which often followed poor choices, was murder in God's eyes, pure and simple. He then stridently argued that the role of the man is as absolute head of the family, his word being inviolate and final. Correspondingly, he pronounced the proper role of women in the family and in the church was to serve. Yet, as Billy delivered his hard sermonettes, his words never seemed to hit a sour note with the crowd. It occurred to Tom, as he watched the people around him lap up Billy's words of eternal life, that the preacher's views on these moral and religious issues were not that far afield from the official positions of the Roman Catholic Church, but he found them unsettling when he heard them declaimed in such stark and hokey terms.

The sermonettes were invariably interrupted by shouts of "Amen!" and "Praise Jesus!" Tom had expected as much. On his drive to the revival, he'd succumbed to the stereotype of tent revivals being peopled by marginally intelligent rabble led by a strutting Bible-thumper. Yet, even if Billy was a stereo-typical Bible-thumper, in spades, the people under the tent looked normal enough and could have been his own earnest parishioners at Sunday morning Mass, as indeed one family was. The old lady next to him, prim and polite, was having a rollicking good time clapping her hands and stomping her foot, albeit out of time, during the last tune of the night, a rousing rendition of "I Saw the Light." Tom clapped his hands and belted out the refrain, "I saw the light, I saw the light; no more darkness, no more night" as it rolled around. The words of Psalm 98, "Make a joyful noise unto the Lord," came to mind, and he enjoyed the music even more and had to admit that listening to the motley group of musicians, the singing, and the little evangelical's homespun liturgies made him feel better than he'd felt in weeks. All in all, he found the revival to be grand theater and enjoyed it immensely.

When Tom checked his watch, he realized Billy had been on stage for over two hours, non-stop, singing and preaching, and it was natural his energy appeared to be flagging. Tom, recalling Billy's thoughtful and discreet response to the news of Naomi's illness, along with now seeing him demonstrate his considerable skills on stage, felt a newfound admiration for the little man, and he decided to wait around after the revival and let him know how much he enjoyed the spectacle.

Billy was not ready to quit, however. The music ended, and the stage was quiet, and the only thing heard under the canopy were random coughs and clearing of throats, the shifts and shuffles of aching backsides in uncomfortable chairs, and spo-radic, unprovoked shouts of "Amen!" or "Praise the Lord!" Crump allowed for the dramatic pause. He then began to walk slowly back and forth along the front edge of the stage, again recognizing regular congregants and thanking strangers and inviting them to regular Sunday meeting. He stopped to wipe the sweat from his face and neck with his handkerchief. There was a quiet but pervasive anticipation moving among the folks in the chairs, and Tom could sense they were wondering what Pastor Billy had planned for a finale. At last, Crump moved to dead center, stood tall in his boots, set his jaw and stared over the heads in the audience and shouted, "Now, looky here, folks, I have something to testify to before you and the Lord, and it is as true a testimony as ever been made! This lowly servant of Jesus Christ has been a witness to a miracle. A miracle, I tell you, right here in this town, and the miracle was performed by a man I know personally."

"Testify, Pastor Billy!" a man shouted.

Another hollered, "Testify! Testify!"

"I've prayed a lot over this, friends. I prayed to the Lord to instruct me in the right way. To set my path straight; you know, for Jesus to show me what I should do with this knowledge. I thought the right thing was to keep it to myself. But the Lord whispered in my ear last night, he says, 'Son, you ain't the type to hide your light under a bushel.'"

"Amens!" rang out under the canopy as Billy stood waiting for confirmation from the crowd that he should proceed in the way he'd already decided to proceed. He paused. More "Amens!" arose from various parts of the tent. Crump stood silently to let shouts and murmurs, which seemed to arise on cue, move about under the canopy until they ceased in expectation of a revelation. Father Tom, however, began to feel a vague discomfort, a prickly hot sensation along his spine, an insidious creeping discomfort rooted in the recognition that Billy's purported "miracle" might well be related to him.

"Brothers and sisters," Crump began, "I personally know a man who is an instrument of God. He healed a woman so filled with cancer she wasn't gonna git better. No, sir. She only had days to live, maybe just hours. I know the woman, and I know her husband. Although they are good folks, both of them, she was sure to be dead by tonight. But about a week ago, this man I know, this instrument of God, filled with the faith of the Lord Jesus Christ and the Holy Spirit, prayed over that woman for days, unceasingly, and healed her!"

"Amen!"

"Praise the Lord!"

"Tell us more," an old voice implored.

"No more to say about that, friends. She's as right as rain, that woman. And I was a witness to the miracle, same as Lazarus's sister."

Father Tom's heart pounded erratically as the heat of anger rose to his face. He began to sweat profusely. This revelation about the healing was a breach, he thought, over the top, even for Billy Crump. How did he find out? Who could have told him? Surely not Theo. But who? And why was he shooting off his mouth about it now, in front of all these people? He was confounded and angry and clenched his fists and pounded them silently against his knees.

"You crazy little bastard," he muttered under his breath. "You crazy little bastard."

"Now here's the kicker," Crump continued. "There are Pharisees and Sadducees among us, right here in Belle City, and these sinners want to run this man of God out of town!"

There were shouts of derision and disgust and anger; there were catcalls bestowing the name of Satan on these Pharisees and Sadducees, along with rabid incantations of Jesus's name, seeking His mercy for this man, this instrument of God who had effected the miracle.

"Hold on, folks," Crump interrupted. "Be assured *I'm* not going to take this lying down. No siree. I'm gonna fight this. As long as God grants me breath. So I'm asking you to pray for me, and for this man, though I can't tell you his name. You just have to trust me on this for now."

"We will, Pastor Billy!" someone in the back near Father Tom hollered toward the stage. "We put our trust in you and the Lord!"

The charm of the event rapidly dissolved for Father Tom. What he'd considered, up to that point, to be harmless theatre had taken an abrupt turn toward the personal, the uncomfortable. He wanted to bolt for the exit, but he didn't want to draw attention to himself. He sat in his chair and seethed.

"And there's other help I need, folks. It costs money to fight the devil. I'm asking for a freewill offering to support me and this mission. Just donate whatever your heart tells you to donate. We'll take nickels or dimes, a dollar or five, ten or twenty. Just drop your money in one of the buckets on your way out."

Tom heard all he was going to hear. That Billy Crump wanted to take credit for being witness to a miracle to boost his standing with these rubes was bad enough, he thought. But to use Naomi's healing as a money-maker for his goddamned church was beyond the pale. He got up and stomped toward the exit. He was so angry he could barely see his way out of the tent. He brushed by a five-gallon bucket near the exit, turned and gave it a hard kick, scattering the handful of seed money across the ground.

Chapter Twenty-Four

As he walked into the cathedral carrying his plastic Walmart bag, the heels of Billy Crump's boots made echoing thuds on the bare tile of the center aisle. He looked around and shook his head at the ostentation. There was an abundance of ornate marble statues, a multiplicity of gold crucifixes, and a polished marble holy water font. He walked through the cavernous nave toward the apse and craned his neck to study the ceiling, which was vaulted in a quadripartite design throughout the building. He stopped at the chancel where there was an ornately carved wooden ambo, a massive cathedra which was overstuffed and covered in a regal, if worn, deep red. He turned around to look at the other architectural features: rows of triforium windows below the ceiling, great marble columns resting on marble plinths, and various works of art on the walls in between the columns representing the Stations of the Cross. He admired them as art but considered them embodiments of vanity and conceit and a waste of money.

As he stood before the altar, he heard someone shuffling about in the sacristy. Out walked an older man, gray and stooped, dressed in a loose black dress shirt and gray trousers.

"Are you the bishop?" Crump asked.

"Oh, my no. I'm Father Gregory. Just an old priest who assists the bishop."

"Is the bishop here?"

"Not at the moment."

"When is he here?"

"He says Mass once a week, at ten o'clock on Sunday mornings."

"I ain't coming back on Sunday. I work Sundays. Where is he now?"

"Well, son, I'm not sure. Did you check next door at the bishop's house?"

"Thanks," Crump replied, and he turned around and clomped down the aisle through the nave.

The bishop's house was a large Federalist-style brick building. Crump stood outside and sized it up. He went up the front steps and tried the door, but it was locked. He rang the doorbell. No one answered the door. He rang the doorbell a second time, getting no response. Finally he pushed the button incessantly until a man answered the door. He was dressed like a priest, so Billy figured him to be a priest.

"Yes, what is it?"

"Are you the bishop?"

"No, I'm not the bishop. And what's all the commotion about?"

Crump knew his type from the days he went door-to-door peddling tracts and pamphlets. A hard sell, this guy. He stuck his leg in the open door so the priest couldn't pull it closed.

"I want to see the bishop."

"That's not possible," the priest replied.

"'But Jesus beheld them, and said unto them, with men this is impossible; but with God all things are possible.' That's from Matthew, Chapter 19," Crump countered.

"I'm aware."

"Well, then, I guess you're aware I'm gonna see the bishop."

Crump pushed his way past the priest. He stood in the vestibule and looked about. Directly across from him was a desk and behind the desk an office door with a frosted glass window. He could hear a single voice coming from the office, as if someone was having a telephone conversation. He pointed to the desk and said, "Who sits here?"

"That's my desk. I'm the bishop's secretary."

"Good, good. Well, you just go on in there and tell the bishop Pastor Billy Crump is here to see him." With that he plopped down in a side chair and held his bag on his lap.

"This is not the proper way to seek an audience with the bishop, Mr. Crump."

"It's Pastor Crump, Grand Hope Nondenominational Family Church. And I don't care a whit about your proprieties. I need to see the bishop."

Exasperated, the secretary let himself into the inner office. After a few minutes, he came back out and informed Crump the bishop had no time to see him.

"I can wait."

"I don't think you understand, Mr. Crump—"

"Pastor Crump. And I don't think you understand. I can wait here all day and all night if I have to. Forty days and forty nights, if I have to. He has to come out of there sometime, and when he does, I'll be right here."

The secretary sat down behind his desk and busied himself moving papers among stacks, occasionally glancing over at Crump, who sat rigidly in his chair, hands on his Wal-Mart bag, staring straight ahead. Finally, he said, "You may as well just leave. You'll not see the bishop today. Or any other day, for that matter."

"You may as well tell the bishop I ain't leaving till he sees me."

The secretary stood up, shaking his head and went back into the bishop's office. He returned quickly, saying, "The bishop cannot see you. And if you don't leave, he's instructed me to call the authorities."

"Hah! Call the authorities? Go ahead and call 'em. The chief of police is one of mine, not one of his. And the chief knows how stubborn I can be when I'm facing down the devil."

"I beg your pardon?"

"You just march back in there and tell the bishop what I

said. Or call the police. One or the other; I don't give a damn."

The secretary returned from the bishop's office and offered to escort him in. When he entered, Crump found the bishop sitting behind a massive desk, ornately carved with seraphim and cherubim, hovering angels and assorted crucifixes of various widths and depths. The bishop was a portly man with a jowly face, thick wet lips, and large hands resting on the center of the desk. He was nattily dressed in a tailored shirt and linen trousers, not in his bishop's regalia, not even in priest's clothes. The bishop, in turn, took time to warily eye up Crump. The secretary stood to the left of the bishop's desk looking Billy over, as well. The scrutiny didn't bother Crump. As always, he was comfortable with himself. He knew that he sometimes emitted an aura of instability or irrationality; it had been that way since his time in Cambodia. And he also knew there were times when his air of unpredictability served to unnerve others, to his benefit, and he reckoned it would serve him well in this interview.

The bishop, in a deep, rumbling voice finally asked, "What is the matter of such great urgency?"

Crump appreciated the practiced tone of the bishop's voice, a tone he also sometimes employed when discussing matters of great consequence. "I want to talk to you about Father Tom Abernathy."

The bishop raised his eyebrows as if to clear his vision and better study his visitor. "What about Father Abernathy?" he asked slowly, and if he were struggling to harness his impatience and incredulity.

"Word on the street is you're taking his parish away from him."

The bishop didn't respond, but focused intently on Billy's face. After about a half minute of staring he asked, "Do I know you?"

"We've never met."

"No," the bishop said after a pause. "I'm sure we've met."

"I would remember."

"What did you say your name is again?"

"Pastor Billy Crump, Grand Hope Nondenominational Family Church."

The bishop sat considering Billy's response and then said, "Now I know. You're the preacher on the billboard on the south end of town."

Crump sensed by the bishop's pronouncement of "preacher" and "billboard" he had a hard, condescending edge, honed by unquestioned fealty that fed his conceit. But Billy didn't care; the bishop's edge was not as hard as his own.

"Anyway, Bishop, I want to talk to you about Father Abernathy."

"My advice to you, Mr. Crump—"

"Pastor Crump."

"As you wish. My advice to you, Pastor Crump, is to not worry yourself about gossip you aptly described as 'word on the street.'"

"It comes from a reliable source."

"Be that as it may, it is none of your business. It is church business."

"I beg to differ, Bishop. It is God's business. I'm merely an instrument of God."

The bishop slid his chair back and put his feet on the desktop in an overt display of condescension. Crump read the imprint on his shoe sole and figured he could feed a hundred people for a month for what those shoes cost.

"Do tell, Pastor Crump, of the Grand Hope Nondenominational Family Church, if I got that right, what business of God's are you an instrument of?"

"Tom Abernathy is a saint."

"A saint?"

"A bona fide saint."

"A saint? Are you an expert on canonization?"

"And he's a faith healer."

The bishop smiled and openly winked at his secretary, as if to confirm for Crump he considered him a crackpot. Billy started to feel anger burn his throat, but he controlled his voice, didn't let it crack, didn't let it quaver.

"And what proof do you have of his miracles?"

"Do you know Theo Swindberg?" Billy asked

"The pastor of St. Paul's Lutheran? Not well, just by reputation. A very good man, I understand."

Billy summoned his own deep voice of authority: "Father Tom cured his wife of cancer."

The bishop dropped his feet to the floor and sat up straight in his chair. "You may have your own deluded reasons for interrupting my day, sir, but dragging Pastor Swindberg and his wife into your fantasy is beyond the pale."

"Call him."

"Don't take that tone with me."

"Listen, you pompous son of a bitch," Crump said sweetly through a smile, "I've been privy to a miracle of God, worked by Father Tom Abernathy. He saved a woman from cancer, through faith and prayer. Now you want to strip the man of his parish, his life's work. It ain't right. Get behind me, Satan!" Billy shouted, jumping up from his chair.

The bishop scrambled from his chair and stood close to his secretary. Crump wanted to laugh at the two nervous emissaries of Rome huddled up in the presence of a crazy little evangelical preacher, yet he kept a grim look on his face as he stared at the two priests.

"Now, if you want to hear the truth, the truth will set you free. You can talk to Theo; you can talk to his wife; you can talk to his wife's doctors; whatever it takes for you to get it through your fat head that Tom Abernathy is a chosen Lamb of God and he should stay right where he is."

"I think I've heard about enough out of you, Mr. Crump," the bishop hissed. "Where Father Tom serves, if he serves, is none of your business. I resent the tone you've taken with me, and I advise you to be on your way."

"I've got a little something for you before I leave," Crump said as he set the Wal-Mart bag on the bishop's desk. The bishop and his secretary eyed the bag apprehensively until Crump said, "It won't bite you, fellas. It's just a little free-will offering from my folks to help you decide the right thing to do about Father Tom." He dumped the bag, and bundles of hundred dollar bills plopped on the desk. "There's five thousand dollars here, Bishop, all in hundred dollar bills. No one needs to know but the three of us."

"Well, I never!"

"Oh, I'm sure you have, Bishop," replied Crump. "And I'm sure you will again," he said over his shoulder as he clomped out of the bishop's office.

Midmorning, the day after Billy Crump's visit to the bishop, Theo called Father Tom and told him the bishop requested he come in, that Billy Crump had told him a wild tale about Father Tom Abernathy and Naomi. The bishop wanted him to come in and clear up the matter. "I don't know what to do," Theo said.

"Don't do anything, Theo. The bishop has no authority over you; you know that."

"He might make trouble for me with the Synod."

"Don't worry about that, Theo. Guys like him are intimidated by Protestants; they're afraid they might be right."

Apparently, Theo didn't think Tom's comment funny. "What do you think Billy told him?" he asked in response.

"Everything, I guess. Look, I didn't ask Billy to talk to the bishop. You know Billy. That's how he plays his hand."

"I want to help you if I can, Tom."

"Just let it go. The bishop probably thinks Billy's a crank. If you get involved, more folks will find out. The Synod will hear about it. You could lose your position. We don't need two unemployed preachers in our poker club."

"I'm sorry, Tom."

"No reason to be sorry, Theo. It's done. Time to move on."

"What will you do?"

"I haven't figured that out. But I'll let you know when I do."

CHAPTER TWENTY-FIVE

Father Tom Abernathy called to order the last meeting of the St. Michael Drinking & Poker Club the Thursday after his telephone conversation with Theo. Theo had taken his advice and refused the bishop's invitation to meet. Subsequently, the bishop's secretary called Tom to confirm that he was to be out of St. Michael by Sunday afternoon. The secretary reiterated the bishop's position, saying a priest's failure to minister to his flock for unexplained reasons could not be tolerated. The diocese was accepting his resignation and retirement, and the bishop wished him no ill will.

The four clergymen gathered in Father Tom's rathskeller and took their usual seats around the poker table. No cards were dealt. No one was in the mood to play cards. Each of the guests was somber, but Tom was lighthearted, entertaining them with his spot-on impression of the bishop, which Crump confirmed, and offering bits of gallows humor regarding his forced retirement. He handed out cans of beer and beseeched the men to have a drink, one last time, in honor of the good times they'd had.

"I should have done something," Metzger said, ending the pensive silence which followed Father Tom's invitation to drink. "I should have gone with Billy. I could have backed him up. I know people, I would have if I'd known—"

"Shoulda, coulda, woulda," Billy said with an edge to his voice. Then he eased back in his chair, sighed, and with a conciliatory tone, qualified his words. "Bottom line, Brian, it wouldn't a done any good. The bishop had his mind made up. And Tom didn't want us to interfere. I shouldn't have done what I did."

"What'd you think was going to happen, Billy?" Father Tom asked jovially. "The Pope make me a saint? It takes three miracles for canonization, and I only have two. Getting you boys together was the first one."

"I probably caused more trouble for you."

"No harm, Billy. The bishop just thinks you're a nut."

"Well, the old fraud kept my money and believe you me, I'm getting it back. For the poor. He's not shed of Billy Crump."

Theo sat sipping his beer, listening to the others talk. "It was my job, Brian," he finally said with tears in his eyes. "Tom saved Naomi's life, and I couldn't even bring myself to speak up on his behalf."

"Don't be so hard on yourself, Theo," Father Tom offered. "I told you not to. Anyway, it's all working out for the best. Things happen for a reason. It'll all work out the way it's supposed to. I want you gentlemen to give me your solemn promises you'll never speak of this matter again, to anyone. And Theo, I'd like for you to tell Naomi that if she has any feelings of gratitude to the Lord for His gift of healing, she won't speak of it either."

Tom surprised himself with his assertions that things happen for a reason and that it was for the best. The sentiment was outside divine intervention and also not part of his personal philosophy. He believed most folks looked at bad outcomes, disappointments, and loss in the light of the changed circumstances, and with no other circumstances being possible, accepted and adapted to the change. They adopted the new circumstances as happening for a reason or happening for the best, because there are no other options. They resorted to platitudes to assuage dire disappointment. His own situation, at least as far as his forced retirement went, was the result of an overweening bishop asserting his primacy. For a reason? Sure, but not preordained. For the best? Likely not.

In all likelihood, and Tom would never share this with the

others, his situation was a result of a malignant alignment of the stars, a negative effect on Aries, the Ram.

"What are you gonna do now, Tom?" asked Crump.

"I'm going back home, where I grew up. Grow roses and vegetables, maybe get myself a cat or two. I like cats; cats have free will." He smiled. "I've been renting out my mother's place for years, figuring I'd retire there someday. Well, it's someday. Besides, my horoscope for today told me to reduce stress by returning to my happy place."

"You can come and work with me," offered Crump. "Think of the folks we could heal, the money we could raise for the poor."

"I appreciate the offer, Billy," Tom replied with a benevolent smile, "but at this stage of my life, I don't want to work as hard as you do."

"The offer will always be on the table, Tom."

"I appreciate that, but I'm tired. I'm going home. I can tell you fellows the only right thing my old man ever did in his life was taking out a paid-up life insurance policy to cover the mortgage on the house before he left town. I was at Benedictine College when my mother got a call from a funeral director down in El Paso, Texas, saying he had my old man's body and wanted to know if she wanted him shipped up for burial. My old man had listed her as next of kin on his last job application. No, she told the undertaker, bury him down there, where he wanted to be. And she wired five hundred dollars to cover the expenses, and another two hundred with instructions to have Masses said at the local Catholic Church for the repose of his soul. She told me later she figured she owed him that much, considering he left her the home place and all. In any event, the insurance policy paid off the home place, and Mother had a place to live.

"I'll tell you boys, for most of my life, I hated my old man for abandoning us. It wasn't until I realized that some men like he and I just aren't cut out to be husbands and fathers. But we still have a purpose in life. His purpose was to provide my mother with her little house and a plot of land to grow her vegetables and roses, and give her me, her son, the priest."

Tom looked into the faces of the men sitting around the table. "Well, that's enough of the sad old stories. All in all, the St. Michael Poker & Drinking Club has been a pretty good time, hasn't it, boys?"

He raised his can of beer in a toast and the three other men took turns clanking their can against his. He could hear Theo softly humming "A Mighty Fortress is Our God," not because it was a proper moment for a hymn, but because he suspected if Theo didn't concentrate on the ponderous melody and difficult words he might break down and cry.

"I always liked that hymn, Theo," said Father Tom. "It's a strong hymn. Don't know why they never included it in our lexicon. Although it might have something to do with the fact it was written by a heretic."

Theo, dour and sad-eyed, made himself smile at Tom's joke. When he could no longer contain his feelings, he lowered his head and wept like a baby. Metzger wiped his eyes as well, while Crump sat in stony silence staring straight ahead, not looking at anyone, lest he too make a scene. True to form, however, he couldn't control himself, got up, and with tears pooled in his eyes, walked around the table and stood in front of Father Tom.

"I swear, Tom, you're the best damned papist I've ever known."

Tom stood up, grabbed Crump in a bear hug, and shook him up and down. "And you, my friend, are the best-looking little evangelical that ever graced a billboard."

When Metzger and Crump had gone, Theo, now composed, stayed behind to clean up the cellar as he'd done after each meeting for months. Tom told him he needn't bother;

there was nothing to clean up other than four empty beer cans. But Theo insisted, saying it was the least he could do, and he wanted to do it one last time. Tom picked up the beer cans, and Theo gently smoothed the tablecloth with his hands.

"I might as well put that away, Theo. I don't think there will be any more card games."

Theo gently folded the cloth in half and smoothed the creases. He then folded it in quarters and smoothed it again. As Father Tom watched, he said, "You know, Theo, that's really not a tablecloth; it's a Catholic altar cloth. I was waiting to spring that on you in front of the other guys, you know, as a joke. But I couldn't bring myself to do it."

Theo picked up the folded altar cloth, gently kissed it, and handed it to Father Tom.

"I've always known what it is, my friend. It was a sign to me from the very beginning. One must always be vigilant; you never know where you'll find an instrument of God."

Acknowledgments

The author would like to acknowledge the fine editing of the manuscript by Mary Ward Menke and Karen K. Snyder.

Author photograph by wphotography, Columbia, Illinois.